A PINCH OF GLUTTONY

GRETA BORIS

Information regarding additional permissions may be found at
www.fawkespress.com

Cover design by Michelle Fairbanks/Fresh Design
Edited by Mary-Theresa Hussey

Print ISBN 978-1-945419-47-8
ePub ISBN 978-1-945419-48-5

Library of Congress Control Number 2020930326

FAWKES PRESS

To my family in celebration of all our wonderful, and not so wonderful, family dinners.

In the third circle of hell:

Large hail and turbid water, mixed with snow,
Keep pouring down athwart the murky air;
And from the ground they fall on, stenches grow.
The savage Cerberus, a monster drear,
Howls from his threefold throat with canine cries
Above the people who are whelmed there.
Oily and black his beard, and red his eyes,
His belly huge: claws from his fingers sprout. . .
And as for the sin of gluttony
I, as thou seest, am beaten by this shower.
No solitary woeful soul am I,
For all of these endure the selfsame doom.

From *The Inferno*
***The Divine Comedy* of Dante Alighieri**

Gluttony is an emotional escape, a sign something is eating us. -
Peter De Vries

CHAPTER ONE

HONEY MARCHED FORWARD into the maw of the mountains despite the growing gloom of the canyon. Despite the persistent feeling she was being swallowed alive. Despite the fact her feet were killing her.

So was her back, her knees, and her lungs. Honey was out of shape. She could stand in a kitchen for hours at a stretch, but hiking up steep inclines wasn't a normal part of her day. She trailed behind Booker, her husband, who was as fit as she wasn't.

Booker was a firefighter, but she bet she put out more fires than he did. If she had his schedule, she'd exercise all the time too. Honey tripped over a rock, put a hand on his shoulder, and righted herself. Okay, she probably wouldn't, but she would exercise more than she did.

"You okay?" He gazed at her with concern. The look in his eyes made her ashamed of her attitude.

"Yeah. Thanks," she added.

"The cut off for the falls is right around the bend."

"But how far to the falls?" She couldn't seem to get the adolescent whine out of her voice.

"We'll take a break when we get to the boulders." Unlike her, Booker sounded energized. He was enjoying his new role as her personal trainer, and anything that made Booker happy these days was something she'd go along with. Which wasn't to say she didn't wish it was something else. Something else like a good movie, dinner out, or wine tasting. Most of the time, she was grateful her husband was a hunk. Not today. Today it was downright irritating.

At the end of last year, Honey's doctor had announced she was insulin resistant, which could turn into type two diabetes if she didn't make changes. Dr. Hillary also said Honey's cholesterol was high. If it got any higher, she'd have to go on medication. The doctor recommended regular exercise and cutting back on animal fats, simple carbs, and sugar.

Of course, Honey didn't do anything about the proclamation before Christmas. How could you bake cookies without butter and sugar and white flour? Booker wasn't happy about it but agreed they could start Honey's lifestyle makeover in the new year. It was now January, the month of resolution hell, hence the hike in Black Star Canyon.

Before they reached the path to the falls, Honey noticed the entrance to another trail branching off the fire road they were on. A barricade decorated with several pockmarked signs stretched across it. The signs read, "Keep Out," "Beware of Dogs," and "No Trespassing." Were those pockmarks made by bullets? Guns were also outside Honey's comfort zone. Guns were one of the reasons she and Booker had left Kentucky fifteen years ago. There were too many of them in Kentucky. Hunters shot up the hills every fall. They aimed for deer but took farmers' cows and even large dogs. It didn't seem like a safe place to raise a family even if she and Booker had made it out of childhood alive. Thinking about Kentucky reminded her of Joe and their lost money. Her mood soured more if that was possible.

"Friendly around here, aren't they?" Honey said.

"Well, you can't blame them. They've had their share of troubles."

"Like what?" She wasn't especially curious, but a story might take her mind off her feet.

"You know everyone thinks this canyon is haunted, right?"

"I heard it was something to do with Native American burial grounds."

"Sort of. Back in the eighteen hundreds, the natives were stealing horses from the Mexicans. Some fur trappers rolled into town and offered to take care of things. They found the natives eating horse meat over there." Booker pointed up the mountain. "They slaughtered everyone who couldn't outrun the bullets, and returned the live horses to the señors."

"On your right." A voice behind Honey made her jump. She turned to see five women in full riding gear pedaling up the hill. She moved to one side and watched them pass, admiring the definition of their thighs. It would be wonderful to have muscles like that. If only you didn't have to exercise to get them.

"Trail angels," Booker said.

Honey glanced around, looking for wildlife. "Where?"

Her husband jutted his chin at the cyclists. "Them. It's a group of mountain bikers. They call themselves Trail Angels. You should look into it. It'd be good for you."

She didn't respond. He couldn't be serious.

Booker made a right onto a dirt trail overhung with branches. The pungent odor of sage and wet leaves pinched Honey's nose, but the shade was pleasant. She was sweating despite the cool weather.

Booker said if you perspired, it meant you were healthy. She strongly suspected Dr. Hillary had exaggerated her condition. Her thoughts wandered to the frittata she'd make when they got home.

"The dead are said to haunt the old mines and trails of Black Star. The story attracts a certain element." Booker's words interrupted the bacon or turkey sausage debate running through her mind.

"Who bothers the locals up here, teens or crazies?" she said, pulling herself out of the kitchen.

"Both." Booker pushed aside a branch that crossed the trail and held it while she passed. "There are the usual ghost hunters, but there's also a fair amount of crime. Two girls were gang-raped and their boyfriends beaten to a pulp."

Honey's foot slid forward. She grabbed a tree branch to stop herself from falling. The past week it had rained for several days in a row, which was great for the environment, but the ground was slick. Honey's tennis shoes didn't have much traction.

Booker stepped around her and resumed his position as leader of the pack. "There are also Satanist wannabes who've been known to steal goats and sheep off local properties and sacrifice them on the rocks."

Why did he sound so cheerful? He'd been as somber as a turkey on Thanksgiving since Joe had disappeared. Honey shook her head. If she'd known all it would take to perk him up was rape and animal sacrifice, she'd have dragged him to a horror movie.

"The Sheriff's Department has cracked down on things," he continued. "But sometimes the locals get a wild hair and take matters into their own hands."

Why were they hiking here? She'd suggested several other destinations. There were so many pretty trails in Southern Orange County. She'd mentioned the one overlooking the ocean north of Laguna Beach, and the walking path near Oso Creek. Even a hike in hilly Whiting Ranch would have been better than this, but Booker was bound and determined to head out into this claustrophobic canyon. Honey shot a glance over her shoulder half expecting to see the bald kid from Deliverance hiding behind a tree. "We should have brought Fury," she said. Their black mutt wasn't big, but he had personality.

"His legs are too short for this hike," Booker said. The comment wasn't comforting. They walked on in silence, picking their way between the large rocks that littered the path. A narrow stream of water rushed past them.

"I bet the falls are really moving," Booker said. "Last time I was here, it was dry." His face darkened.

Honey knew he was remembering when Joe had visited last September. They'd hiked the canyon together. At the time, she'd assumed it was just a brotherly outing, a bonding adventure. Now she knew better.

Honey searched ahead. She couldn't see the falls but noted the path disappeared, broken by boulders. "How are we supposed to get there?"

"We climb." Booker's smile returned.

"Climb? Seriously? This is my first hike in—I don't know—five years. You want me to climb boulders?"

"It's probably been eleven or twelve years since you've hiked. I think the last time was in Mammoth when we went camping with Ash's Boy Scout troop." Ash, their son, was now twenty-two, so Booker's calculations were probably correct.

"You're making my point for me. Twelve years. I don't think I'm ready for this."

Booker gazed at the sky for a moment before responding. "Let's sit, have some water."

Honey shuffled to the closest boulder and collapsed. Booker handed her a metal bottle, and she drank. It was funny, the doctor was after her to drink more water. Eight glasses a day, which seemed a ridiculous amount. But right now, she felt like she could drink all eight one after another. The water tasted like heaven.

After guzzling the entire bottle, she wiped her mouth with her hand. "Gosh, that's good."

"Better than coffee?"

Honey held up a hand. "Don't get carried away now. There's nothing as good as coffee." Wine crossed her mind as a close second, but she was too tired to mention it.

"So here's what I propose. . ." Booker launched into a plan for scrambling over rocks and hauling themselves over boulders that sounded as complicated as it did unpleasant. Honey allowed her mind to wander. If she was going to do this, it was better if she didn't think about it.

Some of the rocks were mottled. Rivulets of rain must have washed their soil covering away. It was kind of pretty. It reminded her of the pastry layers in a mille-feuille. Her gaze traveled uphill, curious to see where the water had come from.

A hiking boot rested on its side in the dirt about five feet away. That's what she needed—hiking boots. She should tell Booker that when he was done with his monologue. He'd love to buy her hiking boots. She would say she couldn't climb those boulders, not in the silly tennis shoes she was wearing. She'd break her neck. She'd promise to come back in the new hiking boots.

"It's not far, half a mile or so." Booker was still talking. "And, it's not all climbing. The path is washed out, but we can—"

A hawk screeched. Honey watched it soar above them and envied it. It would be wonderful to be above this narrow crevasse, to be able to see the surrounding cities hidden from view by the canyon walls.

She had two blisters, one on each foot. A half-mile sounded pretty far. Speaking of, why would someone take off their hiking boots here? When there was so much hiking left to do? Correction, hiking boot. She only saw one.

She pivoted on her rock and glanced around the clearing. No mate. Even more strange. She turned to inspect the lone shoe again. It looked fairly new. It was dirty, but the sole was intact. Even if a couple of teens had hiked in and taken off their clothes to mess around, they'd have had to hike out again.

"You ready?" Booker said.

She looked at him with alarm. "I don't think so."

"Come on, Hon. Just give it a try. The falls will be beautiful." He stood and thrust a hand toward her. She allowed him to help her up.

Booker walked toward a pile of granite swinging his arms. He didn't look the least bit weary. Honey closed her eyes for a moment. She couldn't disappoint him again. He'd tried so many times to get her interested in outdoor activities. Kayaking, stand-up paddleboarding, mountain biking, she'd been a disaster at all of them. At least hiking allowed her to keep her feet on the ground.

She'd make the climb, but she didn't have to like it. She opened her eyes and trudged after him. As she passed the boot, she gave it a kick.

It moved an inch or so, then rocked into its former position. Honey stopped and stared. She'd kicked it hard. It should have skittered into the brush. It hadn't.

She placed the toe of her tennis shoe against the tan leather, and shoved. The boot rocked forward and back again. That's when she noticed something protruding from it she hadn't noticed before because it was the same color as the mud around it.

It was a sock. The top of the sock disappeared into more mud-colored fabric that, on closer inspection, was denim. That leg-shaped piece of denim disappeared into the earth.

CHAPTER TWO

WHERE WAS BOOKER? Honey's gaze returned to the lone hiking boot. The way the leg stuck out of the mud reminded her of Ash when he was a teenager. Ash ran hot and never could sleep at night without pulling the covers up around his chin and thrusting out a foot. She missed her younger child. He was only fifty miles away at Camp Pendleton, but new marines didn't have a lot of free time.

The sun glinted off a centimeter of clean grommet on the hiking boot. She shuddered, despite the warm temperature. It wasn't good to think about what was under the cover of mud as a person. She preferred to think of it as The Leg, to imagine it had sprung from the ground like a shrub or a wildflower.

The crunch of footsteps echoed from the trees. A moment later, Booker appeared. "Sorry that took so long. I had to hike all the way to the fire trail before I got cell reception."

"You called the police?"

"They're on their way."

Honey stood. "Can we leave?" She knew the answer would be no, but she wanted to put distance between herself and The Leg so badly the words had popped out of her mouth.

He gave her a horrified glare. "We have to make sure the scene isn't contaminated. Stay with the body."

She wished he wouldn't call it that. "It's been here a while, don't you think?"

"That's for the ME to say."

Irritation crawled over her skin. She scratched her arm. "My point is, if. . ." she paused, "The Leg was going to be disturbed, or contaminated, don't you think that would have already happened? What's another hour when it's been there for days, or maybe months?"

"It's been buried. Now it's not." His eyes closed to half-mast; lids heavy with stubbornness.

Honey walked to her boulder and sat again with a loud sigh. Booker wasn't a dictatorial man. In fact, he was kind and generous to a fault, but when he made up his mind about something, moving him off his position was like trying to shift a sow away from her slops. Wasn't going to happen.

Her husband strode over to The Leg and squatted next to it. He crouched there for several minutes, not moving. "What're you doing?" Honey finally asked.

He pivoted toward her; eyes glazed as if he was emerging from deep thought. "Huh?"

"I said, what are you doing." Annoyance peppered her words.

He rose slowly. "Just looking."

He had that expression on his face, the one he wore when he wasn't going to tell her whatever it was she wanted to know. She'd seen it when Willow called late on a Saturday night and asked him to pick her up from wherever she was. She'd seen it when he came home after a terrible fire. She'd often seen it as their anniversary or her birthday drew close. Whether it was good news or bad, he wouldn't tell her. She didn't waste her breath asking.

Twenty-five minutes later, two sweaty cops appeared in the clearing. "Kirk," Booker said, apparently recognizing one of them.

"Booker." The cop who replied was short and wiry and bounced on the balls of his feet like an athlete. "Long time."

"Certainly is."

The men stared at each other, blank expressions on their faces. Was it Honey's imagination, or did they dislike each other?

Booker broke the standoff. "When did you get moved to South County?"

"Three months ago. Got tired of Anaheim."

Another silence. This time Kirk spoke first. He gestured to the other officer, a tall man with dark hair. "This is Michael Varma."

Booker and Michael shook hands. "You two know each other?" he said. It was a silly question, since they obviously did.

"We go way back," Booker said.

"All the way to Kentucky," Kirk said.

Honey hefted herself off her rock. "Kentucky? Where in Kentucky?"

Booker tipped his chin toward her. "My wife, Honey."

"Lawrenceburg, like your husband," Kirk said.

Honey gazed at him, trying to imagine his face twenty years younger. She couldn't. "Funny, I don't remember you."

"Kirk was a few years behind us in school, Hon," Booker said.

"I was in the same year as Joe." Kirk's lips lifted in a half-smile. "How is Joe, by the way? I heard he ran into some trouble."

Booker's shoulders tensed, and Honey could feel the anger rolling off him. It hadn't been her imagination. These men didn't like each other at all. "Yeah, well, that got resolved. He's okay."

Okay? Is that what you called it when someone ran off with fifty thousand of your dollars? That's what she wanted to say, but she kept her mouth shut.

Varma must have sensed the animosity between Booker and Kirk too. He stepped forward. "So, what did you find?" His voice held a false, cheerful ring.

Booker led the men to The Leg, and all three gathered around it. Honey hung back. Michael nudged the boot with the tip of his own like she had. She returned to her boulder.

She wished with all her heart she could leave. She needed tea, or coffee, or better yet, a glass of wine. Something comforting and warm to wash away the horror of the morning.

After more discussion about when they'd arrived on the scene, when and how they'd first noticed The Leg, Varma walked toward the trees talking into the radio pinned to his shirt. From what she could gather, the crime scene professionals were on their way.

A shadow fell across her. She glanced up to see Kirk standing over her. "Can I ask you a few questions?"

"Sure. Don't think I can tell you anything Booker hasn't already."

He squatted on his haunches and brought his face level with hers. "You were the first one to notice the body?"

"I saw the boot." Honey went over all the same things Booker had said while Kirk took notes. She'd read somewhere that the police always spoke to everyone at a crime scene separately to make sure the stories lined up. It seemed Kirk had blurred the lines a bit this time. She'd heard everything Booker told him. Must be because of Booker's job. Firefighters and police might compete with each other in softball games or for charity events, but when there was an emergency, they worked together, respected one another.

Kirk stood in a graceful movement. "I think you two can take off. If we need to talk to you again, we know where to find you."

"Ms. Wells." Michael Varma held something out to her. It took her a moment to recognize what it was. Varma had folded a dollar bill into the shape of a cat. He smiled as he saw the light dawn. "A little hobby of mine. Thought you could use cheering up."

She flashed him a smile then jogged after Booker, who was already in the trees on his way to the fire road. As soon as they were out of earshot, she said, "What was that about?"

"What was what about?"

"You and Kirk. It was pretty obvious he didn't like you, and that the feeling was mutual."

Booker shrugged. "He and Joe didn't get along."

That almost made Honey like the officer. Booker was way too protective of his little brother as far as she was concerned. "That was a long time ago," she said.

"Some people don't change." His mouth clamped shut in that tight line that meant he was done discussing it.

The path narrowed, and Honey let him take the lead. As the trees closed around them, she pocketed the origami cat, and a thought struck her. What if The Leg had been killed by a mountain lion? She glanced nervously around her. "What do they think happened up there?" she said.

"They'll know better once they dig up the body," Booker said.

"But, I mean, they seem to be treating this like a crime scene."

"Someone buried the guy. Or girl," he amended.

"Could it have been a mountain lion? Remember that hiker who was killed a few years ago? Didn't the lion drag him off the trail and bury him in the bushes?"

Booker didn't say anything for a minute. "This body was buried pretty deep. I don't think a mountain lion could've done that."

Relief washed over Honey, but it was short-lived. If it wasn't a mountain lion, it was a person. A person who wanted to hide The Leg. If someone wanted to hide someone else, chances are the death of the latter wasn't natural. She picked up her pace and ran into Booker's back. "Sorry," she said.

She felt better when they reached the open fire road. There was a police car parked near the trailhead for the falls. It was empty, but it was a sign of civilization. "So you think it was murder?" she said.

"Why else would you bury a body?"

"Too cheap to pay for a funeral?"

Booker snorted. They walked for a while without speaking. Booker because he appeared to be deep in thought. Honey because she was having a hard time keeping up with him. He walked quickly, as if he'd forgotten she was there, forgotten her legs were about two feet shorter than his. Finally, he said, "There's something I didn't tell you about."

Honey's head snapped toward him. Something about The Leg? Booker couldn't have known anything about it before today. Could he have?

"I heard from Joe," he said.

Her heart, which had been pumping hard from the exertion, skipped a beat. "Really?"

"Yeah, really."

"What does he have to say for himself?" Joe was about the only topic that could drive The Leg from her mind.

"I've never gotten emails like this from him before. He's very reflective. Harkening to the past." Booker shrugged. "He's sorry, of course."

"Of course." She managed to vocalize her sarcasm through pants.

"He said he plans to pay us back."

"I'll believe it when I have it in the bank."

"Don't be that way, Hon."

"How am I supposed to be?"

Booker didn't answer. She jogged a couple of steps to catch up to him. Her blisters and her knees screamed. She slowed, and the distance between them widened again. It had been widening ever since Booker gave his little brother fifty thousand dollars of their money without asking her opinion.

However, she was angrier about the rift in their marriage, the trust and closeness Joe had stolen from them, than she was the cash. She wasn't happy about the cash, though. She'd about killed herself the past few months taking every job that came her way, trying to restore their nest egg. It was one of the reasons she'd agreed to this hike. The stress of her schedule was getting to her. She could feel it pinching and rubbing like an uncomfortable pair of shoes. All the magazines said exercise would help. So far it wasn't working.

Booker beat her to the car and was leaning on the bumper sipping from a water bottle when she caught up. It wasn't like him to leave her in his dust, but whenever Joe got brought up, he didn't act like himself. She knew he felt guilty. There was nothing she could do about that. She'd forgiven him. At least, she'd said the words. But the emptiness in the retirement account echoed the empty place in her heart.

She understood. If her brother or one of her sisters had been in trouble, had been facing jail time, she'd have loaned them whatever she had. But she would've asked Booker first. She wished he'd have done the same.

Booker handed her a water bottle, and she guzzled it, still feeling dehydrated from the hike. When she was done, she said, "So, where is he?"

"He didn't say."

"Is he going to go home?" she asked.

"I don't think so."

Poor Carla. She didn't deserve this.

"He says Carla is better off without him," Booker said.

"But the girls."

Her husband lifted one shoulder and let it drop.

There was nothing more to say. They sat on the bumper together, letting their sweat dry and gazing at the hills. Soon a battalion of dark SUVs roared past them. They watched while the billowing dust obscured the cars from view, the brown cloud growing smaller and smaller until it disappeared around a bend. That was it then. They'd reported what they'd found, and their part in the tragic event was over. She pushed herself up. "Ready?"

Booker stood. "Yeah."

"Hungry?"

"Yeah."

"I was thinking about making a frittata." The morning had been difficult, terrifying, and upsetting in turns. Food was always a comfort.

CHAPTER THREE

HONEY MADE A right onto the long winding drive of the St. Francis Abbey. The sun slanted through her windshield for a moment, blinding her. As she continued along the arc of the drive, her vision cleared, and she hit the brakes.

The statue had sneaked up on her again. How? She couldn't say. St. Francis was larger than life. A bird the size of a small dog perched on his outstretched hand. Today it was the sun, but the same thing had happened on overcast days.

Two novices, one dark, one fair, both in long black robes waited for her near the entrance to the refectory. She parked, opened the van doors, and inhaled the sugar and dirt smell of produce. She handed a box of fresh salad greens, carrots, and celery root from the farmer's market to the young man with coffee-and-cream eyes. She passed an ice chest full of chicken breasts and broth to the fair-haired boy and filled her own arms with bags of rolls and the egg noodles she'd made the night before.

She'd been coming to Trabuco Canyon weekly for the past six months to cook for the soup kitchen and had grown attached to both the religious community and their guests. She hated to give it up but was afraid she'd have to soon. She had no one to watch the shop when she was out since Willow had moved to San Diego. Her daughter had worked at Sweeter than Honey between ten and fifteen hours a week before she'd left. It was amazing how much help those few hours were.

Honey had been raised with two conflicting virtues: never take charity and never pass up a chance to give it. However, if she wanted to stay true to the former, she might have to give up the latter, at least for a time.

Despite what her father had taught her about not taking charity, they'd done it. When Honey's mother died, and the medical bills started rolling in, all seven of them had found themselves at The Assemblies of God Sunday night free dinners. Honey was in high school at the time and still remembered the sting of humiliation she'd felt pulling up next to the town drunk for a plate of chicken and potatoes. It was important to her to show compassion and respect for people in that same predicament.

The large, industrial kitchen of the refectory seemed out of place in the old stone building, but she was grateful for the modern appliances. Friar Philip bustled through the swinging door that led to the dining room, his feet moving so fast he almost appeared to glide across the tiled floor like a gray ghost. "Honey." He stretched both hands toward her.

"Father." She took them.

"How is our illustrious chef today?"

Honey flushed. She struggled with the praise. She was a good cook. Illustrious chef was a stretch. "About that," she said.

The priest cocked his head to one side, a benign smile on his face.

"I'm afraid I'm going to have to turn the task over to Friar Ambrose."

The benign smile faded. "You're unwell?"

Honey had made the mistake of telling Friar Philip about her diagnosis at the end of last year. He'd lit candles for her on a regular basis since. Her Pentecostal grandmother would have a heart attack if she knew candles were being lit for a member of her family. She'd considered Catholics to be heathens at best, idolaters at worst; it was a sentiment Honey didn't share.

"No, it's not that. It's the business. Ever since Willow got the teaching position in San Diego, I've been swamped."

Father Philip opened his mouth, then shut it as if he was going to say something but thought better of it. Honey was pretty sure she knew what it was. Everybody: Booker, Rosie, Ash, and Willow had all been encouraging her to hire somebody new. She would, eventually.

They were far from broke, but knowing that $50,000 was tucked up in its little nest at the bank had given her a sense of security. Its absence gnawed at her. She couldn't bring herself to spend money she didn't absolutely have to spend.

"Give your daughter my congratulations. I'm very happy for her, although we'll be sorry to lose you." The priest dropped her hands. "But we knew it was temporary when you started. You've been so generous with your time."

"I'll finish out the month."

"I'll let Ambrose know."

Honey reached into her bag for her knives. "Better get started then."

"Brothers Owen and Reginald have offered their services as sous chefs." Philip gestured to the salt and pepper twins.

"Wonderful. I can use the help."

Honey got one novice started scrubbing vegetables in the deep metal sink, while the other dumped jars of chicken broth into soup pots. This was the first time she'd actually made soup for the soup kitchen, but the nip in the air had made her long for chicken noodle soup.

Her mother had made big pots from scratch throughout her growing up years. In a large family, soups and stews were a staple. They stretched. Honey's chicken noodle, with its six-hour broth and homemade pasta, was an homage to her mother. It was a special treat that she didn't make often. Booker hated chicken soup.

An hour later, the kitchen smelled like home on a winter day. Friar Philip burst through the swinging door again in a flurry of black robes. "They're lining up. How are we doing?"

"It's ready," Honey said.

The novices carried the food to a long table in the dining room. Honey followed armed with a ladle. She smiled at the regulars at the front of the queue and spoke to them like friends. The old man who lived in a broken-down trailer. The crazy cat lady who had a house, but also had more felines than the county allowed and spent her Social Security on cat food and litter.

A tired-looking young mother with a pallid complexion hiked a baby with a runny nose higher on her hip as she reached for a tray.

"The baby doing better?" Honey said as she ladled soup into bowls.

"Yeah. It was an ear infection like you thought."

"My son got those chronically," Honey said. "Turned out he was allergic to dairy. Stopped giving him milk, and it cleared right up."

The mother pushed her toddler and preschooler forward. "I'll have to ask the doctor about that."

And, on the line went. Honey greeted, ladled, and caught up. She'd miss this community.

"Are those homemade egg noodles?" An unfamiliar voice, bright but raspy, brought Honey to attention.

She looked from her soup pot into a pair of cat-green eyes. "They are."

"I haven't seen homemade pasta since my Nana died. It's not the same when it's dried." The girl who spoke didn't belong here. She was young, mid-twenties maybe, and beautiful. Her teeth were perfect, her skin creamy, her hair as bright as her eyes.

Behind her stood two equally beautiful young men. One about the same age with hair like rich butterscotch. The other was younger, probably a teenager. He had dark hair and eyes, and despite a lanky frame, he was stunning. All three could be models. Honey was speechless both with surprise and that shyness that sometimes hit her when she was in the presence of exceptionally good-looking people.

"That looks like my mama's soup," the teenager said.

"Naw. Mom never cooked like that." Caramel man laughed.

"You haven't been to the kitchen before." Honey finally found her voice.

"We're pretty new in town," the girl said. "My name is Angela." She held out a delicate hand, and Honey shook it. "This is Zach." She gestured to the man. "And Charlie." She nodded to the boy.

"Nice to meet you," Honey said.

"Can we move it along?" A cranky voice broke up the party. Honey was sorry to see them disappear through the throng.

When the last of the line sat at the long wooden tables to eat, Honey poured a bowl of soup for herself and walked to Friar Philip's table.

He scooted over to make room for her on the bench.

"How do you like the soup? It's an upgraded version of my mother's. She was too busy raising six kids to make noodles from scratch, but the broth is hers."

Four pairs of eyes widened across the table from her.

"Oh." Honey put a hand over her mouth. Six months and she still couldn't remember to be quiet. Although there was no formal vow of silence at the Abbey, speaking during mealtimes was frowned on. She put her head down and ate.

When the only ones left at the table were Honey and Friar Philip, Honey lowered her voice and said, "What's with the beautiful people?"

Friar Philip raised an eyebrow in question.

Honey tipped her head toward the three models across the room.

"Oh, Angela and the boys. They are lovely, aren't they?"

"They stick out like sore thumbs in this crowd."

Friar Philip laughed. "Even beautiful people can fall on hard times."

"But they're so young."

"And impressionable, which I believe was the problem."

It was Honey's turn to raise her eyebrows.

The priest's forehead furrowed. "I don't like to gossip."

Honey stayed silent, hoping he wouldn't talk himself out of sharing the story.

He spooned the last of his soup into his mouth, swallowed, dabbed at his lips with a napkin, then said, "They were deceived."

"Really? By who?"

"I believe that's 'by whom.'" Friar Philip mopped up the last of the broth in his bowl with a hunk of bread and popped it into his mouth with finality. He wasn't going to say any more about it. She tried a different tack.

"Angela said they were new in town."

The priest smiled, happy to be on safer ground. "Charlie and Zach grew up in Black Star Canyon. Their father owns a small ranch out there. Charlie's been living at home all along, but Angela and Zach just moved in."

Black Star? Honey thought about the "no trespassing sign" she'd seen that was as riddled with holes as a block of Swiss cheese. She couldn't believe that was the place, although the friar did say the kids were deceived. The signs reminded her of something you might find outside a cult compound. "It isn't the place with the shot-up No Trespassing sign, is it?"

The friar's lips thinned again. "I believe so."

She opened her mouth to tell him about the body, to tell him to warn Angela and the men that there may be a killer on the loose but closed it again. For all she knew, the dead hiker had died in a lover's quarrel, and there was no danger to anyone. Weren't the majority of murders crimes of passion? Although, her best friend Rosie came close to losing her life last October in an incident that was more about envy and paranoia than passion.

Zach and Charlie's father or another Black Star resident might have shot the hiker. Booker had said the locals were on high alert because of the strange crimes that had happened in the canyon. Things she'd read about the shootout at the Branch Davidian Compound ran through her head. The kind of man who hid in the hills behind all those signs couldn't be normal. "Zach's father can't feed them?" she asked.

Friar Philip opened his arms like the St. Francis statue near the gate. "We welcome those who are struggling without question."

Which was all fine and good, but Honey was curious. She watched as the golden girl stood, gathered her own and her companion's dishes, lined them up along her outstretched arms, and carried them to the dirty dish bucket. She must have been a server at some point. Her balance and sure movements spoke of experience in the food-service industry.

A pang of guilt poked Honey. Was she reticent to tell the friar about the body because she didn't think it was relevant, or because she didn't want to get any more involved than she already was? Every time the memory of that leg sprouting from the earth. . . A shiver shook her. She didn't want to think about it. But, if something happened to Angela or the boys because she hadn't said anything, she'd never forgive herself.

"Booker and I were hiking in Black Star on Saturday."
The priest looked at her with mild interest. "We found a
body," she blurted out the words.

Friar Philip's eyes grew wide. "A dead body?"

"Yes, a hiker. He, or she, had been buried. All the rain
we've been having washed away some of the dirt."

He put a hand over his heart. "Was it an accident?"

Honey shook her head. "The police don't think so, but
they haven't done an autopsy yet. I'm only telling you so
you can warn your parishioners-the ones who live out
there."

"Yes. Thank you. I will."

Honey pushed her chair away from the table and
stood. "I'd better be getting to the shop."

Friar Philip inclined his head as if pronouncing a
blessing on her. "Owen and Reginald will take care of
clean up."

As she turned, she noticed Zach only two tables
away. Their eyes met, and he smiled. Honey's pulse
quickened. It was a good thing Willow was safely out of
Orange County. Women weren't safe around a man that
good-looking.

By the time Honey gathered her things and made it
out to her car, Angela, Zach, and Charlie were gone. Why
was she so fascinated by them? It was true they didn't fit
in at the soup kitchen, but Friar Philip was correct, all
kinds of people fell on hard times. She'd seen many a
Mercedes and BMW parked outside the refectory on
kitchen days.

It must be the strange coincidence. Black Star Canyon
had intruded into her life more in the past three days

than it had in the past three years. She loaded her empty crates into her van.

She'd done enough good deeds for one day. She'd fed the poor soup and information that might protect them. Time to get to the shop and leave the mysteries of life and death to the priests and the police.

CHAPTER FOUR

A BRUNETTE IN wedge heels, tight jeans, and a flowing orange top leaned against the window of Sweeter than Honey Gourmet Cooking Supplies, her face buried in her cell phone. The woman's head rose as Honey pulled into a parking space out front and killed the engine.

It was Lisa, no Liza—maybe Lizzy—Fitzpatrick. Whatever her name was had scheduled a home cooking class for that Friday night. Her being here, leaning against the closed store, couldn't be a good thing. Honey plastered on a professional smile. "Hi. . .you."

"I've been trying to call you all morning," Lisa-Liza said.

Honey pulled her phone from her bag. Sure enough, there were three missed calls. "I'm so sorry. I work at St. Francis's soup kitchen on Mondays."

Lisa-Liza didn't crack a smile. No admiration lit her features. "So, anyway, I tried to call all morning. Your website says you're open weekdays from nine to seven."

Honey strode to the shop door. "We are. I mean, we usually are. My daughter, she used to help out in the shop but moved to San Diego, and I had the appointment at the soup kitchen. . ." She let the words *soup kitchen* hover in the air. Maybe Lisa-Liza hadn't heard her the first time. Surely the woman would give her kudos for feeding the poor.

"You should hire somebody else," Lisa-Liza said.

Apparently, she didn't have an empathetic bone in her Pilates body. The door opened with a jangle of bells. Honey flipped on the lights, bustled to the counter, stowed her purse beneath, and turned. "What were you calling about?" she said in as pleasant a voice as she could muster.

"The party," Lisa-Liza said. "I'm going to have to reschedule. My mother-in-law died." This last was uttered with such a complete lack of emotion, Honey's words of sympathy never left her mouth.

Instead, she said, "Did you have another date in mind?"

The doorbell jingled again, and Rosie, Honey's closest friend, entered. Lisa-Liza pivoted and gave her a cold stare. Rosie assessed the situation, nodded, and wandered toward a shelf of casserole dishes she had no interest in.

Honey pulled up her scheduler on the store computer and offered three available dates to Lisa-Liza.

She didn't like any of them. "Can't you do Saturday, January eighteenth?"

"I try not to work outside the store on Saturdays," Honey said, which earned her another incredulous look from Lisa-Liza. Five beats passed before Honey said, "But I do, on occasion."

Before she could reschedule the party in the computer, the phone rang. "Sweeter than Honey," Honey said into the receiver.

"I'd like to do an early dinner," Lisa-Liza said, ignoring the fact Honey was on the phone.

The voice on the phone said, "I'm looking for one of those juicers, you know the ones that are round and you put the fruit in—"

"Hold, please." Honey pushed the hold button. "Five o'clock?"

"I know we were going to do salmon cakes and asparagus, but now I'm thinking a salad. Maybe something with fennel?"

The door chimes sounded again. A dark-skinned woman with glossy black hair and a lanky teenage girl entered. "Welcome to Sweeter than Honey's," Honey called out. "I'll be with you in a minute." The woman smiled. Her daughter didn't, but she was a teen, so that was to be expected.

"Take your time," the woman said.

"Mom." The teen sounded like a leaky balloon. "I'm supposed to be at swim practice."

"Chicken and fennel. Maybe something with strawberries for dessert," Lisa-Liza said.

Honey's heart stopped beating. Just for a second, but when it started up again, it was as if someone stepped on the gas and wouldn't let up. It raced like it was competing in the Indy 500. Honey sucked in air and tried to exhale it slowly.

The phone rang again. She picked it up. "Sweeter than—"

"I know. Don't put me on hold again. Just tell me if you have one of those juicers. They look like a garlic press on steroids. You know which ones I mean?"

"Yes," Honey managed to get the word out.

"Yes, what? Yes, you know what I'm talking about? Or, yes, you have them?"

"Both."

"What time do you close?"

"Seven." But even as Honey said the word, she wasn't sure she'd make it until seven. Something was wrong. Her heart galloped in her chest. Her breathing was shallow. Nausea made her salivate.

The teen's mother approached the counter with an electric kettle in her hand. "Do you gift wrap?"

Honey's mouth dropped open, but no words came. What was happening to her?

"Yes, we do." Rosie walked up from behind and plucked the kettle from the woman's hand. "I can take care of that. What's the occasion?"

Rosie led the mother and daughter to the back wall of the shop where the gift-wrapping supplies were kept, and Honey sank onto the stool behind the counter.

"Strawberry tarts would be nice," Lisa-Liza said.

Honey agreed to everything she suggested. She'd call and change the menu later. Strawberries weren't in season, and tarts were too complicated for a party class, but she didn't have the strength to take on Lisa-Liza at the moment. All she could think about was getting her out the door, which she did.

Rosie reappeared with the mother-daughter duo and a wrapped box. "Want me to ring it up?"

Honey nodded and disappeared into the relative quiet of her office. She sank into her chair, closed her eyes, and breathed deeply. Dr. Hillary's serious face played on the dark screen of her mind. *For many people, the first symptom of a heart problem is an attack and sudden death. You need to take this seriously, Honey.* The words she'd poo-pooed at the time suddenly seemed grave.

Rosie interrupted her thoughts. "You don't look good."

Honey opened her eyes. "I don't feel good."

Rosie rummaged in the small refrigerator, pulled out water and string cheese. "Maybe it's your blood sugar. What have you eaten today?"

Honey waved away the cheese but accepted the water gratefully. After she polished off half the bottle, she leaned into her chair. "I'll be okay. Just had a busy morning. What brings you in?"

"I came to tell you about a catering job, but I'm reconsidering."

"No, don't reconsider. What's the job?"

"Peter is having an opening at the gallery. It's for a new artist. He wants to make a splash."

Honey reached for her laptop and flipped it on. She could check the desktop computer in the front of the shop, but that would mean getting up. Her heart rate had slowed to a trot, but she didn't want to rev it up again. "What's the date?"

"January seventeenth. Less than two weeks away, I know, but he says people are chomping at the bit to see this guy's work. I can't imagine why."

"Why's that?"

"You know Peter's taste. It's a horrorfest. The artist specializes in landscapes with dead bodies hidden somewhere in the scene. It's like *Where's Waldo* meets *Dexter*."

Honey laughed. She felt better. Rosie was good medicine. "I have that open. Want me to schedule it?"

"Are you up to it?"

"Of course. I told you, I'm tired. That's all."

"Finding a body is a shock. I know."

Rosie did know. She'd had the same unpleasant experience less than six months ago.

"This was different," Honey said. "All I saw was a shoe. I didn't know it was attached to anything at first."

"Sounds familiar."

Honey was sorry she'd mentioned that detail. "Yes, but I don't know who it belongs to. What happened to you was much more traumatic, Rosie. This was upsetting, but I wouldn't call it a shock."

"I think you're making light of it."

"I could try to work up a case of hysteria if it would make you feel better."

Rosie pinched her lips, and changed the subject. "When are you going to replace Willow?"

Honey closed her laptop and pushed her chair out. "Not for a while."

"Why would you put that off?"

"We're in a tight place. I need to bring in more income, not spend it."

"You have to spend money to—"

Honey waved her words away. "I know, to make money, but this is a temporary situation."

"How do you figure? Booker shelled out a lot of cash. You're not going to replace it in a couple of months. You're not going to replace it in a couple of years."

"Joe emailed Booker," Honey said.

Rosie's mouth dropped open. "He did?"

"Yeah. Booker says he's very circumspect. His emails are long and thoughtful. That's not his usual MO."

"Does that mean he's going to make amends? Pay you guys back, go home and face the music?"

"Booker seems to think so, but I don't know," Honey said.

A line creased Rosie's forehead. "Did he tell Booker why he embezzled the funds in the first place?"

Honey shook her head. "No. Book said something about Joe being in an investment club, but stealing from a church fund for that seems like a stretch. Carla pays the bills. The girls get free tuition at their private school because Carla is the principal. I happen to know her daddy bought them that big house. They were doing okay."

"Does he gamble?" Rosie asked.

"I don't think so, but I guess I don't know Joe very well. You'd think with all his trips out to California, he and I would've gotten close. We didn't though. He was happy running around doing whatever he was doing, going for hikes with Booker, and eating my food. I was happy he was busy. Honestly, I've never liked him all that much. Always seemed so impulsive. I think if it wasn't for Carla, he might have ended up in jail a whole lot sooner."

"You think he's going to end up in jail?"

"Not if Booker has anything to say about it. My husband is a hero. A real one. He's rescued children from burning buildings, but that's not enough for him. He's on-call twenty-four seven for that ne'er do well brother of his." Honey heard the bitterness in her own voice.

"Look who's talking. You're as bad as he is. Maybe not with Joe, but with everybody else. You've been working yourself to the bone lately. I'm worried about you."

The doorbell jangled, and Honey stood. "Gotta make hay while the sun shines, as Daddy used to say whenever he opened a bottle of Jack Daniels."

After she helped two middle-aged women purchase a pressure cooker, she returned to Rosie who waited in the office.

"Work is therapy. When I get mad at Booker, mad at Joe, I take it out on my cutting board." Honey continued the conversation as if it had never been interrupted.

"How long are you going to be able to keep it up?" Rosie said.

"I'm pacing myself." Which was a complete lie and both of them knew it.

"I just signed with a new client, but I could bring in my laptop and help manage the shop here and there." Rosie was an interior designer. Her career had taken off thanks to recent circumstances that had landed her in the news. Infamy, or fame, whatever she had now, it was working for her.

"No." Honey shook her head. "You've got your own business to run. I'm fine. I really am. Stop fussing."

Rosie searched Honey's face so intently, Honey looked away. "Okay, but you have to promise me that you'll at least think about getting someone in the shop part-time."

"Yes, ma'am," Honey said, but she didn't intend to keep that promise. An echo of the nausea she'd felt earlier cramped her stomach. She would keep her promise to Booker, though. As soon as she got home, she'd look for that diet plan Dr. Hillary had given her.

CHAPTER FIVE

FURY LEAPED AROUND her then darted to the hook where Honey kept his leash and back again. "You don't know how tired I am," she said to the dog. He grinned and wagged. Apparently, he didn't care either. "Oh, alright, but only around the block. You hear me?"

He scampered to the leash hook again, showing her he did hear. Honey clicked on the leash and walked out in the chilly evening air. It was only five-thirty, but it was almost dark. A half-moon hovered on the horizon.

Fury led her around the corner to his favorite block. There were homes on one side of the street, but the other was an unbuilt hillside. It was the perfect place for neighborhood dogs to leave messages for one another. Fury raced to a cape honeysuckle, its orange flowers neon under the streetlights, and lifted his leg.

Honey and Booker had inherited the dog from one of Rosie's former clients. He came at an opportune time, seven months after Bruiser, their old boxer, went on to that great dog park in the sky.

Honey's phone jangled in her jacket pocket. She fished it out, glanced at the screen and answered. "Hi, baby," she said.

"Hi, Mom. What're you doing?"

"Walking Fury."

"You have a minute to talk?"

Honey smiled at the ridiculous question. When did she ever *not* have time for her daughter? Willow had stayed close for college, getting a master's in music from UCI, but last fall she was hired to teach at a private school in San Diego. It wasn't far, only about an hour and a half away, but Honey missed her terribly. "Of course, what's up?"

"I heard you and Dad found a dead body. How come nobody tells me anything?"

"Someone told you that."

"Ash did."

"How did he find out? I thought he didn't talk to anyone outside the base."

"Conner told him." Conner was Rosie and Eric's youngest child and Ash's best friend.

Honey exhaled in frustration. "How do any of you know about it? Your dad and I weren't going to say anything until we knew the details."

"You still don't know who it was or how they died?"

"No. We don't."

"Poop. That's why I was calling."

"How did Conner hear about it?"

"He has a friend who works in the Sheriff's Department. I guess your names were on the police report, so he called Ash."

"It's impossible to keep anything quiet in this family."

"Conner said the police released it to the press today. You should turn on the local news. I don't think it's big enough to go national."

"I will."

"I talked to Kort today," Willow said, losing interest in the body.

Honey inhaled slowly. Kortney was Joe's oldest child. Honey had been meaning to call Carla for weeks. When she first heard about Joe's disappearance, she'd called at least once every few days for an update, but as time went on, it almost seemed cruel. Carla never had anything new to tell her. "How is she doing?"

"Not good. She misses Uncle Joe a lot. I think she needed to vent, and she can't talk to her mom about it."

A shadow rustled the bushes. It was probably a tree rat. There had been a lot of them in the neighborhood lately. Fury darted toward it instead of away as Honey would've preferred. "Why can't she talk to Carla?"

"Because Aunt Carla doesn't want to talk about it. She's really mad."

"You can't blame her."

"I don't know. Kortney thinks the church would have tried to have her dad sent to jail no matter what. She believes he's innocent, of course, thinks he's hiding out somewhere waiting for them to find their bookkeeping error like they did last time."

Honey didn't know what to say. She couldn't tell Willow about the money they'd loaned her uncle. She'd promised Booker she wouldn't say anything to the kids. She pulled Fury out of the bushes and strode up the block as if she could outpace the conversation.

"Mom? You there?"

"Yeah. I'm here."

"What do you think?"

"About Joe?"

Honey heard a frustrated exhale through the phone. "No, about global warming. Yes, of course, about Uncle Joe. What have we been talking about?"

"I'm sorry, sweetheart. Fury was after a tree rat."

"You should take him to obedience classes."

"I know," Honey said. "He's getting better, though. Dad took him to the dog park last week. He didn't let him off the leash but—"

"You're changing the subject." Willow was too smart for her own pants.

It was Honey's turn to sigh. "I think Joe is gone. I don't think he's coming back."

"Do you think he took the money?"

Honey waited one beat too long before answering. "I don't know what to think." She hated lying to her children.

"Aunt Carla does."

"How do you know that?"

"Kortney said they were going to get divorced even before this whole thing happened. She said they've been fighting for at least a year."

"About what?" Honey snapped her mouth closed as soon as the words exited them. She shouldn't be gossiping about Booker's brother with their daughter, but she needed to know what was going on. It was her retirement account that was at stake.

"Aunt Carla won't talk about that either, but Kort thinks it was another woman."

Honey turned the corner onto her own street. "What?" Joe had never been her favorite person, but she hadn't thought of him as a philanderer. "I don't think—"

"Kortney knows more than we do, Mom."

Honey pulled her keys from her pocket and let herself into her house, flipping on lights to avoid stumbling on the piles of things she left lying about whenever Booker was at the station. It was a bad habit. She always had to race around before he came home straightening up shoes, mail, books, whatever had come into the house since he'd been gone.

"So, how'd your date go last week?" She was tired of thinking about Joe and didn't want to waste any more of her precious Willow time on him. He'd cost her too much already.

"Okay. He wasn't a complete loser." As Willow filled her in on the evening, Honey rummaged in the refrigerator for something for dinner. She didn't cook when Booker was at the station either, which didn't mean she ate healthfully. Instead of chopping veggies for a salad or stir fry, she tended to make a grilled cheese or hot dog, neither of which were doctor-approved.

A memory of the heart palpitations at the shop sent her into the vegetable bin to retrieve a head of lettuce, peppers, and a cucumber. "Are you going to see him again?"

"I don't know. I don't think I'll like him any better the second time." Willow promised to call and let her know if the not-complete-loser called her again, and they hung up.

Honey fed Fury, made a salad for herself, and walked into the living room. She pushed a stack of cooking magazines off the coffee table to make room for her plate, picked up the remote, and clicked on the TV.

She scrolled through the channels until she came to the local news channel. She was as curious as Willow to find out the identity of The Leg now that she wasn't sitting next to it on a boulder in the wilderness.

A story about a mudslide in Laguna Beach ended, and the station went to a commercial break. She pondered her schedule as she poked at the salad in her bowl. She had to get a hold of Peter to discuss catering for Nightshade's art show, rethink the menu for Lisa-Liza's cooking party, decide what she needed to get in stock at the shop for spring and summer, and start the orders. Maybe Rosie and Booker were right. Maybe she did need to hire someone.

"Two hikers found the body of an unidentified male in Black Star Canyon on Saturday," a woman on the television said. Honey turned the volume up. "The medical examiner's office estimates he's been dead for two to three months. Someone had buried the body, but recent heavy rains unearthed it."

The pretty brunette touched her ear as the screen split and displayed an anchorman in the studio. "Do they know how he died, Regina?"

"They haven't released that information yet, Bart, but have said they believe there was foul play."

Bart furrowed his smooth brow as much as the Botox would allow. "A tragic circumstance, and a little scary too."

"Absolutely. The Ranger's department has put out a bulletin reminding hikers to stay alert and hike in groups whenever possible."

"Always a good policy," Bart said.

"Yes, and especially now. I can tell you; I won't be hiking alone until police know exactly what happened to this poor unfortunate individual."

Bart nodded solemnly. "Thanks for the update, Regina. Keep us posted."

"Will do, Bart." Regina's side of the screen closed.

Honey flicked off the TV. She hadn't learned anything she didn't already know, other than that The Leg was male.

She stood and carried her bowl into the kitchen, her imagination running hot. A scene played through it like the opening of a movie.

A young man, who looks a lot like Ash, wears new hiking boots. He and a tough-looking guy hike up a steep hill. They're headed to the falls. Ash is smiling, happy to be out hiking with a buddy.

They stop near a pile of boulders for a short rest before continuing on to the falls. The tough guy wants Ash to do something Ash doesn't want to do, maybe a drug deal, maybe a robbery. They argue. Tough guy gets in Ash's face. Ash shoves him away. He grabs Ash's shoulders, pushes him to the ground. Ash is throwing punches but they're wild, not making contact. Tough guy—

Fury whined at the cupboard door where the biscuits were kept. "Thank you," she said as she reached into the box and gave him one. She didn't need those thoughts in her head, not this close to bed. Not when Ash was an hour's drive away.

Honey liked to think empty nest was a thing of the past, that she was proud and happy her children were out on their own. All that was true. Most of the time. But whenever she heard a deadly news story about a young man or woman her own children's ages, fear pierced her like an ice pick.

She hated the idea that Willow was meeting men online. She got hot flashes whenever she thought about Ash being deployed to some dangerous corner of the world. She rinsed her dish and put it into the dishwasher. The truth was she had no idea how old the hiker was, and she had no idea how he died. Fury pawed at the cupboard door again. She bent to offer the dog another biscuit. "Last one."

As she stood, a package of chocolate chip cookies caught her eye. She shouldn't. Sugar never fixed anything. It only made things worse. If she ate the cookies, she'd feel sick and guilty. Cookies were right up there with bacon as far as Dr. Hillary was concerned. Honey pulled the box from the cupboard, set it on the counter, and stared at it.

One wouldn't hurt. She popped a cookie into her mouth whole. Booker would be home in two days. She'd cook something healthy then. She ate two more. And, maybe he'd have learned what really happened to the dead hiker at the station. She ate another cookie. Maybe he'd have learned the hiker was sixty-five and had a heart attack. Another cookie disappeared into her mouth. Hopefully he'd learn something that would stop the bad movies playing in her mind. Honey polished off half the box before closing the package.

Her stomach roiled as she padded through the house, turning off lights. Why had she done that? Probably because she'd promised herself she'd go on that diet. Diet. The word made her feel rebellious and hungry.

Fury followed her from room to room. When Booker was gone, she let the dog sleep at the foot of the bed. As soon as he sensed she was done for the night, he stuck to her like glue fearful he'd miss out.

She closed the blinds on the sliding door that led onto the backyard and heard a quiet growl behind her. The dog had stopped. His head was low, his hackles high, his nose pointed toward the glass.

"What's the matter?" she said.

The deep growl rose in pitch.

Honey paused, unsure of what to do. There was probably a cat in the yard. Fury didn't share her love for America's other favorite pet. Or a possum. He didn't like them either. But cats and possums were about most nights, and he'd never behaved like this before.

She could open the door and let him run off whatever was outside. She placed a hand on the handle, then paused. What if the creature in her yard was dangerous? Or rabid?

She dropped her arm to her side and turned to Fury. If she took him upstairs, he'd forget all about it. She bent to lift him. Before she got a grip, he charged the door, his growl now a threatening bark.

Honey pushed the blinds aside with a finger and peered into the dark yard. There was nothing visible outside the small circle of light shed by the bulb at the back door. Fury's sense of smell must detect something her eyes couldn't.

Pressure in her chest grew to match the volume of her dog's clamor. She leaned on the couch, trying to catch her breath. It was happening again. Her heart thudded like it had in the shop earlier today.

She shouldn't have eaten the cookies.

The thought trotted through the noise in her head, although a rational part of her knew a handful of cookies, even a big handful, wouldn't cause a reaction like this. She promised herself she'd start following the doctor's orders anyway. Tomorrow. She'd start tomorrow.

She repeated the words to herself as Fury's bark became a growl then quieted, and as her pulse slowed and the weight on her chest lifted. When the dog stopped pacing and dropped to his belly, she said, "Are we done here?"

She shoved off the couch and headed toward the stairs, flipping on a small lamp in the kitchen as she walked past it. She usually turned off all the lights, but leaving the downstairs in darkness didn't seem like a good idea tonight.

CHAPTER SIX

Email dated: December 29th

Dear Booker,

HAVE YOU EVER wished you were somebody else? Stupid question. I know you never have. You're everyone's hero.

I, on the other hand, wish I was somebody else all the time. Especially now that things have gotten so screwed up. By now you know I've taken off, left Carla and the girls. And by now you also know I never paid off the church with the money you sent. Despite what you must be thinking, both of those decisions were good ones.

I did borrow money from the church. I admitted that to everyone concerned when they confronted me last August. I intended to pay it off with the cash you sent, but once I had the check, I rethought things.

Four years ago, when the church accused me of siphoning money from the mission fund, it ruined my reputation. I was innocent, but that didn't matter. I know the pastor and the elders reinstated me as treasurer as a sign of good faith, but people believe what they want to believe. I guess it was the old "where there's smoke" thing, or maybe a hangover from my younger years. I don't know.

I tried to fix it, Book. I really tried. I ran the board without pay. I donated money to the church—money I couldn't afford to donate. I built houses with Habitat for Humanity in Mercer County, helped on local church projects, attended mission conferences around the country on my own dime. I brought new ideas to the table, introduced the board to all kinds of charities. I outlined a plan to start a home for troubled teens. It didn't seem to matter.

I felt like I was pushing a boulder up a never-ending hill. Every time I stopped to rest, it slid to the bottom again. Didn't that happen to some guy in a Greek myth? I wonder what kind of sadist thought up that punishment. It's terrible, especially if it's totally undeserved. You were smart to move away. Rumors never die in small towns.

I'm not making excuses, just explaining. I feel like you deserve the whole story, since you have skin in the game.

The fact is, one year after the first incident I was in debt up to my eyeballs, and it was the church's fault. My boss at the tool and die shop was an elder. No way I was moving up in that company. I was fraying. Coming unraveled. I wanted to leave Lawrenceburg, start over somewhere nobody knew me, but I had nothing to start over with.

I was stuck. I couldn't atone for my past sins. Nothing I ever did was ever going to be good enough. The church had no intention of letting me off the hook even if I repaid what I'd taken. In fact, I could tell it was as if they now felt justified about accusing me four years ago, like somehow their mistake was my fault.

I realized right then and there my responsibility was to my family. Family are the people who have your back. Family are the ones who bail you out. Not these jerks.

I decided to do what I should have done a long time ago. Leave. I'm starting over with the money you gave me, Booker, but I'm going to pay you back with interest. You're family, and you deserve it. As for Carla and the kids, I can only say I believe they're better off without me. They shouldn't have to pay the price for the prejudice against me in Lawrenceburg. Her daddy will take care of them better than I can right now. If you talk to her, tell her she needs to forget me and move on. It's for the best.

I keep thinking about all those great hiking trips we took the past couple of years, Whiting Ranch, Top of the World, Black Star. Those were good times, bro. When all this settles, we'll do it again.

Love,
Joe

CHAPTER SEVEN

HONEY RACED AROUND the house scooping up magazines, shoes, sweaters, and jackets. Why was she such a slob when Booker was gone? Maybe it was rebellion. He was so neat she felt the pressure. It was one of the only things they'd ever fought about, until recently.

Of course, now they fought about Joe. Well, not directly. He'd asked her to let it go, forgive him. He'd acknowledged he should have talked to her about it before he'd written the check. She'd agreed, and she didn't bring it up anymore. Instead, she worked.

In the past when Booker got home after a stint at the station, she'd have taken the morning off, made him a big breakfast or lunch. Maybe they'd pop upstairs for a little dessert afterward, but no more. She was too busy. Was that rebellion too? Maybe, but she didn't have time to analyze it.

After dumping a load of magazines on the table in her home office and running the castoff clothing up to her side of the bedroom closet, she headed outside. She had an appointment with Peter at the gallery at noon and wanted to open the shop for a few hours first.

Booker pulled into the driveway before she reached her car. She tightened her lips in annoyance. Now she'd be late. Shame quickly followed that thought. Annoyance? Really? That was her reaction when her husband arrived home after three days away? She tacked on a smile and tried to make it genuine. "Hey there."

He got out of his car and closed the door, his movements languid. His shoulders sloped. There were dark circles under his eyes. He looked exhausted.

"Was there a fire?" she said, her shame increasing.

"Nothing big. Grease fire in a kitchen yesterday. Couple of false alarms and a heart attack the day before. Pretty quiet."

"Why. . ." She was going to ask him why he looked so drawn, but thought better of it. She knew the situation with Joe was wearing on him, and she didn't have time to get into a big conversation.

"Why?" he said.

"Nothing." She put her hands on his shoulders and gave him a kiss. "There's cold cuts in the fridge. I can't cook. I've got to open Sweeter."

"You need to hire somebody to replace Willow." Booker sounded like a petulant child.

"Hm," was all she said. She clicked open the van door with her key fob, which reminded her of using a remote, which reminded her of the story on the news Monday night. "Oh." She pivoted. "I heard the body we found was a man's."

He nodded, a slow laborious movement as if his head weighed more than it usually did. "Yeah. They don't know who he is yet. They're checking the missing persons database. They'll release a sketch when the artist is done, see if anybody knows him."

"Do they know how he died?" Honey wanted to put her horrible imaginations to rest. Maybe the death was awful, maybe it wasn't, but not knowing was the worst.

"Head injury, I believe."

Honey felt a trickle of relief. It might not be murder after all. "Could he have fallen?"

"No. He was hit. Probably a rock. There are plenty of them up there."

The relief dried up, replaced by something cold. Honey had stood on the spot where a man was murdered, walked where his killer walked.

Booker covered a yawn with one of his large hands.

"Were you up all night?" She didn't think murder was all that boring.

"The grease fire was called in at ten-thirty. By the time we put it out, got back to the station, and cleaned up our gear it was at least one. Then I couldn't sleep. You know how it is when your adrenaline is pumping. I couldn't shut it down. I ended up watching old movies until three."

Honey could relate. The past couple of nights hadn't been much better for her. Fury had been restless, patrolling the house and snarling at the dark windows. "Why don't you take a nap?" Booker hugged her and ambled toward the front door reminding her of a bear heading to his lair to hibernate.

* * *

The shop was blissfully quiet. Honey caught up on all her paperwork. At noon, she put an "Out to Lunch" sign on the door, set its paper clock for one-thirty, and headed to Laguna Beach. When she crested the hill on Crown Valley Parkway and saw the sun sparkling on the ocean and white puffs of clouds floating on the crisp air, her spirits lifted. She was suddenly very glad to be alive.

Perhaps it was seeing the face of death, well, the foot of death anyway, that brought on the feeling. She'd been so focused on Joe and the money she'd forgotten all she had to be thankful for. She'd spent too much time peering into the dark looking for lost things and not enough time enjoying everything the sun shone on.

Honey was a perfectionist, although few would guess it. Those who didn't know her well looked at her messy house and assumed her brain looked the same. It didn't.

She carefully created and followed her own recipes. Cooking was more than an art, it was the science of salt, fat, and acid. She considered baking the oldest form of chemistry. Although the rest of her home was disorganized, the tools of her trade were not. Meal planning was an orderly event carried out with great attention to detail. Nothing drove her crazier than to stand at the counter, all ready to cook and discover she was missing an ingredient.

That's how she'd been feeling lately—like she was missing an ingredient. It wasn't the money, although that bothered her. It wasn't that Joe had disappeared, and no one knew where he'd gone. It was, she now realized, that her control had slipped.

Booker took control away from her when he gave their savings to Joe without asking. According to Dr. Hillary, Honey's body was out of control. And, she had to admit, her eating habits had spun out of control as well. Enough was enough. She might not be able to replace every missing ingredient, but she could create a new recipe. It was time to regain control of her life.

Her Pollyanna mood followed her into Nightshade, then died a sudden death. Things hidden in the dark should be the tag line for Peter's gallery. Most of his paintings were pleasant enough at first glance, but second, third, and fourth glances revealed things she wished she hadn't seen. Rosie, who was closer to Peter than Honey was, described the gallery as *The Nightmare on Coast Highway*.

She entered through the rear door, which led to a large room Peter used as his office and tried not to look at the paintings leaning against the walls. "Peter." She called out to him instead of wandering through the gallery.

"Coming." His voice traveled from the showroom. A moment later, he appeared. Peter was small and pale, his pallor emphasized by the shades of black and charcoal gray he always wore. Eric, Rosie's husband, was convinced he was a vampire.

"I've procured a repast." He spread his hands to emphasize the sandwiches and salads set out on the long table between them. "It's nothing like the fare you create, but we mere mortals do what we can."

"It looks great." It did. Honey realized she'd skipped breakfast again. They sat, and Peter handed her a paper plate. She helped herself to half a turkey sandwich even though she wanted the Italian, then rewarded herself for her virtuousness with a large scoop of potato salad. "Tell me about the art show. Do you have a theme in mind?"

Peter launched into an explanation of the new artist's work. As he spoke, Honey had visions of bloody meats; fish and fowl served with their heads; and chocolate-covered insects for dessert. He wrapped up his monologue with, "Tex-Mex, maybe? What do you think?" Nothing about what he'd described said Tex-Mex to Honey. "Marco hides bodies and, of course, skulls in every piece of art."

"Of course," Honey said around a bite of sandwich.

"I know it's the wrong time of year for *El Dia de Los Muertos*, but the theme fits. Marco's largest work is a desert scene, sort of a *Breaking Bad* thing. A dead drug dealer behind a cactus."

A light bulb clicked on in Honey's mind. "Oh, good idea." It certainly was better than what she'd imagined.

"I ordered a bull's skull complete with horns. We could use it for a centerpiece."

"I like that. How about we serve an assortment of tamales? I could do savory and sweet."

Peter clapped his hands together. "I love it. I'm so over taco bars."

They finished planning, and Honey looked at her watch. It was one-fifteen. She pushed her chair away from the table. "I have plenty to work with. I'll run recipes by you through email, but call me if you have more ideas."

"Wonderful. One more thing, a buffet table is fine, but I'd like to have at least one server moving through the guests with finger foods and drinks. Can your lovely daughter come?"

Willow had helped Honey out at another gallery's Christmas party last year. Peter had been in attendance and was obviously impressed by her. "I don't think so. She's living and working in San Diego now. She couldn't make it in time. Not with traffic."

"Too bad." Peter's mouth turned down, but only for a second. He smiled as quickly as he'd frowned. "I'm sure you can find someone."

Honey said she would and left. Her mind churned through possible candidates all the way to the shop. Everyone she thought of was either too inexperienced, or too expensive, or didn't live close enough for a Friday night party.

The image of the young blonde from the food kitchen balancing plates along one arm popped into her mind. Angela. If the girl was eating at the soup kitchen, she must need cash. But Honey didn't know anything about her. Nothing other than that she moved like a pro and wasn't hard on the eyes. Peter would be thrilled to have a walking, talking *objet d'art* serving his guests.

Honey could tell Friar Philip knew more about the three young people than he'd been willing to share. Perhaps he'd also know how to get a hold of the girl and if it would be a good idea to hire her. Honey decided to call him as soon as she returned to the shop.

CHAPTER EIGHT

BY THE TIME she closed up Sweeter for the evening, Honey was humming to herself. It had been a good day. She'd resolved Lisa-Liza's menu. She'd sold three casseroles, five of those new pressure cookers everybody and their brother wanted these days, and an entire seven-piece set of stainless-steel cookware.

Friar Philip thought Angela would be an excellent choice for Peter's party. He assured Honey that Angela had arrived in her current situation through no fault of her own. He'd contacted the girl as soon as they'd hung up the phone, then called back to say she'd be in for an interview the next day. Things were coming together, even without Willow.

Honey was in such a good mood she made a detour to a fancy butcher shop and bought an overpriced piece of salmon for Booker's dinner. He loved her blackened fish. Then she made another stop for vegetables.

She pushed open the front door with a hip—her arms filled with bags—and called his name, but the house was dark. Fury was the only one to greet her. "Hey, baby." Honey high-stepped her way around the dog, walked into the dim kitchen, and deposited her bags on the counter. "Booker," she called again.

His pickup was in the driveway, so he had to be home. He couldn't still be asleep, could he? She climbed the stairs to their bedroom, turning on lights as she went. She paused with her hand on the bedroom switch. If he was sleeping, she wasn't sure she wanted to wake him. Her eyes adjusted to her surroundings, and she could see that the bed was empty.

She trotted down the stairs, a tickle of anxiety traveling with her. She had no reason to be anxious. Booker was an adult. He probably took a walk, but then why hadn't he taken Fury? Maybe he was at the neighbor's. Magda, the widow across the street, had a longer honey-do list for him than Honey did. She reassured herself with these words, but unfortunately her mind and her body weren't on speaking terms these days. The Leg injected itself into her mental images. Her good mood was slipping away.

Anxiety had plagued her on and off since her mother's unsuccessful fight with cancer. Her mother's untimely death was only the first in a cascade of curses that had descended on her family. Her father's grief led him to the bottle. His alcoholism brought pain and poverty down on them all. Some of her siblings had never recovered. Their lives were littered with broken marriages, broken children, and broken bank accounts.

Honey had managed to overcome her childhood trauma. She'd graduated from cooking school with honors, worked in some of the best restaurants in Louisville, married a handsome, responsible firefighter, and they'd had two great kids. Now she had her own business and a home in Southern California. Life had been good to her.

There was no logical reason for anxiety to rear its dark, ugly head from the grave she'd shoved it into. But it was whispering in her ear again. *Grab, get, and guzzle because there may be a famine tomorrow.*

If the empty bank account had revived it, finding the hiker's body had given it new language. *Life is fragile. Life is dangerous. There are no guarantees.* Not for her, not for her children, not for Booker. Her heart tripped and thudded.

She'd call him and find out where he was. That would calm her. Honey perched on the edge of the couch and punched his number into her cell phone. One ring. Two. Three. Four. His voice mail popped on. Honey's heart raced. She didn't leave a message.

Water. Water would help. She was probably dehydrated. The last glass she'd had was at Peter's gallery at lunchtime. She moved to the kitchen, leaning on the counter for support, and filled a glass at the sink. She downed it in four gulps, refilled her glass, and returned to the couch. A cold sweat broke out on her forehead. Nausea rolled through her gut.

Maybe it had been the potato salad. The mayonnaise must have been old. Honey preferred to make her own aiolis for this very reason. She rested her head on the couch and propped her feet on the coffee table, knocking three library books onto the floor in the process. She didn't care. Her breath was coming in short gasps now. Where was Booker?

Honey wasn't sure how many minutes had passed when she heard the rattle of the front door and Fury's happy yelp. "Hon?" He was home.

"In here." She forced the words through lips that felt thick and clumsy.

"Magda's garbage disposal is broken. She's going to have to get—" He stopped short. "You okay?"

"No. I think it was the mayonnaise." Her response was a mumble.

A moment later, Booker's cool hands were on her face, turning it to his. "Tell me your symptoms." His paramedic training came to the forefront.

"I think I'm going to throw up." She spoke in gasps now. "And I can't breathe. I feel like an elephant is sitting on my chest."

Booker lifted her from the couch in one abrupt motion.

"What are you doing?" she said.

"Taking you to the emergency room."

* * *

Two hours later, the doctor entered the room where Honey lay hooked to a heart monitor and IV. Booker stood nearby. The doctor, a woman with a straw-colored ponytail and a space between her front teeth, looked too young. She could be one of Ash or Willow's friends. "I have good news," she said. "You didn't have a heart attack."

Booker exhaled and dragged a hand through his hair. "Thank God."

Before Honey could ask what had happened to her, the doctor said, "My guess is it was a panic attack. The symptoms are very similar. I've written you a prescription for benzodiazepine that should get you through this until you see a psychiatrist." The child doctor ripped a page off a prescription pad and handed it to Booker.

"A psychiatrist?" Honey tried to sit up, but her head spun. Whatever they'd put in her IV made her woozy. "I don't need a psychiatrist."

"Panic attacks need to be diagnosed by a mental health professional so the correct protocol can be determined," the doctor said.

"I did not have a panic attack," Honey said.

The doctor chewed her lip.

Booker spoke up. "What do you think that was, Hon?"

"I told you, I think it was the mayonnaise."

"It wasn't mayonnaise," Booker said.

The child doctor spoke in the calm voice kindergarten teachers and dog trainers often use. "The best way to settle the argument is to see a psychiatrist. If you don't have one already, the front desk can give you a referral."

"I certainly don't have a psychiatrist," Honey said.

"That would be great," Booker said.

They didn't speak on the drive home. Honey was too drowsy from the medication to argue. Booker pulled into the driveway, turned off the engine, and pivoted in his seat to face her. "There's nothing shameful about going to a psychiatrist. Firefighters, police officers, welfare workers, we all see shrinks after bad cases."

"You've never gone to a shrink," Honey said.

"I have. You just didn't know about it."

"When?"

"Two years ago, after that house fire."

"When the baby died?"

Booker nodded. "It was just so darn sad. I couldn't get it out my mind."

"Did you take drugs?"

"No. I talked it out, but I would've taken them if I'd needed them."

She thought about that for a minute. "But nothing happened to me," she finally said.

"You found a dead body. That's not a common occurrence in Southern California."

"True," she said. She didn't tell him this wasn't the first time her heart had tried to fight its way out of her chest, only the worst.

He continued his assessment of her situation. "When the kids left, you started working way too hard too. You've been running on adrenaline—adrenaline, caffeine, and sugar—for a long time. Add to that a shock like we had on the hike and bam, your body reacts. Look at this as a wakeup call, babe."

It was very convenient how he'd completely ignored the very thing that had knocked her off-kilter in the first place—the damn money. She couldn't talk about it anymore, though. She was exhausted. "I need to head to bed."

Booker wrapped an arm around her shoulders, pulled her close and kissed the top of her head. "I love you. Please, start taking care of yourself. Okay?"

She would as soon as she didn't feel like she'd keel over.

Fury was ecstatic when they entered the house, leaping and flipping in the air. "It's okay, boy. It's okay," Booker tried to calm him. "He was worried about you."

"He didn't get dinner." After she said the word dinner, she groaned. Booker turned a worried gaze on her. She held up a hand. "I brought salmon for you. It's sitting on the counter. It'll have to go into the trash now."

"That's okay. I can grab a sandwich. Want me to make you one?"

"No, thanks. I'm too tired to eat." Honey headed toward the bedroom. Twenty minutes later, she was asleep.

CHAPTER NINE

A BREEZE TICKLED Honey's nose. She sneezed but didn't open her eyes. Her bed was soft and warm, too soft and warm to leave. She burrowed farther under the covers. She couldn't remember the last time she'd slept so deeply and dreamlessly. She'd like a bottle of whatever they'd given her at the hospital.

Her eyes flew open. Hospital. The events of the night before galloped into her head. She threw off the covers and padded into the bathroom. Lying there thinking about having a panic attack would give her another one.

When she got downstairs, she found Booker in the dining room sipping a cup of coffee and working on his laptop. He shut it as soon as he saw her. "I was going to make oatmeal. Want some?" His tone was nonchalant.

He knew she hated oatmeal. "No, thank you. Can I make you eggs?"

"How about an egg white omelet?"

He was so transparent. He hated egg white omelets almost as much as she hated oatmeal. "White is an unnatural color for an omelet." She parroted his words.

"Hon, after last night. . ."

"Last night had nothing to do with my cholesterol unless it was the stress from having to change my eating habits that got to me." Honey strode into the kitchen and began pulling the things she needed for a cheese omelet from the refrigerator and cupboards and slamming them on the counter as loudly as possible. Neither she nor Booker had dinner the night before. In her opinion, they needed something substantial. It turned out she was correct. Despite his protests, Booker devoured his eggs.

"Can you clean up?" she said when they were done eating.

"Sure. You go rest."

"Rest? I'm going to work."

"Do you think that's wise?"

"I have an appointment with a possible hire."

Booker's eyes widened. "To replace Willow?"

"Not sure about that. I need someone to help with catering. We'll see how she works out there before talking about the shop."

Booker stared into his coffee cup. She could tell by the furrowed brow and the thin line of his lips that he was trying not to lecture her. He'd said it all before.

She put a hand on top of his. "I hope she works out. I'm starting to think maybe you're right. I need help at least a couple of hours a week."

His face relaxed, and his eyes lifted to meet hers. "Just don't work too hard today."

"I won't. Promise." She pushed away from the table and went upstairs.

Honey took extra time getting dressed. She washed her hair, blew it dry with a round brush, and applied her twelve-minute face. She had a seven-minute face for everyday use and a twelve-minute one for fancier occasions. Although she wasn't going anywhere fancy, the twelve-minute face might give her more confidence.

Her hand shook as she applied eyeliner. She was still weak from the day before, but she was also nervous about meeting with Angela, which was silly. Honey was in the power position, the employer not the employee, but there was something about the girl Honey couldn't put her finger on. Maybe it was just her stunning good looks.

It could be that, or it could be that Honey hadn't ever hired a stranger before. The only people who'd worked at the shop were her daughter and her best friend. Hiring a stranger seemed a daunting task, but she had to face it.

She gave her hair a final poof in the mirror. The heart palpitations she'd experienced on Monday, coupled with the completely debilitating symptoms she'd had the night before, had scared her more than she liked to admit. Booker wasn't the only one who'd thought she was having a heart attack. Thank God she hadn't. A panic attack was embarrassing and no picnic, but it wasn't a heart attack.

Booker flipped his laptop closed as she entered the dining room. He'd been doing that a lot lately. "Looking at porn?" She didn't believe that was the reason, but it was starting to bug her.

He made a lecherous face. "What am I supposed to do if you leave me home alone all the time?"

"How about the lawn? It needs mowing." Honey kissed the top of his head and left.

* * *

Angela arrived at Sweeter at ten forty-five. The door chime jangled and sunshine entered. Everything about her was bright: her eyes, her hair, her smile, her pale skin that was only a shade darker than the plain white shirt she wore like a designer dress. "I'm a little early," she said in a husky voice that didn't quite fit her appearance.

Honey felt the stress she'd been under lift. The dark mood that had been flapping its wings around her head like a vulture flew away. "That's fine," she said, using the word the way her Granddaddy had. When he'd said "fine" it evoked china or dining. It was as far from the dismissive "okay" that fell from other people's lips as Kentucky was from Southern California.

"I was so excited when Friar Philip called," Angela said.

Honey gestured toward her office door. "Why don't we sit and talk?"

Angela's head swiveled as she walked through the shop. "I love your place. I'm a total kitchen gadget junkie."

"You like to cook then?" Honey sat behind her desk, and Angela took the chair opposite. She smelled of summer—of lemons and of laundry that'd been dried in the sun.

"When I was a kid, I read cookbooks instead of comic books." She pushed a typed resume across Honey's desk with a slender hand.

"Tell me about your experience. I could see by the way you cleaned up your friends' plates the other day that you've worked in the industry."

Angela sat straight up in her chair and folded her hands in her lap as if she was getting ready to recite a lesson for school. Honey found it charming. "I worked in a restaurant in San Francisco—that's where I'm from originally—for a couple of years. It was a small, family-owned place, so I got to do a bit of everything; sous chef, waiting and busing, dishwasher."

"It says here," Honey lifted the resume, "you moved from food service to marketing in 2016. Tell me about that job."

Angela blinked twice. "It was a startup in Irvine. I was responsible for booking and running our booth at events."

Honey didn't recognize the company name Angela had written on the resume. "What kind of business was it?"

"Health and wellness products," she said.

"I imagine that required the ability to think on your feet?"

"Yes, that was it exactly. It sounds mundane, but it was actually a creative position. I enjoyed it." She laughed, and her laugh was Willow's, breezy and unselfconscious. "Most of the time. There are always difficult people."

"That's a given when working with the public." Honey set the resume aside. "This all sounds like great experience for the catering business. Why did you leave your last position?"

A cloud dimmed the light in Angela's eyes. Honey almost regretted asking the question, but she had to know.

"Went out of business," Angela said.

Honey liked this girl. She reminded her so much of a blond-haired, green-eyed Willow, which meant she wasn't exactly objective. She had to ask some of the hard questions, resist making an emotional decision. "Friar

Philip mentioned you're living in Black Star Canyon with one of your friends' fathers. How did you end up there?"

"Zach and I worked together. When the business failed, Zach said we could stay with his father until we got our feet under us again. I was ready for a change of scenery."

Honey tried to line up Friar Philip's assertion that the kids had been deceived through no fault of their own with the story Angela was telling her. Was Angela deceived by the people who'd owned the health business? Or was Zach's father the problem? An image of the No Trespassing sign's bullet holes appeared in her mind. "Do you like living up there? It seems a bit remote," she said.

"It's okay." Angela seemed reluctant to say more.

"What about Zach's dad? Is he happy to have you guys?"

Angela tipped her head to one side. "Happy? That's hard to say. He's a little. . ." She paused as if searching for the right word. "Eccentric," she said. "But it's fine."

"Eccentric how?" Honey asked.

Angela shrugged her delicate shoulders. "He's a prepper."

"Prepper?" Honey hadn't heard the term.

"You know, one of those guys who thinks the apocalypse is coming any day, so they live out in the middle of nowhere. He's got stockpiles of food and water, a generator, carries a rifle everywhere he goes, that kind of thing."

That didn't sound like a good atmosphere for a young girl, especially not one as fragile seeming as Angela. Her makeup was very natural, but on close inspection Honey could see the carefully covered circles under her eyes. Her motherly instincts were snapping with electricity. She wanted to do more than hire Angela, she wanted to rescue her.

"Do you have transportation?" That was another question she had to ask. If Angela had no reliable way to get to Laguna Niguel, Honey couldn't hire her. She had to be practical. Compassion was what had gotten her and Booker into the financial situation they were in.

"Zach has a car. I can borrow it, or he'll drive me," Angela said.

"Last question, are you looking for something more permanent?"

"Yes. I've been job hunting, but I haven't found the right position yet. I was excited when Friar Philip called. It seemed so. . ." She paused again. "You know, like a God thing."

A God thing? Honey was beginning to believe it was. "To be honest, I've been a tiny bit stressed since my daughter moved. She used to help in the shop. I guess I didn't realize all she did."

Angela leaned forward, just an inch or two, but it was enough for Honey to sense her interest. She continued. "You see, I teach in-home cooking classes as well as. . ." She waved a hand toward the front room. "I have to prep for those, develop recipes, shop, you know?"

"Everything takes more time than you think it will," Angela said.

"Right," Honey said. "There's never enough hours in the day."

Angela inclined her head encouragingly, but didn't speak. There was something regal in the movement. She seemed a neglected princess, a frail Cinderella. Hiring her suddenly seemed of paramount importance. Not only for Honey's sake, but for Angela's. "I went to the emergency room last night." Honey blurted out the words, and her cheeks blazed. Why had she said that?

"Oh." Angela's mouth formed a surprised circle, her forehead creased.

"It wasn't anything serious." Honey felt as if she had to explain. She couldn't let the girl be scared away by the idea that she was severely ill. "The doctor said it was a panic attack."

Panic attack. Had she really uttered those words to this child? "I mean, not a panic attack, per se. More like stress. I was stressed out."

Angela's head nodded like a dashboard bobblehead's after a speed bump. A long, silent moment stretched between them. The obligation to fill it prodded Honey. "The point is, I need to off-load—" She'd better rethink that phrase. She cleared her throat. "Find someone I can train to run the shop while I'm otherwise employed."

Still, Angela didn't speak. The desire to hire her filled Honey with a sense of urgency. "That person would work under me until they were ready." Honey coughed. "Would you be interested?"

After a beat, Angela's face broke into a smile that was so lovely it was contagious. "I would."

Honey's shoulders relaxed. She hadn't realized how tight they'd become. "Can you come in tomorrow? Start training?"

"Yes, ma'am."

They shook on it, and Angela trotted out of the store. Honey trailed behind her and through the shop window, watched her get into a battered, blue Honda Civic. Charlie, the handsome teenager, was behind the wheel. He must have been there all that time. She wished she'd known. She'd have invited him inside, offered him a cup of coffee, or a glass of water. But he didn't seem any worse for wear.

His face lit up with unfiltered delight after hearing what Angela had to say. Honey watched as he lifted his fist and waited for her to bump it before starting the car. It was a childlike gesture, and she found herself grinning in response. She liked him. She liked Angela. A warmth she hadn't felt since Willow moved to San Diego filled her. She turned and walked to her office, ready to face the rest of the day.

CHAPTER TEN

HONEY LEFT THE shop fifteen minutes early. She hadn't had a customer for an hour. She called Rosie on her way home.

"Hi." Rosie's voice came through the car speakers.

"Are you home?"

"Yeah, why?"

"Want to walk the dogs?"

"Wait, who is this?"

"Ha ha. I walk Fury every day. Well, the days Booker isn't home anyway."

"But Booker is home."

"So you don't want to walk?"

"Yes. Just teasing you."

"I'll be home in ten minutes."

"Text when you're ready."

Seven minutes later, Honey pulled into her driveway. Fury greeted her at the door. She pushed past him and rounded the corner into the dining room. Booker slipped the lid of his laptop closed and smiled at her. "You're home early."

"A little." She kissed him. "Rosie and I are going to walk the mutts."

"Are you feeling up to it?" His forehead crinkled.

Honey put her fists on her hips. "I thought you were my live-in personal trainer? Do you want me to exercise, or not?"

Booker stood and wrapped his arms around her. "You scared the heck out of me last night, darlin'."

Honey relaxed in his embrace. "Yeah, well, I was pretty scared too." She pushed away and headed toward the stairs. "So, I'm doing something about it," she said over her shoulder. "I'm exercising. I haven't had any sugar or any white flour today. I drank more water than coffee. And," she yelled from the top of the stairs, "I'm training someone to help out at the shop."

She could hear Booker's surprised exclamation from the closet as she grabbed her sneakers. He was standing at the foot of the stairs when she returned to the top. "That's great. Tell me about it?"

She jogged down. "Can I tell you when I get back? I already texted Rosie to meet me out front."

"Sure. Can't wait to hear."

Rosie was waiting by the crepe myrtle tree in her front yard when Honey emerged from her house. Fury and Peach, Rosie's Golden Retriever mix, greeted each other with brief butt sniffs and wags. "What's up?" Rosie said as they plowed down the block, Fury straining at his leash, Peach heeling by Rosie's side.

"What do you mean?"

"You left work early. You called me—instead of me calling you—to walk. This is unusual behavior."

"I guess I'm celebrating."

"Celebrating what?"

"I hired somebody today." Honey told Rosie about meeting Angela at the soup kitchen. "Her friend's father has a home in Black Star Canyon. He's letting her live there, but I get the feeling she'd like to move."

"She's not working anywhere? Isn't that a little odd?"

"She had a marketing position with a business in Irvine that went defunct. She'd been looking for work, but hadn't found anything yet."

"Are you going to look into it?"

"How am I going to get a referral from a business that's been shut down?" Honey felt genuine confusion.

"I don't know, but you have to check her out somehow. She could've manufactured a fake job with a nonexistent company."

Defensiveness rose up inside Honey. "I'm sure she didn't. She's a sweet girl. Besides, I told you I could tell at the soup kitchen she had serving experience."

"You could at least check the restaurant in San Francisco, unless they're out of business too," Rosie said.

"I'm sure they're not. I'll call them tomorrow." Honey's words came out more aggressively than she'd intended them to.

They strode on in silence for a quarter of a block, then Rosie said, "Last year taught me people aren't always what they seem. It's best to do your research."

Honey couldn't argue with that. Her friend had lived through a nightmare. She softened her tone. "I'm sure you are right, but I'm glad for the opportunity to give Angela a chance. I think she's had some tough times. I can't imagine any other reason a girl like her would move to a prepper compound."

"A prepper compound? We have those around here?" Fury pulled Honey to a halt at a tuft of tall grass that must have contained fascinating smells. "Out in Black Star Canyon on one of the back roads," she said to Rosie's back.

Rosie stopped and turned. "And she's living there?"

After what she thought was long enough, Honey yanked Fury forward. "That's what I'm saying. Why would she live there if she wasn't desperate?"

Rosie didn't respond for several steps. "That's a weird coincidence, don't you think?"

"What's a coincidence?"

"That you and Booker found a body in Black Star, and now this girl who lives there on a prepper compound, no less, shows up on your doorstep."

Honey thought about her answer. It wasn't that she hadn't recognized the coincidence, of course, she had. She'd lived in Orange County for fifteen years and had heard about Black Star on maybe five occasions in all that time. Three of them were within the past week. "But Angela doesn't know we were the ones who found the body. Our names haven't been released to the media."

"I'm not saying she does. I'm just saying it's a strange coincidence, that's all." Rosie stopped walking, and Honey realized they were standing in front of her house. "Be careful, will you?"

"Careful about what?"

"This girl. I know you like her, feel sorry for her, but her story makes me nervous. Where's her family? Why is she living on someone else's charity?"

Honey could feel her hackles rising. It was fine for Rosie, a New England aristocrat, to be judging people. She'd never had to take charity. She came from money, married money, and now made a boatload herself. Honey knew what it was like to be taken advantage of by people with more resources and power than she had.

"I gotta go feed Booker. He hasn't had a decent meal since he's been home," Honey said.

Rosie's voice dropped. "Don't be mad at me, Honey."

Honey's anger leaked out of her. "I'm not, but you don't know what it's like, Rosie, to live from hand to mouth. I do. It's rotten."

"You're right, I don't. Thank God, I've always been well taken care of. I'm probably just gun-shy."

Honey knew she was referring to the events of last fall again. She reached out and pulled Rosie into a hug, grateful for her friend. "I'll be careful," she said.

* * *

The smell of grilling meat met Honey's nostrils when she entered the house. She found Booker in the yard flipping tri tip on the barbecue. She walked up behind him and slipped her arms around his waist. "You are so sexy when you're making dinner."

He waggled his eyebrows and deepened his voice. "I have potatoes baking and broccoli waiting to be steamed."

"Oh, baby." She was glad he liked to cook. When you did it for a living, you needed a break.

"Tell me about your new hire," he said.

"Yes." She released him. "Let me get a glass of wine first. Want one?"

"No, thanks. I have a beer going."

Honey opened a bottle of wine Rosie had brought her from a recent trip up to the Central Coast. Vibrant red splashed into her glass and filled her head with aromas of chocolate and berries. She swirled the liquid, sniffed, and took a small sip. It was delicious. She picked up the bottle and read the label, Red Ravish. She'd have to remember that.

Booker sat at the wood picnic table in the yard, butt in one chair, feet on another. Honey sat across from him. "She's a lovely girl. Her name is Angela, and she reminds me of Will." Angela was a fair version of their brown-eyed, olive-skinned Willow.

"Where did you find this Angela?" Booker said.

"At the soup kitchen."

He raised his eyebrows, and Honey filled him in on the day she'd met Angela and the boys. She ended with what she'd learned about the prepper compound.

"Preppers, eh?" He rocked his chair onto two legs and took a swig of beer. "I'd heard some of the Black Star locals were nut jobs. I didn't know the particular brand of nuts."

Honey's lips tightened. Booker tended to segregate people into two categories: People who saw the world as he did, and nut jobs. In this case, he happened to be right, but still. . . "It's nice of the man to take her in regardless," she said.

"It's nice of you to give her a job, considering."

"She's not a prepper." Why was Honey having to defend Angela again? "I don't get you and Rosie. First, you nag me about hiring someone, then when I do, you second guess me. I guess I could tell her forget it."

"No, no, no." He dropped his chair onto all four legs. "Forget I asked. It's just strange, that's all. Especially after..."

He didn't finish his sentence, but he didn't have to. She knew what he'd been planning to say. *Especially after we found a body in Black Star.*

Honey didn't want to think about that. She was happy with her hire, and she was feeling relaxed for the first time in a long time. There was a steak on the grill, her handsome husband was cooking for her, and she had a glass of Red Ravish. All was right with the world. A timer went off. Booker sprang to his feet. "Dinner is ready."

* * *

Booker fell asleep after dessert, but since dessert had nothing to do with food and had taken place in their bedroom, it was okay. Honey pulled on a bathrobe and wandered downstairs. They'd left all the dirty dishes on the counters in their haste to get upstairs. She rolled up her sleeves and got to work. She hated to clean, but she didn't mind doing dishes. Setting the kitchen to rights after a meal had a way of setting everything to rights.

She wiped the stainless-steel counter with a soft cloth one last time and glanced around. White cupboards smiled at her from the walls, the dishwasher hummed a happy tune, and the wine beckoned from its corner. She poured a splash and took it to the dining room.

Booker's laptop was on the table where he'd left it. She placed a hand on its lid. It was warm. She shouldn't open it, shouldn't pry. But married couples shouldn't have secrets from each other either. Should they?

She lifted the lid. The screen came to life. A cursor blinked, demanding login information. Honey's hands hovered over the keyboard but only for a moment. Images of Booker snapping this lid shut four or five times over the past few weeks invaded her thoughts. It was suspicious, and the curiosity was killing her.

She typed Booker's birthday into the login line. Wrong password. She tried her own—nada. Then she tried Ash's. Voila, open sesame. First, she checked Booker's browser history. She really didn't think she had to worry about porn, but you never knew. She'd heard plenty of stories about men who you'd never imagine indulged but did.

No porn. All she found were grill times for tri tip steaks, an online class entitled Common Combustibles, and an article about the dead hiker from Black Star. She perused the article, but there wasn't anything in it she hadn't already heard on the news.

Next, Honey opened Booker's email. She did feel guilty about this, but he'd been very closed about his correspondence with Joe. She had a right to know what was happening. Didn't she? Hadn't she paid for it, and paid dearly?

She scanned the messages. Joe Wells' name appeared five lines down from the top. She ran the mouse over it and gave it a defiant click.

CHAPTER ELEVEN

Email dated: January 5th

Hi Book,

THANKS FOR WRITING. You're my lifeline, you know that? You always have been. You've pulled my fat out of the fire more times than I can count. You've taught me what family is all about. I'm here for you too, Book. At least, I will be when I get my stuff together.

I've been thinking a lot about when we were kids. I guess that's what leaving home does for you, makes you take stock of life. I realized how lucky I am to have you for a brother. Nobody would've taken care of me the way you did, not a dad, not anybody.

I know Mom relied on you too much. You had to be her son, my brother, and the man of the house when you were way too young. I didn't appreciate how much responsibility that was until I moved out on my own. I know I didn't understand the risk you took with the whole Vic thing. You could've lost everything you'd been working for.

Nobody knew what happened, not the details, but they suspected. I could tell things were different as soon as the news got out. It was like some kind of cosmic curse descended on me. Walking into school was like walking into a sci-fi movie. Nobody would talk to me. They just stared; their faces blank. Made me think of *Invasion of the Body Snatchers*. Remember that movie? We watched it when Mom was working late one night. It scared the piss out of me.

Anyway, when everybody turns their back on you, it changes you. Again, not making excuses, just explaining. I may have made mistakes, but at least I had the smarts to learn from them. One thing they taught me is you can't rely on anybody but yourself. And you, Book. You're the exception to the rule.

Enough of this nostalgia stuff!

In answer to your question, things are going good. I'm starting to find my groove again. I don't want to say where I am, not yet. Let's say things are looking up, but I won't jinx it by telling you any more than that.

I understand you want me to go home, face the music, and I respect your opinion. But next time I see Lawrenceburg, it's going to be through the windshield of a brand-new Ford Super Duty with a fat checkbook in my pocket. Unfortunately, due to crap luck, I'm one of those people who have to buy honor. But I'm working on it.

In fact, that's one of the reasons I'm writing. I've been introduced to a new investment opportunity. This could be the one, Book. The one that launches me into the career I've always dreamed about. I hate to ask you for more money. You've been so generous, but this one wouldn't be only for me. We could be partners like we always talked about when we were kids, only you don't have to do any of the work. You'd be the banker. I'd manage things. We'd split fifty-fifty. I hope you'll give me the chance to prove I'm not a loser.

I'll send another email with the details when I hear from you. Just promise me you'll think about it, but don't think too long. We only have two weeks to decide.

Love,
Joe

CHAPTER TWELVE

HONEY SAT IN the light of the computer screen. It seemed her entire world had been reduced to its small circle of illumination. How dare he. She could feel her blood pulsing in the veins of her forehead.

She left the glow and walked to the kitchen. The prescription the emergency room doctor had given her sat on the counter. Booker had filled it. She'd never have done it herself, but now she was glad he had.

She poured a glass of water, popped a pill in her mouth, and swallowed it. She inhaled deeply, blew out the breath, and returned to her island of blue glare.

Did Joe honestly think Booker would throw his money, their money, into some sketchy business venture? She'd always known Joe was bad with money. Booker's mom said he had holes in all his pockets. Booker had saved. He had after-school jobs. Bought his own car when he turned sixteen. Joe was his opposite. It was generally believed in the family that he'd still be living with his mother if he hadn't married Carla. She came from money and knew how to manage it.

Being bad at managing money wasn't the same as being dishonest, however. Honey hadn't thought of Joe as dishonest, but what did she know? This email proved Joe wasn't who she'd thought he was.

I know I didn't understand the risk you took with the whole Vic thing. You could've lost everything you'd been working for. What on earth did that mean? Who was Vic? What had happened to him or her? Booker had never mentioned anyone named Vic.

Honey thought back to the day she and Booker had discovered the dead man in Black Star. There'd been animosity between that cop, Kirk Wickett, and Booker. She'd felt it. Booker had said it was because of Joe. That Joe and Kirk hadn't gotten along.

What kind of person brings animosity forward into their adult life from their high school days? Even bullies are usually forgiven when the spotlight of time shines on the past.

Jacqueline Rogers had made Honey's life miserable in high school all because Derek King asked Honey to the winter formal. Honey didn't even like Derek King. She told Jacqueline that, but it seemed to throw fuel on the fire.

Jacqueline started a campaign to turn every girl in the sophomore class against Honey. Honey never knew what the rumors were. Her sister Lilac, who was one year older, heard it had something to do with the football team. Honey figured that was right because she suddenly became as popular with the boys as she was unpopular with the girls.

She hated Jacqueline for years, until one day after Honey and Booker were married, she bumped into her and her father in the grocery store. Jacqueline's father's nose was covered with a map of bright red broken blood vessels. His eyes were bleary. He shuffled through the store hanging onto the grocery cart for balance.

Jacqueline walked toward the cart with a box of crackers. Before she could drop them in, he snaked out a hand and slapped them to the floor. The snap of flesh on flesh rang through the aisle. "Wrong brand." His words were a growl. "How stupid are you, girl?"

Jacqueline's eyes met Honey's, and her face colored. As she passed the pair, Honey heard the old man mutter, "You're just like your mother. Stupid women run in the family." She forgave Jacqueline her high school cruelties on the spot.

But Kirk Wickett obviously hadn't forgiven Joe. Maybe it had something to do with Vic, whoever Vic was. She'd ask Booker. Find out what was going on. As soon as that thought crossed into her mind, she realized it wasn't going to happen. To question Booker, she'd have to admit to him that she'd read his emails.

An angry sound erupted near her. It voiced the emotion reverberating within her so perfectly it took her moment to realize she wasn't the one making it. Fury's eyes were fixed on the window. His lips pulled into a snarl.

What was wrong with him? Honey had assumed he'd been on high alert when Booker was at the station because in his doggy mind Alpha was gone. But Booker was upstairs.

She pushed out of the chair and walked to the window. It was a sheet of obsidian. As she drew close all she could see in its glass was her own figure in its white bathrobe. She was blind to what lay beyond it, but whatever was outside had a perfect view of everything within. A chill shivered over her. She hugged herself.

When the light of the computer flickered off behind her, the outlines of the yard became visible. She saw the silhouette of the barbecue, the new wicker chairs she'd purchased last summer, the bushes Booker hated to trim. There was nothing out of. . .wait. A potted plant, a Christmas cactus she'd set outside after its winter bloom, lay broken on the cement. Something, someone, must have knocked it off the table she'd set it on.

She stared for a long moment at the shards of pot and exposed roots. The leg growing from the mud in Black Star flashed in her mind. She shook her head. She wouldn't think about that.

A cat, a possum, not the wind. The plant was too heavy for the wind to upend. That's all it was. The dog's growl stopped as abruptly as it had begun, and he curled into a doughnut at her feet.

Fury must have picked up on Honey's feelings. She'd become suspicious. Dark things, like mistrust and insecurity, had entered her comfortable existence. She felt like she was standing on the deck of a small boat in a big storm. The sensation made her want to grab at everything within her reach, to find something, anything she could hold onto.

The kitchen had always been her place of safety. She'd taken over the role of chief cook and bottle washer when her mother had died and that had led to a career. Food had provided emotional and financial security, until now, and she didn't know how to navigate the change.

She turned to the table and the dark computer. She had to stop it. She couldn't allow Joe to infect their marriage with his disease. He was insatiable. If he was allowed, he would take and take and take until there was nothing left in their bank accounts. She ran a finger across the mouse pad and brought the computer to life again. The email lit up the screen. She hit reply.

Her hands, poised over the keyboard, shook a little. With anger, or nerves, she wasn't sure. Probably both. What should she say?

Her hands dropped into her lap. Did she plan to take Booker's reply away from him, answer for him? Wasn't that what he'd done to her?

She stood abruptly and walked to the kitchen. She rummaged through the junk drawer, found a pad and pencil, and carried them to the dining room. She copied Joe's email address. She would think about what she wanted to say then send him an email from her own account.

Honey yawned. Whether it was because she'd decided, or because the pill she'd taken had kicked in, exhaustion dropped on her like a heavy blanket. She shut down Booker's computer and made her way up the stairs in the dark.

* * *

The next morning, Honey opened her eyes and had a moment of disorientation. The sun streamed through the blinds on her bedroom window. It was late.

She rolled over, wiped the sleep from her eyes, and tried to focus on the clock. It read nine-forty-five. *Nine-*

forty-five. The shop should have been opened forty-five minutes ago.

She rose and staggered into the bathroom. What was wrong with her? She felt like she'd drunk a fifth of whiskey the night before. Of course, she'd never actually drunk a fifth of whiskey. That was something her father used to say on mornings after a long night at the bar, but she imagined this must be what it felt like.

She climbed into the shower and turned the water as cold as she could stand it. She needed to wake up. When was the last time she'd slept so late? As she washed her hair, she tried to remember. Maybe two years ago on New Year's Day? They'd gone to a party at Rosie's house the night before, stayed up until two.

By the time she stood at the coffee pot watching the brown, life-giving liquid drip into her cup, she'd worked it out. The last time she'd slept this late was the March before last when she'd had the stomach flu and was up all night puking.

Booker entered the kitchen. "Glad to see you're still alive."

"Why didn't you wake me? I should have been at work an hour ago."

"I did. You told me you were getting up, so I left." Honey gaped at him. She had no memory of that. "How much of that wine did you drink last night?" he said.

"Two glasses. That's it." Her gaze fell on the bottle of pills. "It must have been the pills."

"I'm sure you shouldn't take them with alcohol."

"I didn't. I took one with water."

Booker tipped his head to the side and flattened his expression. "You know what I mean. You shouldn't have taken them after you'd been drinking."

Honey stirred cream into her coffee. "Not a problem. I'm not going to take them at all."

"Now, Hon—"

She held up a hand to stop his words. "I don't need those pills. I'm fine. And, I can't take anything that knocks me out for ten hours. I have things to do. I have a life."

"When you see the doctor, you can ask—"

"I've had enough of doctors." She put a lid on her mug, kissed Booker and headed toward the front door. "I'm catering a party at Peter's gallery next Friday night. When are you going to the firehouse next? I could use your help loading the van."

"I'm all yours," he called after her.

When Honey pulled up to Sweeter, she was surprised to see the lights on. Nobody had the key but her, Booker, and Rosie. She couldn't imagine why Rosie would be inside. She pushed open the front door, nerves jangling with the bell, and poked her head inside. "Hello?"

Angela's head popped up from behind the counter. "Oh, hi."

"Angela?" Honey had completely forgotten it was the girl's first day.

"Your friend Rosie let me in. I hope you don't mind. You said to come in at nine, but no one was here, and there was a customer waiting. Rosie rang her up and showed me how to do it because she had to get going."

"What was Rosie doing here?"

"Looking for you, I guess. She said something about the gallery opening next week."

Before Honey could respond, the bell pealed behind her and two women entered.

"Welcome to Sweeter than Honey's," Angela said. "Let me know if I can answer any questions." The women smiled and headed for the cookbook aisle.

Angela handled herself well. Honey made a snap decision. She'd listen to the girl from the other room. If things started to head in the wrong direction, she'd step in. Booker and Rosie were concerned about Angela's resume. What better way to see if the girl had been truthful about her experience than to watch her in action? "Looks like you've got this. If you need help with the register, call me. We'll do some training this afternoon." This afternoon when I wake up, Honey thought, but didn't say.

"I know where you are if I have any questions."

Honey escaped into her office, collapsed into her chair, and dropped her head into her hands. The night before she'd been so sure she should email Joe and tell him to back off, but now she wasn't. If she did and Booker found out, wouldn't it seem that she didn't trust him?

When you weren't sure what to do, doing nothing seemed the best policy. She would think about it. When she had time. Right now she had plans to make and a new employee to train. And she had to pull herself out of this stupor.

CHAPTER THIRTEEN

ONE WEEK LATER, Angela, clad in Willow's white serving jacket, floated through the dark night of Peter's gallery like a bright star. Most of the guests were dressed in cocktail black, which fit the mood of Nightshade. Honey had been curious to see what kind of people would attend a show for the type of art Marco created. They looked like the guests at every other gallery event she'd attended.

She wasn't sure what she'd expected, fangs, or scars, or hunched backs, but it was the usual crowd of beautiful people. Angela fit right in. Honey smiled as she watched heads turn to follow the girl's progress across the room. She was good for business.

Not just the catering side of the business either. She'd been a blessing in the shop the past week, better than Xanax for Honey's stress levels. Angela learned fast, had great customer service skills and was fun to be with. Honey hadn't looked forward to going to the shop this much since Willow left.

Seeing Angela in Willow's old jacket did make Honey's heart squeeze, however. Nobody could replace her daughter, that was definite, but having Angela around was a little like having Will home. Apart from their coloring, they looked a lot alike, and they had the same quick wit.

Tonight's featured artist, Marco, held court next to the largest of his horrible paintings. He was younger than Honey had imagined him to be, which might explain his tremendous ego. Having a gallery opening when you were only in your early thirties must be heady stuff. When she was working the restaurant scene, she'd found the younger the head chefs were, the more insufferable they were.

Two women and three men gathered around a framed desert. Blue-brown hills, naked but for a sprinkling of cacti, filled the canvas. The sun was setting, and the colorful sky contrasted with the stark landscape. It was well executed, the colors beautiful, but the bloodied corpse half-hidden behind a Joshua tree drew Honey's gaze like a magnet.

"It's the mystery of the desert." Marco's voice was loud and nasally. "It may appear barren but is actually teaming with life." He opened his arms, palms to the ceiling. "Where there's life, there must be death."

Honey shook her head. He seemed so pleased with himself, stating an obvious truth as if it was a great revelation. She turned to check on the buffet table, but stopped when she heard him say, "Lovely girl, would you please bring another round of champagne for my friends?"

Lovely girl. He didn't have a right to address Angela that way. Someone his age should know better. Honey had some leeway for older men who'd grown up in an era when being a gentleman meant complimenting a woman on her appearance, but the rules had changed. She couldn't believe Marco wasn't aware how rude he sounded.

While she debated whether she should bring the champagne herself and save Angela the embarrassment, Angela drifted over holding a full tray of flutes. "Here you go." She smiled as if she hadn't noticed the slight.

Marco shot the cuffs of his charcoal gray jacket, took the glasses two at a time and handed them around with a flourish, then took one for himself. Angela turned to go. He reached out with his free hand and touched her low back. She froze. Honey took a step forward, but Angela slid away from him without comment.

Honey exhaled. She was used to working with her daughter. Will didn't suffer fools, which was exactly what Honey's dad used to say about Honey. She'd have probably made a snarky comment to Marco *after* she decked him.

She'd called that morning, as promised, to fill her mother in on the second date with the not-a-complete-loser. They'd gone to a micro-brewery and ordered flights of ale. He knew his beer, and that raised his status in Will's eyes. He'd gone from not-a-complete-loser to Jonathan. He had a name, which was promising.

Angela's and Honey's gaze locked from across the room. Angela waggled her fingers to let her know everything was under control. Honey returned the waggle and headed to the buffet table.

The tamales were a hit. They were disappearing fast. She replaced an empty tray of mushroom, one of potato, and then checked the beans and rice.

"Delicious." Peter's voice was so close she jumped. He was like a cat, slipping silently into rooms, sneaking up on people. She wished he'd knock it off.

"Thanks. Seems to be going okay."

"Okay? You've started a new Laguna fad. Out with the taco bar. In with the tamale party. You're stealing some of Marco's thunder. He's not thrilled, let me tell you."

"I'm not sorry about that. Your Marco needs to be taken down a peg or two."

Peter tipped his head like an inquisitive dog.

Honey stirred the beans before explaining. "He's a bit too hands on with my help."

Peter walked to the doorway and gazed at the crowd in the main room for a long moment. "She looks like she can take care of herself," he said as he rejoined Honey at the buffet table.

Irritation ran up her spine. "She shouldn't have to."

Peter patted her arm. "Don't be upset with me, Honeysuckle dear. It was only an observation."

Honey pulled her arm away. "You don't know her."

"You're correct, of course. I don't know her. But she reminds me of others I once knew."

Honey shot him a glance. "Others?"

"Did she grow up here? In Laguna?" He didn't answer her question.

"I don't think so. I believe she grew up in San Francisco, although I don't know much about her past."

Peter's eyes glinted in the overhead lighting. "San Francisco, eh?"

"That's right. Why?"

He gave her a thoughtful nod, but before he could say more, a crash and a cry came from the other room.

Peter and Honey rushed toward the noise. Marco was posed by his painting, arms out, chest covered in blood, bright red and dripping. Angela stood before him, a tray dangling by her side.

"You did that on purpose," Marco stuttered. He sounded angry, not wounded.

"It was an accident." Angela's voice was calm, apologetic.

Honey pulled her cell phone from her pocket as she crossed the room, her finger on the emergency services button, but when she reached them, she noted the blood had chunks of tomato, onion, and peppers in it. She pocketed her phone.

Marco looked at Peter. "She threw salsa on me."

Honey reached for the tray Angela held. "I'm sure it was an accident." As she took it, she lowered her voice and said, "Why don't you go get a rag."

Angela walked toward the kitchen with an unhurried stride.

Peter took a cocktail napkin from one of the guests and began brushing mango salsa from Marco's shirt. "Now, why would she do that?"

Marco opened his mouth to speak but closed it again with a clack of teeth. He must have had a sudden insight. There was no way to explain why Angela would pour salsa on him without incriminating himself. *I was aiming for her back, but I guess I grabbed her butt by mistake.* What could he say? It was best to shut up.

Angela returned with a rag and a tray of champagne. The champagne was a good touch. Honey took the rag, and voices resumed as flutes were handed around. Marco disappeared into the men's room while Peter and Honey mopped up the dribbles of salsa he left in his wake.

They returned to the small kitchen at the back of the gallery together. As they washed their hands, Peter said, "I told you she could take care of herself."

"I'm sorry about that. I wish she'd have—"

Peter interrupted her apology with a wave. "She did exactly the right thing. Marco shouldn't be allowed to get away with bad behavior."

"I know, but if she'd come to us, we could have handled it."

"My guess is she's used to managing her own problems."

"So you said, and I wish you'd explain. If you don't know Angela, how do you know what she'll do or not do?"

He reached for a dishtowel, dried his hands, then handed it to her. "I've spent time with people from disadvantaged circumstances. They have a wariness the rest of us don't. Angela has that wariness."

Honey hung the towel on the oven door. "When were you around disadvantaged people?"

He answered her question with a question again. "Your childhood wasn't a bed of roses either, was it?" Honey blinked. He continued. "Now our mutual friend Rosie is a hothouse flower. You can tell within minutes of meeting her she's never gone a day without a meal or a night without a safe place to sleep."

Strange, she'd had the exact same thought about Rosie the other day, which made her feel guilty now. "Rosie is no wimp." Honey defended her.

"I didn't say that." Peter looked affronted. "She's one of the toughest women I know, but that is a recent development."

Honey agreed with him but was saved from having to admit it by Angela's entrance. "Do we have more dessert tamales?" she asked.

"We do." Honey opened the oven door and pulled out a warm tray. "Do they want apple habanero or chocolate cinnamon?"

"I don't know. I'll take out some of both."

Honey loaded the tray, and Angela whisked them from the room. A moment later, a guest entered the kitchen looking for a clean serving spoon. The one that had been in the rice had fallen on the floor. Peter bustled out with the spoon and the guest, and Honey returned to work.

Two hours later, the gallery was empty except for Peter, Marco, Angela, and Honey. Angela puttered around the room, picking up discarded plates and glasses while Marco did his best to avoid her.

"It was a good night," Peter said. "We sold three paintings."

"I was hoping to sell *Death in the Desert*." Marco's lips fell into a pout.

Peter placed a hand on his shoulder. "There was interest."

"But no sale." The artist sounded like a spoiled child.

Peter made soothing noises and steered him toward the door. When it shut behind Marco, Peter raised his eyes to the ceiling. "Deliver me from self-important artists."

Angela laughed. She'd been in a cheerful mood ever since the salsa incident. Honey wasn't sure whether she needed to address the issue of dousing patrons with food or let it go. Marco had deserved it. Either way, she was too tired to bring it up tonight.

Honey had been going to ask Angela to come to the house to help her prep for Lisa-Liza's event the next day. She'd been considering bringing her along to the party as well. Honey didn't need the help but thought it might be good training. However, after the temper flare tonight, she was no longer sure that was a great idea.

She didn't know Angela very well. Not yet. She hoped that over time the girl would open up to her, but meanwhile Honey would take things slow. Angela might remind her of her daughter, but she wasn't Willow. Honey needed to remember that.

CHAPTER FOURTEEN

CHARLIE OPENED THE door of Sweeter. Angela entered with a jangle of bells, walked straight to where Honey stood at the checkout counter and deposited a paper bag in front of her. "They're high protein."

"Made with coconut oil, so healthy fat." Charlie came up behind her.

"And they're sugar-free," Angela said.

"Gluten-free too." Charlie grinned; his teeth shone against his tanned complexion. "My mom had cholesterol. We didn't know about gluten though."

"There's no cholesterol in gluten." Angela sounded annoyed.

"Then why does everybody say it's bad for you?"

"Just because something isn't healthy doesn't mean it has cholesterol."

Charlie's mouth lifted on one side like he didn't believe her.

"And, there's good cholesterol and bad cholesterol," she said.

"No." His dark hair swung side to side. "I don't think so. I definitely think you're wrong about that."

Honey peeked inside the bag, consternation tuning out the argument. She hated sugar-free, gluten-free baked goods. At least, she had the few times she'd tried them. "You shouldn't have," she said.

Angela gave her a shy smile. "I know your doctor doesn't want you to eat simple carbs."

"Or cholesterol," Charlie said.

A lovely smell wafted from the bag when Honey raised it to her nose and sniffed. She reached inside, pinched off a piece of a grainy looking bar, closed her eyes, and popped it into her mouth.

It wasn't bad. Good texture. Nice flavor. "Are these date bars?"

"Date and walnut. Walnuts are really good for you too. Do you like them?" Angela fidgeted with the strap on her purse. She looked like she was waiting for test results.

"They're good." Honey took the rest of the bar from the bag. "Hard to believe there's no sugar in them."

Angela exhaled. "Want a cup of coffee? I think they'd be good with coffee."

"Sure."

Angela bustled into the office, and a moment later emerged with a steaming mug. "I also brought you a bottle of liquid stevia for your coffee. I know you like sugar."

Angela handed Honey a small, glass bottle along with the mug. "Don't use too much. It's really sweet."

"Very sweet," Charlie agreed.

Just the idea of fake sugar gave Honey hives, but she didn't want to seem unappreciative. Angela had obviously gone out of her way to please her. It was endearing. She squeezed a couple of drops into her coffee and took a tentative sip. It wasn't as bad as she'd expected. Better than black anyway.

"You're spoiling me," she said.

"I wanted to make up for last night."

"Make up for what?"

"Dousing that guy with salsa. I hope I didn't get you in trouble with Peter Stiller."

Honey laughed. "If you hadn't dumped salsa on that jerk, I might have. And don't worry about Peter. He's had to deal with worse."

"You're not mad at me?"

"No, I'm not mad at you." To emphasize the point, Honey took a second date bar from the bag. They were good, and she probably wouldn't have time for dinner.

"I told you so." Charlie fixed his brown eyes on Angela. "I knew she wouldn't be mad. Honey is a nice lady." Angela didn't answer. He looked at his shoes for a long moment as if unsure what to do next. "See you at six?" he finally said.

"Great. Thanks." She waved him away, and he headed toward the door. Honey caught him glancing over his shoulder at her as he exited, his expression wistful. He seemed smitten. She wondered if Angela knew he had a crush on her. It was none of Honey's business. What was her business, however, was the salsa incident.

"So about last night, I'm not saying I approve of your tactics, but I understand the sentiment." Honey had planned out what she'd say that morning. "I had a boss once who made my life miserable. In retrospect, I wish I'd have stood my ground."

"Really?"

"It was right after I graduated from cooking school. I was young and broke, that's my excuse. Anyway, I got a job at a French-Southern fusion restaurant in Louisville. The chef was well-known, and I was in awe of him."

Angela settled onto a stool like a kid settling in for story time.

Honey rested her elbows on the counter. "Chef Fabien was a class A chef and a class A jerk. He had this way of making people want to please him. He did it by doling out favor in tiny sips. . ." She held up two fingers to show how tiny they were. "Like it was Hennessey cognac, you know?"

Angela nodded.

"It was fear too. We were all afraid of him. He wielded humiliation like a butcher knife."

"I know somebody like that," Angela said. Honey waited a long beat before continuing her story hoping the girl would share more, but she didn't speak.

"Six months into my apprenticeship, Chef Fabien broke up with his girlfriend. Honestly, I was relieved. The nights she showed up at the restaurant generally ended with the two of them screaming at each other in the alley behind the kitchen."

A dark cloud passed over Angela's bright face. "I don't like it when people scream at me."

The words seemed obvious. Nobody likes getting screamed at, except maybe one of those radio shock jocks. But something in the way she said them made Honey believe it wasn't a throwaway statement, that Angela had an intimate experience with a screamer. Honey finished the second date bar and washed it down with the dregs of her coffee. She'd added too much stevia. The last sip was overly sweet. She grimaced, then said, "At least she had the sense to break it off with him when she did."

"True. What happened after that?"

"He changed. For the better, I thought. He was less angry, had more patience. But after a couple of weeks, I realized I was the only beneficiary of his new-found charm."

Angela's eyes widened with understanding. "Oh, no."

"Oh, no, is right." Honey stood straight. "One night, I was closing with the dishwasher and Chef Fabien. Fabien sent me to the front of the house to turn chairs. When I was done, I walked into the kitchen to get my purse and say goodnight. The dishwasher was gone, and Fabien was in his office."

"Let me guess," Angela said. "He grabbed you."

"Not that bad. He called me into the office. I could see the candlelight from across the kitchen."

Before Honey could finish her story, the front doorbells chimed. A forty-something man entered with a confused look on his face.

Angela hopped off the stool. "Welcome to Sweeter than Honey. What can I help you with?"

Relief washed over his features. He lifted his phone and read from the screen. "I'm looking for chorks. Do you know what they are?"

"Of course." Angela led him to the gadget bin, pulled out a set of four fork-handled chopsticks and began explaining how to use them.

Honey watched her with a critical eye. She was good with female customers, but this was the first time she'd seen her with a man. After the fiasco at Peter's, she was worried.

She hadn't been angry as Angela had thought. No, she was sympathetic, but that didn't mean she didn't have concerns. She'd decided to share her own story with Angela today to see how she reacted.

She looks like she can take care of herself. Honey wondered how Peter had decided that. Looking at Angela this morning, she noted how thin she was. There was a circle under her right eye so dark it almost looked like she'd been punched. She didn't look strong. She didn't even look especially healthy.

Honey stood in one swift movement, no longer comfortable sitting. She was going to head to the shelf where Angela and the man were now discussing bamboo rolling mats for sushi construction, but they pivoted and walked toward her.

"I can ring him up," Angela said.

Honey checked her watch. Lisa-Liza's party was in two hours, and she had things to do. She'd wanted to finish her story, maybe get Angela talking about her past, but it was late, and suddenly she was too jittery for conversation. "I'll leave you to it then. Set the alarm when you close up?"

"I will," Angela said.

Honey ran to the office to retrieve her bag. This was the first time Angela would be closing alone. She'd gone over the procedure with Honey several times. She was smart, responsible, and personable with patrons, so why did a niggle of worry run up Honey's spine? She hadn't been worried when she'd scheduled it. The salsa fiasco. That was the problem. The look on Angela's face—serene, undisturbed, no anger or passion—as she stood in front of Marco, popped into her mind. Honey would have understood if Angela had been in a rage, red faced and yelling but she wasn't. That was confusing. *I don't like it when people scream at me.* She didn't like being screamed at, and apparently didn't scream at others. At least she was consistent. But the niggle became a band that tightened around Honey's chest. She crossed the shop but paused with her hand on the front door. Did she trust Angela enough to leave her alone in the store?

What could go wrong?

That didn't bear thinking about. A myriad of things could go wrong. Angela could insult a client, steal money from the till, break the breakables. But would she? Maybe a better question was why would she? Why would she sacrifice a job she seemed to enjoy, one she needed and wanted?

Honey should have asked herself these questions days ago. If she changed her mind now, sent Angela home and closed herself, she'd be late for Lisa-Liza's party. Honey was controlling. That was her problem. She had to loosen her grip on her business, or she was going to lose the grip on her health. Her jumpiness was unreasonable, silly.

The man took the bag of chorks and walked toward the door. Honey opened it and followed him out into the evening air.

CHAPTER FIFTEEN

HONEY ENTERED THE half-circle drive and parked in front of Lisa-Liza's house. It was obese—a tract home that thought more highly of itself than it ought. It reminded Honey of a popular reality show that revolved around over-coiffed, over-dressed women. Everything about it was large. The fountain, the palm trees, the double front doors with oversized lion-head knockers.

Honey lifted one of the felines and let it drop. A moment later, she heard the clack of heels on wood and Lisa-Liza opened the door. Silhouetted against the bright chandelier behind her, Honey couldn't read her expression, but she felt waves of irritation streaming from the woman. "I hope you don't need help," she said by way of greeting. "My husband left early."

Honey could tell from Lisa-Liza's toned arms, she worked out regularly. She was certainly fit enough to lend a hand. But Honey said, "I can make a couple of trips."

Lisa-Liza spun on her heel. Honey followed her through a wide entryway, down a hall and into a spacious kitchen. Crackers, cheese, vegetable sticks, and hummus were laid out on a horseshoe-shaped counter. Five women gathered around the spread, glasses of white wine in their hands.

"Our instructor is here," Lisa-Liza said.

Five faces turned toward Honey, and her heart thudded. Honey acknowledged the loud beat with a combination of dread and surprise. She'd been teaching in-home cooking classes for years. She'd taught in condos, in mansions, and in modest, suburban three bedrooms. She'd taught for lawyers, doctors, and kindergarten teachers. Before this moment, she'd have said nothing could make her nervous anymore.

Shake it off, girl.

"Hi, y'all. My name is Honeysuckle Wells, but everybody calls me Honey."

She was annoyed Lisa-Liza hadn't introduced her by name, but she really couldn't complain. She'd been mentally calling her hostess by the wrong moniker for weeks. Honey knew her name was actually Liza, but she seemed like the kind of woman who should have two. Like her house, Lisa-Liza was pretentious.

Honey placed a cold storage bag on the counter and turned to retrace her steps.

"Do you need help?" An older, less fit woman than Lisa-Liza, but more attractive by Honey's way of thinking, offered.

The earlier thud in her chest repeated itself. Honey didn't know what was wrong. She was jumpy, jittery, nerves tingling. She hadn't been happy about leaving Angela in the store alone, but she didn't think that was her problem. The words "panic attack" hovered in a dark corner of her mind. She drew a curtain between herself and them, smiled, and said, "I could use a hand."

"I'm so looking forward to this. My doctor said I should go on the Mediterranean diet, but I don't know what that is. I mean, I've been to the Mediterranean, but I ate at tourist places mostly. They gear all that food for Americans. It's not authentic. Are you making authentic food tonight?" She gave an embarrassed laugh.

Before Honey could answer, the woman answered herself. "Of course, you are. You're a chef. Chef's know what they're doing, don't they?"

She continued her monologue about chefs she'd known, and Mediterranean food, and European travel all the way to Honey's van and back to the kitchen not giving Honey a chance to get in a word edgeways. That was fine with Honey. She was finding it hard to catch her breath. Speaking would have been more work than it was worth.

Honey began setting ingredients out on the large granite countertop. The menu included dolmas, falafel, and a Greek salad with feta cheese and kalamata olives. She'd been looking forward to the meal herself. Her talkative assistant, whom she'd learned was called Bets, wasn't the only one who'd had the Mediterranean diet suggested by their doctor.

Honey had been experimenting with her own versions of Greek food for a month or more. Problem was she tended to be attracted to the festive, less healthy, recipes. Lisa-Liza had insisted tonight's meal stay within a certain calorie allotment, which forced Honey to think outside the meat and cheese box. She'd been pleasantly surprised by the results.

"What else can I do?" Bets gazed at her through eager eyes.

Honey glanced around herself searching for a task she could hand off. Her thoughts, normally as neatly organized as her kitchen when she taught, were coming in short bursts. They flew at her from all directions. "Can you give me a minute?" she said and instantly regretted it. Her tone was filled with irritation. She never snapped at class members.

Bets' open expression slammed shut. "Certainly." She turned her back on Honey and walked to the other side of the counter. The thudding in Honey's chest became the rapid rat-tat-tat of a machine gun. "I'm sorry. I didn't mean. . ." She mumbled after Bets' retreating form, but the woman either didn't hear or ignored her.

Rice. She needed to get the water boiling. She could have asked Bets to do that.

Why hadn't she brought her pills? Why was she so stubborn? Because she'd fall asleep on Lisa-Liza's oversized couch, that's why. But she couldn't work like this either.

Wine.

Honey walked to the corner of the kitchen where the wine and glasses had been set up and poured herself a generous glass of Chardonnay. She took a large sip as she moved to her workstation again.

She pulled the packet of recipes she'd printed for the group from her purse. As she laid them out, she reread the first for the dolmas and struggled to organize her thoughts.

She should call the women to order, begin the class, but a buzzing in her ears had joined in the list of other symptoms she was experiencing. She was dizzy, disoriented. Honey gripped the edge of the counter to steady herself.

"We should get started." Lisa-Liza was at her elbow. The perpetual look of irritation she wore deepened. "Are you okay?"

A cramp in Honey's gut answered the question. "Where is the restroom?"

Lisa-Liza furrowed her brow and pointed toward the hallway. "Left."

Honey darted from the room. She made it into the softly lit powder room just in time. After using the toilet, she felt better, but weak. Food poisoning. Maybe she had food poisoning. She thought through everything she'd eaten in the past forty-eight hours but couldn't think of anything out of the ordinary.

When she stood to wash her hands, dizziness broke over her like a wave. Beads of sweat broke out on her forehead. She needed to lie down.

She couldn't let Lisa-Liza or Bets or the other guests see her like this. No one wanted to eat food prepared by a diseased chef. If only she could lay down for a minute, get some blood into her head.

The bathmat was soft and cream colored and probably cost more than the duvet on Honey's bed. She collapsed onto it, curled into a fetal position and rested her hot cheek on the cold tiled floor.

She took short sips of air, panting like Fury after a session of fetch. She'd make an appointment with Dr. Hillary tomorrow. She couldn't go to a shrink. The idea was too embarrassing, but she needed help. Nothing was as embarrassing as this.

A knock jarred her. "Are you okay in there?" It was Lisa-Liza.

"Yes. Sorry. Be out in a minute." Honey dearly hoped that was a true statement.

"If you're not feeling well. . . "

"No, I'm fine." Honey sat up. The world spun, but only for a second. "I'm coming." She stood with the help of the sink. "Just washing my hands." She turned on the tap to reinforce the statement.

After splashing cool water on her face, she dried it on a hand towel, then adjusted her chef jacket. She was okay. She could do this. Honey drew a deep breath and opened the door.

No one was in the kitchen when she got there. Where had they all gone? Maybe Lisa-Liza had moved them to the dining room? Maybe she'd decided to skip the instruction part of the evening and wanted Honey to cook and serve them.

She stepped into the hall and heard voices. She followed them to the right toward the entryway. By the time she got there Lisa-Liza was ushering out the last of her guests. She closed the front door and faced Honey.

"Why?" Honey said, but she knew the answer.

Lisa-Liza's lips twisted into a grimace. "You're obviously not well. I wish you wouldn't have tried to hide it from me. We could have rescheduled."

"It's not. . .I'm not sick."

Lisa-Liza crossed her arms across her chest.

"Really. I wouldn't expose you or your guests to anything. I think it's—" She stopped talking. She'd almost said, "food poisoning." That was worse than the Avian flu for a chef.

"It's what?"

Honey couldn't make herself say panic attack. It sounded so weak. So crazy. "I'll get my things."

Honey packed up the food she'd brought and made three trips to the car. Her heart was beating frantically against her ribs, but the dizziness had passed, replaced by anger.

If Lisa-Liza was so worried about Honey's health, why hadn't she helped her? After glancing around the kitchen to be sure she'd gotten everything, she went in search of her hostess.

She found her in a colossal living room seated on an equally colossal white couch, legs crossed, *Architectural Digest* in hand. She didn't glance away from the pages. "You done?"

"Yes. I'm leaving. I'll call you."

Lisa-Liza tore her gaze from the glossy pictures in her lap. "You needn't bother. I won't be rescheduling."

Honey's throat tightened. She wanted to cry, but a vision of Marco with salsa dripping off his shirt flashed into her mind. *Toss the salsa.* Lisa-Liza, like Chef Fabien before her, wasn't worth the grief. "Right," she said and left. By the time she climbed behind the wheel of her car, her only thought was: who was going to eat all this Mediterranean food?

CHAPTER SIXTEEN

THE COFFEE SMELLED wonderful. In Honey's half-dream state she saw an amorphous, cartoon finger traveling up the stairs and into her room. It came to rest below her nose and beckoned her. She opened her eyes. The coffee finger disappeared, but the smell drew her to the kitchen.

Booker sat at the counter, sipping a cup and reading something on his phone. He looked up as she entered. "Sleep good?"

She took a cup from the cupboard. "Like the dead."

"They've released more information about our hiker," he said.

She'd begun to think of the man they'd found as "their hiker" as well. It was kinder than thinking about him as The Leg. "Hmmm?" She hummed a question mark.

"He was middle-aged, probably in his forties. They don't know who he is yet. He was pretty decomposed so they can't compare his face to pictures on the missing persons database. They plan to have a forensic artist do a reconstruction."

"They can do that?" Honey added a few drops of stevia from the bottle Angela had given her to her coffee, and then a splash of cream. She sipped. Not bad. Tasted a little like licorice. She could get used to that.

"Yeah. It's not perfect. I mean, the artist has to guess at the features based on the bone structure. The hair is hard too, especially if there isn't much of it left."

A gruesome skeletonized skull with tufts of hair sprouting from it flashed into Honey's mind unbidden. She shuddered. "What an awful job."

"I don't know." Booker stood, walked to the coffee pot, filled his mug, and leaned against the counter. "It could be very rewarding. I've heard stories about people finding loved ones who'd been missing for decades because they recognized an artist's rendering."

"But they're dead."

He inclined his head. "It's closure. They know the person isn't being held captive in horrible circumstances. They often know how they died."

"It wouldn't make me feel better to find out one of our children had died. I'd rather imagine they were alive somewhere, that they might escape, come home. It would be the death of hope."

"Everybody's different." Booker slugged his coffee and put the cup in the sink. "I've got to get going."

"How long will you be at the station?"

"I'll be home Wednesday morning." He crossed the kitchen, placed his hands on her shoulders, and kissed the top of her head. "You take care of yourself while I'm gone. Get some exercise, get some rest. Right?"

She nodded. The events of the evening before cascaded through her mind. She hadn't told Booker what had happened and didn't plan to. Lisa-Liza's party was one of the most humiliating moments of her life. A close second only to the job interview at Le Chien Affame.

After she left Chef Fabien, she'd sent her resume to five restaurants in Louisville that were hiring, but her heart was set on Le Chien Affame. The chef there, although not as well-known as Fabien, was a respected, Cordon Bleu-trained professional. Honey's interests were in southern comfort foods and fusion cooking, but learning traditional French cuisine for a chef was like learning classical music for a jazz musician. It would be an amazing foundation.

The day of her interview dawned hot and sunny. Honey fretted over what to wear. She'd planned on a conservative dress with long sleeves and a boat neckline. But it was ninety degrees outside, and the temperature was rising. She ended up in a sundress with wide straps. It wasn't sexy, but later she wished she'd worn something that covered more flesh.

Chef Antoine sat at a table in the empty dining room. She waited while he went over the specials *du jour* with his head waiter. He beckoned to her as the waiter walked away and watched her progress across the room with cold, blue eyes. "Fabien called me this morning."

Honey stumbled to a stop in front of his table. "Chef Fabien?"

"I don't think you'll be a fit here."

Disbelief filled her. "Why?"

Antoine shook his gray head. "What do they teach girls these days?"

Honey found her voice. "What did he say?"

"I am a married man with a daughter your age. I cannot afford a scandal. *Vous comprenez?*"

Honey's face grew hot. "I'm married too. I wouldn't. . . I don't. . ."

Antoine waved a hand toward the exit. "I hope you've learned a lesson through all this."

"What do you think I should have learned?"

He gave her a small, sad smile. "If you have to ask that. . ."

"Wait a minute." Anger bubbled through the embarrassment. "I don't know what Fabien told you, but he and I never had a thing. We never dated, nothing. I'm a married woman."

"Are you accusing Fabien of lying?"

She saw Fabien's candlelit office, the two glasses, and the open bottle of wine on his desk. She'd been reluctant to enter, but Fabien intimidated her.

Honey had once read that human beings are the only species that will override their own instincts to abide by social norms. Many women have been raped because they were too polite to refuse a man's offer for help. "If he said what I think you're implying, yes. He's lying."

"Why would he do that?"

The scene behind her eyes continued to play. Fabien came out from behind his desk. He poured two glasses of wine and handed one to Honey. "You'll enjoy this," he'd said, and she wasn't sure if he meant the wine or what was about to transpire.

"I need to head out," she'd said.

"What's the hurry?" He reached out, stroked her cheek, and tucked a strand of hair behind her ear.

Honey stepped away. He stepped toward her. They continued this dance until there was nowhere left to go, her back, literally, against a wall. The rest of the memory came the way it always did in snatches of movement, scents, sounds, and colors. Fabien pressing himself against her. The smell of onions and sweat. His grunt of pleasure. The sound of a zipper. The paleness of his flesh.

Honey shuddered. "Vindictiveness. He made advances. I rejected him," she said.

Antoine stood. "Fabien is my daughter's fiancé. I don't believe he'd be disloyal to her, not with. . ." He let his words trail off.

Poor woman, was Honey's thought. She must have taken him back after the breakup. Technically, Fabien hadn't cheated on her, but not because he hadn't tried. He hadn't cheated on her because Honey had bit and scratched and clawed her way out of his office.

She turned on her heel and left Le Chien Affame. It took her six months to find a decent job in Louisville after that. The food-service industry was close-knit.

Orange County was a larger, more cosmopolitan community, but today there was Yelp. Honey dearly hoped Lisa-Liza wasn't the vindictive type.

Honey held her head with her hands. It felt heavy, thick. She'd been afraid she wouldn't sleep after the stress attack, so she'd taken a Xanax. It had knocked her out, and she was having a hard time waking up.

She refilled her coffee mug and stared out the kitchen window onto her broad backyard. This couldn't go on. She couldn't dope herself to sleep at night or to remain calm in tense circumstances. Honey had always prided herself on keeping her cool even in chaotic situations. It was an important trait for a chef. She'd hired Angela to help with the store so she could do more cooking classes. She couldn't give them up.

Helplessness oozed from her head and made her limbs weak. She sat on a stool. What was she going to do?

She sat for a long time. Two minutes turned to ten. The coffee in her mug grew cold. She dumped it in the sink. She didn't need caffeine. She needed to act.

Stress is a killer. You need to exercise, lose weight, stop working so hard. Her doctor's words floated through her stupor.

When the new plan hit her, she stood so quickly she nearly knocked over the stool. She strode into the kitchen, pulled a garbage bag from under the sink, and threw open the cupboard door. Cookies, sweetened cereal, the box of chocolates she'd been nursing since the holidays, powdered sugar, white sugar, she tossed all these things into the bag.

Next, she grabbed the chips, potato and corn. They joined the sweets. She moved to the refrigerator. Ice cream, coffee cake, white bread, hot dogs, salami, all went into the bag. She was in a frenzy. When all that was left in her cupboard and fridge were Dr. Hillary approved items, she took the trash outside and dumped it into the can on the side of the house.

Afterward, she marched upstairs, put on a pair of yoga pants and the sneakers Booker had made her buy. Ten minutes later, she and Fury were on a trail near her house that resembled a roller coaster. She trudged up, slogged down, enjoying the pressure in her lungs and the sweat that rolled between her shoulder blades. She'd get in shape, get her health under control. And she was going to get her life under control.

Dr. Hillary was right, stress was a killer, but diet, lack of exercise, and overwork weren't the only things causing Honey stress. The idea that Joe might be able to weasel more money from Booker darkened the edges of her mind like the threat of a hurricane. It kept her up at night. It drove her to work fifty and sixty hours a week. When she wasn't at the shop, she felt guilty.

Like today, Sunday. Honey was raised to respect the Sabbath. Although it wasn't common practice in Southern California, she closed up shop on the first day of the week. It had never worried her in the past. She'd been proud of the decision, but now she doubted her own principles.

It had to stop. She was sick of it and sick from it. When she got to work on Monday, she'd email Joe. Booker would have to deal with it.

CHAPTER SEVENTEEN

INSTEAD OF HAVING coffee, Honey went for an early Monday morning jog, then headed in to work. The shop smelled warm and comforting. Honey loved the cool, dim space before she turned on the lights, before the first customer of the new week jostled through the door, before the scents of other people's perfumes and soaps muddied the air.

Ignoring the overhead lights, Honey padded to her office at the rear of the store. Here the smell was strongest. It was a combination of the glue used for packing boxes, catalog ink, old coffee grounds, and the basil and lemon-scented candles she bought in bulk. It was the scent of her nest. Honey loved her home, but it wasn't hers alone. It was Booker's home and had been and would always be Willow and Ash's home.

She eased herself into the old desk chair she'd used for ten years. The chair bore her stamp. It had formed itself around her dimensions. What would happen when she lost the weight Dr. Hillary wanted her to lose? She'd hate to replace it. It seemed a part of her.

Honey flipped up the lid of her laptop and booted it up. As she waited for it to wake, she shuffled through the stack of mail that had been growing on the side of her desk like a wart. Maybe sorting mail was something she could give to Angela? Three-quarters of it was trash anyway.

The laptop sprang to life, Honey logged in and opened her email. Nothing of interest today. Newsletters from vendors wanting to sell her new products, spam, reminders of upcoming bills. She was about to hit delete all when she saw a familiar name, Bets Anderson. At least, the first name was familiar. A flicker of hope ignited inside her. She clicked it open.

Dear Honey,
It was so enjoyable meeting you the other night. I was sorry you were taken ill and couldn't teach the class. As I mentioned, I'm very interested in learning to fix some Mediterranean dishes and would love to book you for the same menu you'd planned for Liza's party. Many of the girls who were there that night would come. We're not all as persnickety as Liza :)
Best,
Bets

Honey smiled at the old-school emoji and use of the word "persnickety." She'd have used another adjective to describe Lisa-Liza. She'd been so sure she'd offended Bets and the other guests. What a relief. She typed up several dates she was available over the next month, a short apology, her heartfelt thanks, and hit send.

Now she would email Joe. Something hard bounced around in her stomach, but she ignored it. This was necessary for health and sanity. It was necessary for

Booker too, even if he wouldn't agree with her. She opened a new email and began.

Dear Joe,

I read your recent email to Booker. Maybe I shouldn't have, but I did. He doesn't know it, and I'd prefer to keep it that way for both our sakes. The way I see it is Booker has an Achilles heel. It's you. My job as his wife is to be strong where he's weak. It's what defines a good marriage.

I know you've had your troubles. Not all of them are your fault, but many are. I don't approve of what you're doing with your life. You've hurt a lot of people, and based on your last email, you don't intend to stop.

What you're doing to Carla and the girls is none of my business, but what you're doing to Booker is. You prey on him, Joe. You always have.

He sees you as the weaker brother and rises to your defense. I think he's wrong about that. You're not weak, except in your morals. You want and want and take and take and are never content. You trick good people like Booker and Carla into helping you satisfy your cravings.

It's got to stop. No more, Joe. You stay away from Booker. You stay away from me. We will not be investing in your crazy schemes. If you have a single, ethical fiber left in your being, you'll return our money, go home to your family, and man up.

Honey

She hit send before she could change her mind and stared at the computer screen for a beat, then spun her chair. The mixing bowl clock's wooden spoon hands pointed to the nine and the twelve. Time to open the shop. At ten-thirty she had to leave for the soup kitchen.

The next hour and a half passed in a blur of activity. Business was picking up. Except for returns, it had been dead after the holidays. She hadn't been worried, not exactly. It was a familiar trend, but coming on the heels of their disappearing dollars, it had stressed her out.

At ten-thirty, her final customer of the morning left. Honey saw her to the door, posted her *Out to Lunch* sign, and headed for St. Francis Abbey. She would rather have remained open, but Angela had called in sick, a migraine. Honey was grateful she'd never had to deal with migraines.

Her phone rang as soon as she pulled into the parking lot of the refectory. It was Willow. "Hey, Mom. Any word on the corpse?"

Honey grimaced. "Nice greeting. Not really. They still don't know who he is. Your dad says a sketch artist is going to do a rendering."

"Wasn't he buried in mud for a month?"

Honey opened the door of her van and removed the donated bags of bread she'd picked up at a local bakery on Sunday. Today's menu was an easy one, salads and sandwiches. Rather than prepping and bringing food from home, Honey had called in her ingredient order to Father Philip. This was part of the new Honey. She was simplifying her life, getting rid of the stressors.

"Mom?" Willow said.

Honey gripped the phone with her chin and walked into the building. "I think it was more like two."

"He must be pretty decomposed."

"You know, that's something I'd rather not think about. I sat with him for close to forty-five minutes while I waited for your dad to call the police."

"That's pretty creepy."

"Exactly." Honey nodded a hello to Brothers Owen and Reginald, who took the bags from her hands. "So, what's going on with you?"

"I went on a third date with Jonathan." Her voice fizzed like champagne. Using a form of sign-language, Honey gestured directions to the novices. They were used to nonverbal communication and jumped into action. One removed salad ingredients from the industrial-sized refrigerator, while the other washed vegetables.

"And?" Honey said.

"And I think I like him."

"Really? Where did you go? What did you talk about? I want the scoop."

Willow talked for ten minutes while Honey chopped salad vegetables. She hadn't heard her daughter sound this excited since she'd gotten the news about the San Diego job.

"He's a foodie, Mom. You'll love him. He even likes to cook."

"That's good because you don't."

"I know. He wants to cook for you and Dad, but he's nervous. I told him he shouldn't be. You cook so much you love having other people take over the kitchen."

Which was true, and it wasn't. Honey did like having other people cook for her, but not in her kitchen. When anybody other than Booker pulled a saucepan from her cupboard, it made her itch.

"We were going to come see you soon. Maybe we could meet him then?" Honey said.

"We'll be headed your way in the next couple of weeks. His parents live in San Clemente, and his dad is having health problems. I said I'd keep him company on the drive. We could kill two birds."

"Visiting me is a chore now?" Honey pretended offense.

"You know what I mean."

"I do. I was just teasing you."

"Jonathan says his parents' house has a panoramic ocean view. I guess they're really rich."

Honey slid cucumbers into a big bowl of lettuce Reginald had broken. "What do they do?"

"His dad had a software company that did really well. Aviation software, I think. He sold it for a *bajillion* dollars and retired two years ago."

Honey washed her hands at the kitchen sink. She raised her voice above the sound of the running water. "Well, you two are getting serious pretty fast."

"Why do you say that?"

"He's telling you all about his family. You're telling him about yours. He wants to cook for us. That's a lot of ground to cover in three dates."

Willow's voice flattened a bit, like she was trying to sound nonchalant. "We talk on the phone a lot."

"Oh, yeah. You got it bad. I went through quarters like nobody's business when your dad and I were dating."

"Quarters?"

"That was before cell phones, back in the prehistoric era. I had to sit on the payphone in the dorm hallway at school to talk to him."

Willow laughed and the bubbles returned to her voice. "I'd better go. I have a class in fifteen minutes." They each made kissing noises into the phone and hung up.

Honey hummed while she assembled ham and turkey sandwiches. She was feeling good. It was only twelve o'clock and look how much she'd accomplished. She'd hiked the hills near her house, booked a cooking class, sold quite a bit of inventory, talked to Willow, and emailed Joe. She'd gone through the terrible stack of mail, and now she was feeding the poor.

She didn't love it when Booker was at the fire station, but she'd grown accustomed to the rhythm of their life together. She worked hard when he was gone, trying to clear space for the days he was home. At least, that's what she'd done for most of their marriage.

It had changed last November when she'd discovered he'd sent money to Joe. Some of her reaction had been panic. She hadn't felt she could afford the time off any longer. But the bigger issue, she now realized, was bitterness. She'd been angry at Booker, and she'd been punishing him.

Honey's sister Lilac was the martyr of the family. When they were all still at home, and the fights over whose turn it was to do dishes ensued, Lilac was the one who'd always flounce off to the kitchen, shouting, "I'll do them," over her shoulder. She'd wanted everyone else to feel guilty, to come running after her, but it hadn't worked. Siblings don't feel guilty in those circumstances. They feel relieved.

Joe didn't feel guilty either. Honey was sure of it. It didn't matter how big a martyr Booker became; he wasn't going to do the right thing. He was a sibling.

Father Philip floated into the kitchen with a nervous smile that told Honey people were lining up for lunch. "It's ready," she said and placed the last sandwich onto the platter Brother Owen held out to her. "Let's go feed the masses."

* * *

Two customers entered the shop behind Honey when she returned to work. It was a busy day. She wished Angela had been able to come in, but now she could afford to give the girl an extra day next week when Booker was home from the station. She and Book could drive to San Diego for the day. Spend time together. Have dinner with Willow and Mr. Foodie. Dr. Hillary said time off was important for Honey's health.

At three o'clock, the stream of customers dried up. School was out, which meant the soccer moms were chauffeuring the kids to their after-school events, then helping with homework and making dinner. She remembered the routine well. The shop would be quiet until closing.

She walked to the office, sat at her desk, and opened her email. A frisson of tension made the muscles of her chest tighten. Joe had responded.

CHAPTER EIGHTEEN

Email dated: January 20th

Dear Honey,

I WISH I could say it was good to hear from you, but your email was painful. I'm sorry I've been such a burden and disappointment.

My intention in inviting you and Booker to invest in the venture I'm currently involved in came from a place of deep caring and concern. It's a good opportunity, a sure thing. Whoever gets involved will make money. If it's not us, it'll be someone else.

As far as my relationship with Carla and the girls goes, you're correct—it's none of your business. I will fill you in; however, just so you understand I do have one or two ethical bones in my body.

If I were to *man up*, as you put it, Carla would be in the unfortunate position of having to hire a lawyer. The church could and would go after our house, our private bank accounts, everything we've built over the years. I believed, rightly, that they wouldn't go after my family if I left town. So, you see, leaving was the responsible thing to do.

You and I have had a rocky relationship for a long time, and I wish it weren't so. I've always admired you. You're a good wife to Booker and a good mother to Ash and Willow. I'd like to mend fences, Honey. How can we do that? What can I say or do to earn your trust?

I am sorry you feel the way you do about the money Booker advanced me. I had no idea he didn't run it by you before he sent it. I assumed, since you two are so close you have access to his private emails, you knew all about it. Either way, be assured I intend to pay it back. All of it. With interest. In fact, I'm trying to help you double, maybe even triple, your initial investment.

I wish you'd rethink your silly stand against me and consider the business opportunity with an open mind. I owe Booker far more than the money he lent me. This is the only way I can think to repay him.

Don't worry; I won't be visiting. I'll stay out of your hair. But I can't promise I won't contact Booker. He may be your husband, but he's my brother. Family is everything to me.

Best,
Joe

CHAPTER NINETEEN

THE URGE TO call Booker and confess she'd emailed Joe made Honey so uncomfortable, she couldn't sit still. She closed the shop fifteen minutes early and headed home. When she got there, she walked straight to the kitchen cupboard and stared at its depleted interior like a cow at a new gate. What had possessed her to throw out perfectly good food?

The refrigerator didn't yield anything better. Who felt like eating carrot sticks when stressed out? She returned to the cupboard. She rummaged around on the bottom shelf and found a bag of pretzels she'd missed in her cleaning frenzy yesterday morning. There were chocolate chips in her baking supplies. She made piles—one pretzel, three chips—and arranged them on the counter. She set her cell phone at the end.

As she ate, she debated. If she told Booker she'd emailed Joe, he'd be angry with her. He'd already asked her to let him handle his brother. *I know him, Hon. You don't.* She could hear his voice in her head.

Booker did know Joe better than she did on one level, but he also had blinders on when it came to his little brother. Booker's dad had left the family when the boys were young, and his mother had her hands full. Joe was impulsive, hard to control, probably would have been diagnosed with ADD today.

Booker's mom had relied on Booker. She became the breadwinner for the family, and Booker became Joe's keeper. Booker took his job seriously, probably too seriously. In many ways, he was more like a parent to Joe than a brother.

Honey saw Joe through the eyes of a peer, and she'd never liked what she'd seen. Joe was handsome. Joe was charming. But there was something missing. He wasn't self-absorbed, but he didn't often think of others. He wasn't greedy, but he manipulated people to get what he wanted. He was missing the self-control chip.

Joe never met a temptation he didn't like. He over-ate and over-medicated until he was old enough to over-drink. He had sex with half the age-appropriate females in Lawrenceburg until he settled down with Carla, and who knows what he'd done since. If Honey had to describe Joe in one word, it would be hungry. He consumed but was never satisfied.

I owe Booker far more than the money he lent me. What had he meant by that? It was true. Lord knows Booker turned himself inside out for that man, but she didn't think Joe realized it. He'd never seemed to appreciate Book in the past.

Could it have something to do with Vic? Honey ate a pretzel creation. Kirk, the cop from Kentucky, popped into her brain. He didn't like Joe because of something that happened in high school, that's what Booker said.

Vic happened in Joe's past. She couldn't seem to shake the idea the two things were connected.

Honey walked to the front door and fished in the bag she'd left on the floor for her laptop. She brought it to the kitchen counter, pushed her phone aside, and set it down. The impulse to call Booker had passed, deadened by curiosity and carbs.

She fixed herself ten more chocolate pretzels while she waited for the laptop to boot up, then sat at the counter munching. She typed: *Lawrenceburg, KY, Vic, 1982.* She included the year Joe had graduated from high school.

Ads for old Crown Vics were the first thing to come up. That wasn't helpful. She chewed a pretzel and pondered. She added the word "accident" to the search bar. Whatever had happened to Vic couldn't have been pleasant. If it was an unwanted pregnancy, she'd never find it on the Internet, but a car accident might show up.

A website listing Kentucky car crashes appeared. It reported recent Lawrenceburg accidents, but only went back about five years. She returned to the search page and stopped chewing. There were several funeral parlor and obituary listings beneath the accident site. Could Vic, whoever he or she was, have been killed? Could it have been Joe's fault?

She clicked on the obituary site, but in order to get any information you had to know the person's first and last names. She slapped the lid of her laptop down. It was hopeless. She wasn't a detective.

Honey nibbled on another pretzel. Detective. Now that was a thought. Maybe she should hire a detective to find Joe. She and Booker could confront him in person, demand their cash.

No. She discarded the idea. That would be throwing good money after bad, as her Grandma Grace used to say. What good would it do? Chances were Joe had already spent the money. He was asking for more, wasn't he?

She felt frustrated and restless. She should get out, walk Fury, do something productive. If she sat here much longer, she'd finish the bag of pretzels.

Her phone buzzed and began vibrating across her stainless-steel counter. She scrabbled for it before it bounced off the edge. "Hello," she said breathlessly.

"Hi, Honey." It was Angela. "Don't think I'm a ditz, promise?"

"Okay," Honey said.

"I forgot if I was supposed to come in tomorrow. I know you have that cooking class, but I can't remember if you need me to close."

"No, actually, I don't. The party isn't until seven."

"Oh. Okay, then."

"I guess you're feeling better?"

There was a pause on the other end, then Angela said, "Yeah. I slept it off."

Honey had an idea. "I'm planning to test recipes tonight. I know you said you'd like to learn some of my techniques." This wasn't entirely true. All the recipes she was bringing with her were tried and true ones, but Angela had sounded disappointed, and Honey needed a distraction tonight.

"You wouldn't mind?" Now she sounded happy.

"Not at all. I'd like the company."

"I can be there in a half hour."

They hung up, and Honey got to work cleaning up her snack and setting up her cooking supplies. The doorbell rang twenty-five minutes later.

Fury charged as only a small male dog can, throwing himself at the door in a barking fit. It was how he'd gotten his name. Angela seemed to shrink into herself as he sniffed her legs. She obviously wasn't a dog person. "He's a harmless blowhard," Honey said.

Angela put out a cautious hand. Fury gave it the once over and allowed her to enter. "Guess I passed the sniff test," Angela said.

Honey led her to the kitchen. "I thought we could make spanakopita. I'm not going to teach the party guests how to make it but wanted something for them to nibble on while we cook."

As they laid out phyllo dough and basted it with butter, thoughts of Joe melted from Honey's mind. At six-thirty, she opened a bottle of Sauvignon Blanc. By seven the two were laughing and joking. It made Honey miss Willow and Ash, but especially Willow.

Angela was up to her elbows in spinach and feta cheese, which Will would never have been. Willow would sit on a stool, sip wine, and sample while Honey cooked, but the feeling of camaraderie was the same.

The spanakopita was a success. Honey watched as Angela cut the pie into small squares. "Another splash of wine?" she asked as Angela handed her a piece. "Or are you driving?"

"Yes, please. I'm not driving. Charlie's taking me home."

Charlie again. He was awfully attentive for a non-boyfriend. Honey topped off their wine glasses, took her dish into the living room, and sat in an easy chair. Angela followed and settled on the couch.

"He seems like a good friend, always willing to chauffeur," Honey said.

Angela's lips thinned in a tight line. "He hasn't been driving that long. It's still fun for him."

And he has a crazy crush on you, Honey thought, but she said, "What's it like living up there on the ranch? Lots of beef jerky?"

A laugh tripped from Angela's lips. "We eat normal stuff. Rick goes to the grocery store every week or two."

"I thought he was a prepper?"

"Oh, he is. He's got stockpiles of dry and canned food, barrels of water, a generator, gasoline. You name it, he's got it. He's saving up for the big one."

Honey took a bite from the steaming spanakopita and almost groaned. It was delicious. Angela had suggested a pinch of nutmeg, which wasn't in the original recipe. It was excellent. Honey planned to include nutmeg from now on. "The big one?" she said around her bite.

"Earthquake, World War III, alien invasion, whatever comes first. He's given up on Y2K."

"'Bout time."

"You think?"

"He's a little strange then?" Honey was fishing for information. It was such a different lifestyle; she couldn't imagine it.

Angela gazed at the ceiling as if gathering her thoughts. "He's not a bad guy," she said lowering her gaze. "Just sad. Zach says he wasn't always like this. He got weird after his wife died."

Honey stopped eating, fork in midair. "What happened to his wife?"

"Cancer. It was long and painful. I guess watching her go destroyed Rick's faith. He used to be a Catholic. Now he believes he has to take care of himself because God isn't going to."

"I hate to hear those stories."

"Yeah." Angela tipped her head. "I understand where he's coming from though. I've always had to take care of myself."

"Have you?" Honey said in a measured, nonchalant tone. She thought about Peter's assessment of the girl; that she'd had a rough start in life. Honey was curious, but she hadn't wanted to pry. At least, she hadn't wanted to be obvious about it.

"I lived with my aunt from about age eleven until I moved out at eighteen. She didn't have kids, didn't want kids. She kind of treated me like a stray cat she decided to feed but not actually take responsibility for."

Honey's mothering instinct took hold as she imagined a young Angela fending for herself in the home of an unloving aunt. "I'm so sorry."

"It wasn't that bad. She wasn't mean or anything. I got to do pretty much whatever I wanted, which seemed awesome at the time." The right side of Angela's mouth rose in a half-smile. "I lived."

"What happened to your parents?" Honey asked.

Angela's answer was quick, brittle and dismissive. "I never had a dad, and Mom's boyfriends either didn't like me, or they liked me too much."

Honey didn't know what to say. She'd lost her mother and her father didn't cope well with that death, but she'd known she was loved. She couldn't imagine a parent choosing a selfish, perverted partner over their own child. They ate in silence for a long moment. Angela inhaled her spanakopita and asked if she could have another piece before Honey ate half of her first. "Help yourself," Honey said.

Angela went into the kitchen and reappeared with not one, but two wedges of pie which disappeared as quickly as the first had. Honey was tempted to have another small piece, but after all the pretzels and chocolate chips, she didn't dare. She was sure she had exceeded her daily calorie allotment.

Angela stood. "Can I use your restroom?"

"Sure." Honey waved in the direction of the guest bathroom, headed into the kitchen, and began loading dishes into the sink. When she turned off the tap, she heard Angela enter the kitchen behind her. "I'd better get going. Charlie likes to get to bed early. Rick has him on goat duty," she said.

"You guys have goats?"

"Rick does. And it's Charlie's job to rise with the sun to milk and feed them every morning. Glad I only got cooking duty."

Honey grabbed a towel and turned as she dried her hands. "Want a little more pie? You've got time before he gets here. Black Star is at least fifteen minutes away."

"He's here," Angela said.

"When did he get here? I didn't see you call." Honey was confused.

"He's been waiting out front." The girl set her wine glass on the counter. "He didn't think it would be worth driving all the way back to the canyon. By the time he got there, he figured he'd have to turn right around."

"He could have come inside. Had something to eat." Everything about this sent distress signals to Honey's inner hostess. "Why don't you call him in now." She bustled into the kitchen pulled out another plate and began heaping spinach pie onto it. "Is he old enough to drink wine? I have beer and soda too. I could pull together—"

"He's fine." Angela's voice was cold. Honey shot her a surprised glance. The girl's face had molded into hard lines. "He's shy. He didn't want to come in. I asked him."

Honey looked at the plate in her hand. "I could wrap this to go."

"I don't think he eats spinach."

"Well, I feel bad that he was in the car all that time. Make sure he knows that, would you? I don't want him to think he wasn't invited."

"I will." Angela drummed her fingers on the counter, a sign of impatience. Honey noted her knuckles looked bruised. Honey's gaze searched Angela's face. The dark circle below her eye had faded, but she could still make it out under the makeup. A thought struck her; was someone abusing Angela? Was that why she reacted so strongly to Marco's flirtatious behavior at the gallery?

Honey's work at the soup kitchen had brought her into contact with abused women. She knew the symptoms: closed faces, reticence to have people get too close or come to their homes, so quick to apologize. And, the bruises. The bruises blamed on clumsiness. They were always bumping into doors and slipping in the shower.

"Next time, I'll take you home, so he doesn't have to wait," Honey said on impulse. She'd like to take a look at what was going on in the canyon. Maybe giving the girl a ride home wouldn't reveal much, but it might. At least, it would be a tangible way to let Angela know she was on her side.

"That's nice of you, but kind of difficult," Angela said. "You have to have keys to all the gates."

A vision of the pockmarked "No Trespassing" sign she'd seen on her hike with Booker played behind her eyes. It was the perfect setting for a story about abuse and imprisonment, like a horror movie. Angela reached into her purse and held up a small bottle. "Oh, I forgot. I brought you more stevia. The bottle I gave you before was mostly empty."

"I'm good. I've been monitoring my caffeine intake."

"Because of the panic attacks?"

"Yeah."

Angela paused. She seemed to be trying to think of something to say but was unsuccessful. She dropped the bottle into her bag again. "See you day after tomorrow, then."

"Right. Thanks for the help tonight."

A bright smile broke out on Angela's face. It was like the sun coming from behind a cloud bank. Honey smiled too. Things had gotten so serious tonight. She had intended it to be fun.

"Thanks for the lesson," Angela said. "It was great."

After Angela left, Honey wandered into the kitchen and surveyed the mess. Willow might not have cooked with her, but Willow would have done the pots and pans.

CHAPTER TWENTY

THE NEXT MORNING was overcast. A fine drizzle fell from a cast-iron sky and covered Fury's dark coat with glitter. Honey pulled her jacket hood up to cover her hair, but it was too late. Her hair was a frizzy, wet mess.

She was proud of herself. The weather hadn't kept her from her morning workout. In the past, she'd have rolled over in bed when she'd seen the gray clouds.

Fury did his business, and she made a U-turn. They'd skip the park today. He trotted alongside her, not seeming to mind. When she turned the corner, her house, windows glowing gold in the dull day, looked warm and inviting. She found herself wishing she could stay in, bake cookies, and watch old movies. They'd have to be low fat, sugar-free cookies. That thought made her feel better about going into the shop.

She walked straight to the kitchen and poured herself a second cup of coffee. She'd cut back on caffeine since the party at Lisa-Liza's house, and it seemed to be doing the trick. She hadn't had another attack. However, this morning's weather begged for hot coffee. She'd splurge. One more cup was all.

Honey put several drops of stevia into her cup. She'd been cheating, using agave nectar, but since it was her second cup she should stick with the sweetener. She topped off the coffee with coconut milk—she'd given up cream—and walked upstairs to dry her hair. When she shut the dryer off, she saw she'd missed a call from Booker.

She sat on the edge of the bed to return it. As she waited for him to answer, she wiggled her foot into a black boot. It only rang twice. "Where are you?" Booker said.

"Home."

"Stay there."

"I have to open the shop." She stuck her other foot into the second boot. "Can you meet me there?"

"No. Just wait for me. I'll be home in a couple of minutes."

"Why—" She didn't finish her sentence because he'd already hung up. She looked at her blank phone screen as if it might have the answer to the question she hadn't asked.

Fury sat at her feet panting. "You want breakfast?" she asked him. He spun around twice. "Is that once for no, two for yes? Or, the other way around?" He barked three times. "Oh, that was clever."

The dog followed her down the stairs and into the kitchen, not taking his eyes off her until she put his filled food bowl on the kitchen floor. Honey drained her coffee mug, glanced at the pot, and sighed. She wanted more. The weather was bad. She had to wait for Booker, but she'd already exceeded her one cup rule. A half. She'd only have a half, she'd use Angela's stevia not agave, and she'd have one of her gluten-free date bars to counteract the caffeine.

By the time she'd finished, washed and dried her mug, and placed it on the shelf, she heard the front door open and close. Fury tore into the front hall to greet Booker. "I thought you weren't coming home until—" her mouth clamped shut. Booker looked terrible. His eyes were red-rimmed. His hair stood in tufts on his head as if he'd been tearing at it. His face was gray beneath his tan. "What it is?" she said, alarmed now.

He took both her hands in his, drew her into the living room, and pulled her onto the couch next to him. "It's Joe." His brother's name caught in his throat. Honey didn't speak. She waited for Booker to get his emotions under control.

He cleared his throat. "He's dead."

Dead? The word raised so many questions; she didn't know which to ask first. And, God help her, it didn't bring the sense of grief and horror she knew it should. She mentally adjusted her tone and her face to express those emotions. "Where? How did it happen?"

"I don't know how to—" The doorbell rang. Fury raced toward it almost drowning out Booker's next words. "That's the police." He stood and followed the dog.

Why were the police at her door? Honey's brain was a muddle of confusion. Her heart began to do a drum dance. She pressed a hand against her chest.

Booker returned. Kirk Wickett and Michael Varma, the two cops she'd met in Black Star Canyon, were with him. Trailing behind all three was a dark-skinned woman in khaki pants and a sweater. Despite the casual outfit, everything about her from her athletic build to the intelligence in her eyes screamed detective.

What was happening? Had Joe gotten in an accident on his way to see them? Maybe her email had angered him, and he'd decided to bypass her and see Booker in person.

"Inspector Sylla," the woman said and held out a hand to Booker, then Honey.

"Would y'all like coffee?" The Kentuckian in Honey came out when she was nervous, and she was unaccountably nervous.

"No, but thanks, ma'am," Michael Varma didn't look as relaxed and confident as he had on the trail. Kirk Wickett's face was unreadable.

"Sit down," Booker said, and they all sat.

"We have some questions." Kirk's eyes were hard.

Booker held up a hand. "I haven't told her."

Honey struggled to understand what was happening. A car accident didn't explain the tension ricocheting around her like a pinball. Booker's grief, yes, it explained that, but not the presence of a detective, two officers, Kirk's anger, or Varma's discomfort. "What happened to Joe?" She blurted out the words.

Booker looked at his hands. "The body we found in Black Star. . ."

"We believe it to be Joseph Wells of Lawrenceburg, Kentucky," Inspector Sylla said.

The dance in Honey's chest picked up speed. She couldn't catch her breath to speak. She stared at the hands in her lap, willing them to unclench, to relax. She'd read somewhere that if you could relax a muscle, any muscle, it would help your entire body to relax. Just like smiling when you didn't feel like it put you in a better mood. Easing the tension from a muscle group sent signals to the brain.

"I recognized the artist's rendering," Kirk said.

"Those things are approximations. They're not proof," Booker said.

"What I want to know," Kirk said. "Is how you two knew where to find his corpse?"

Honey's head shot up. "How did we know? We didn't know there was a body there. We had no idea."

Kirk's chin dropped to his chest. He exhaled long and loud.

Sylla raised a hand. "We're not accusing you of anything, Mr., Ms., Wells. However, it is an unusual coincidence. You must admit."

Booker stood to his feet and raised his voice. "It can't be him. I keep telling you that. As of last week, Joe was alive. That body had been there weeks."

"Months," Varma said.

"Okay, months." Booker flipped his hands to the ceiling. "The point is Joe was alive and well as of last Wednesday."

"Actually." Honey's voice sounded weak after Booker's booming one. She tried again, a little louder. "Actually, he emailed me yesterday."

Booker glared at her. "Emailed you? You didn't tell me that? Why did he email you?"

"Sit, please, Book. You're making me nervous standing over me like that," Honey said. Booker sat. "I did something I'm not proud of." She paused, trying to think of the right words. "I read your emails. Not all of them," she added quickly. "Just the ones from Joe."

Her hands had balled into fists again. She straightened her fingers and rubbed her hands together, hoping the release of tension would transfer itself to her chest which was getting uncomfortably tight. "I shouldn't have. It was an invasion of privacy. But," she met his eyes, "I had to know what was happening with our money. If he was going to try to soak you for more."

"I told you I wasn't going to give him more." Booker's voice was soft now.

"I know that, Book, but—" She couldn't finish the sentence. What was she going to say? *You betrayed my trust once, and I was afraid you'd do it again. You have a weakness when it comes to your little brother.* Both were true, but why hurt him now? If Joe was dead, it didn't matter anymore.

But Joe couldn't be dead. The police had to be mistaken. "He did ask you for more money," she said. "I couldn't stand by this time. I was mad. Real mad. I emailed and told him to stay away from you. I told him he wasn't going to get one more dollar."

She drew in a shaky breath. Her heart fluttered against her ribs. She didn't feel well. She looked at the police officers and opened her hands like the St. Francis statue at the Abbey. "And he emailed me back. So, you see, that body can't be Joe's."

"You may have gotten an email, but Joe didn't send it," Kirk said.

"He sent the ones I got," Booker said. The cop looked at him as if he was the town fool. Booker kept talking anyway, "He referenced things nobody else knows about."

"Really? Like what?" Sylla said.

"It doesn't matter," Booker said.

"We're going to take both your laptops in as evidence so you might as well tell us," Kirk said.

Honey sat straighter. "Take our laptops? How am I going to manage the business?" Kirk didn't look concerned about Honey's business. "I want to see some paperwork. A warrant, or whatever it is you guys have to get," she said. "I don't believe you can take my laptop if you can't prove the body is Joe's."

"The dental records are a match." The detective's voice was calm and soothing.

Kirk pulled a piece of paper from a pocket. "I called the police in Lawrenceburg and found out Joe left town three months ago. His wife hadn't heard from him since. No one knew where he was. We requested dental. It's him."

CHAPTER TWENTY-ONE

BY THE TIME the police officers left, the dance in Honey's chest had become a frantic, whirling dervish. She leaned into the couch, closed her eyes, and concentrated on her breathing like she was in labor. She would not have another panic attack. She *would* control her stress.

Booker paced on the other side of the coffee table wearing a rut into the carpet. "Who has been emailing us?" He'd asked the same unanswerable question six times now. She'd counted.

"The police can trace the email, can't they?" She murmured.

"It depends on how tech-savvy the person is. The police can figure out the IP address, but that doesn't always tell you a whole lot."

Honey didn't know anything about IP addresses, and at the moment she was too consumed with what was happening inside her body to worry about it.

"Why would someone pretend to be Joe?" That was the second unanswerable question.

"Maybe they didn't want anyone to know he was dead," she said without opening her eyes. She heard him halt in his tracks.

"You're right. You're exactly right." He said the words as if they were a new idea. Honey was pretty sure she'd said it one of the other four times he'd asked the question. He continued as if she hadn't though. "If everyone thinks Joe's alive, no one is looking for him. There's no murder investigation."

There was another reason that emailer had impersonated Joe—money. Joe got fifty grand from Booker once. The killer must have known that and thought: Why not go after more? Those thoughts went through Honey's mind but never made it out of her mouth. She didn't want Booker to blame himself for Joe's death, even though it was most likely inevitable. He had a healthy sense of shame and guilt when it came to Joe.

"It must be the killer. Don't you think? Who else would—" he stopped short. Honey cracked open her eyes. "You don't look good," he said.

A cold sweat had broken out on Honey's forehead. She was pretty sure if she stood, she'd faint. Her thoughts and her heart were moving at such a rapid rate it took all her focus to stay calm. She felt as if she was driving a race car, body still, but mind going a hundred miles an hour.

"Where are your pills?"

"It'll pass," she said.

"It will once you take a pill."

"I can't drug myself up. I have to open the shop."

Booker disappeared from the room. When he reappeared, he held a glass of water in one hand and a tiny white pill in the other. "Take it," he said.

"Who's going to handle the store?"

"I will. You take this, and I'll go in."

"You don't know a slow cooker from a punch bowl." Nausea joined her mix of symptoms. She slid into a prone position.

"How about that girl you hired? Angela. That's her name, right?"

Honey nodded. It was easier than talking.

"I'll call her."

"It's so last minute."

"Where's your phone?"

Honey pointed toward the kitchen. She was fairly certain she'd left it on the counter. A moment later, she heard Booker's one-sided conversation as he circled the house. "I'm sorry. So last minute. . . had a shock. . . sure she'll be fine by tomorrow."

He stood at her side with the pill and water again. "She'll be there in half an hour. She's happy to open and close. Take this now."

Honey propped herself on an elbow, swallowed the tranquilizer, and waited for it to take effect. Fifteen minutes later, a down blanket dropped on top of her. The sharp edges of anxiety became soft and padded. The shape of her distress was still there—Joe was dead—but that knowledge no longer stabbed and poked at her. Thirty-five minutes later, she entered a restless, dream-filled sleep.

Fury barked. Voices. The sounds brought her to consciousness. She heard them, but it was as if she sat on the bottom of a pond and had to push her way to the surface before she could understand the words properly. "So nice of you." That was Booker's voice.

"Oh, it's okay." That was Angela.

Angela? She should be at the shop. Honey pried open one eye, then the other, retrieved her phone from the coffee table, and looked at the screen. It was noon. She'd slept all morning. Angela must be on a lunch break.

Honey heaved herself off the sofa and shuffled toward the voices.

"I'm learning so much from your wife. She's an amazing cook." Angela's praise sent a dull glow through Honey. She wasn't great at accepting compliments, but this one was helping her wake up.

"She is, but she needs to slow down," Booker said.

Honey sidestepped into the kitchen where she could hear the conversation without being seen.

"She works a lot." Angela sounded concerned.

"Too much." He paused, then said, "Maybe you can help me out?"

"Of course. Anything."

"If you see her getting stressed at work, having trouble breathing, looking faint, would you let me know? I think she's hiding things from me, and I'm really worried about her."

Of course, she was hiding things from him. If Booker knew how frequently Honey's heart jigged, he'd make her see the doctor again. There was nothing the doctor could do other than give her drugs, and she hated drugs. She was so groggy at the moment; she couldn't think straight.

Honey was handling it. She was exercising in the mornings, and even though she'd cheated on her diet now and again, she was eating better than she had been. Diet and exercise took time, but she was beginning to see the effects. Her clothes were looser. Her pace was faster when she went out to walk. So why didn't everyone leave her alone and give her time?

"You mean spy on her?" It sounded as if Angela's enthusiasm had diminished. Good. Honey knew she liked the girl.

"Not spy on her, not exactly. More like keep an eye on her. For her sake. We don't want her keeling over." He barked a disingenuous chuckle. He was attempting to make light of his request.

There was a long silence, and Honey held her breath, waiting to hear how Angela would respond. "I guess. If it's for Honey's health."

Honey exhaled a rush of breath. They were ganging up on her. She cleared her throat so they would know she was there and walked into the front hall.

Angela stood in the doorway with a white plastic bag in her hand. She wore a red wool jacket. It was covered with moisture droplets that glinted in the dull daylight. Her normally straight hair waved around her lovely face in the humidity. Booker leaned against the wall a few feet away, arms crossed over his chest, a funny smile painted on his handsome face.

Their heads swiveled her way. Booker's pleasant expression transformed into a guilty one. He looked so much like Ash when Ash had broken some rule or other, Honey almost laughed. She didn't however, because the situation wasn't funny. Her husband and her employee were in cahoots.

"Angela brought you chicken soup," Booker said. Angela held out the bag.

"How thoughtful." Honey took it from her.

"It's from that deli you like," Angela said.

Honey took the bag. It was surprisingly heavy. "You brought enough soup for a village. Why don't you have some with me, then we can go to the shop together."

"Hon, I really think—" Booker said.

She cut him off. "I'm okay. I got a good nap. I feel great." Which wasn't true. She didn't feel great. She felt like she was swimming through molasses. Maybe the soup would help.

"I brought lunch. I'm going to eat it at the shop." Angela backed out the door with rapid steps.

"I'll be there in an hour," Honey called after her.

Booker followed Honey into the kitchen and sat on a stool. He watched her ladle soup into a bowl and set it in the microwave. "Can't you take one day off?" He asked.

"I did. I took Sunday off."

"Joe is dead." Booker's voice filled with pain.

Honey dropped her chin to her chest. How could she be so callous? Booker's little brother was dead, and all she could think about was herself. She circled behind her husband, wrapped her arms around him and set her chin on top of his head. "I'm so sorry, Book."

He gripped her arms, and she felt his broad shoulders heave. They stayed that way, her holding him, him holding her, until his silent sobs ceased. He released her arms and wiped his face with his sleeve. "I know he wasn't your favorite person. . ."

"He was family," Honey said. "I'm not proud of myself for the way I've been acting."

"I get it. He hurt you. Hurt us. In some ways that's harder, you know? I can't fight it out with him. Get to the other side of it."

Honey understood. Her mother hadn't been an easy woman. Maybe she'd been overwhelmed by having six children so close together. Maybe it had been her hormones, but most of Honey's memories of her included sharp slaps and even sharper words. Consequently, Honey had avoided her mother as much as possible. Sometimes Honey would venture into the garden if she saw her there. The only time she seemed happy was when she was planting or pruning or cutting roses or hollyhocks to bring into the house.

One day when Honey was thirteen, her mother came down with a cough. She went to bed, and Honey took over the kitchen. That cough turned out to be lung cancer. Honey buried herself in soups and stews and breads and biscuits. Cooking dulled the confused emotions that jockeyed for dominance inside her: anger, grief, fear, and eventually loss.

Eight months after her diagnosis, her mother died. Honey never said goodbye. It left a hollow place in her gut no amount of crème brûlée could fill.

"He knew, Book. He knew you loved him."

Booker untangled himself from her embrace and left the kitchen. He returned a moment later, eyes red but dry. "You have to take care of yourself, Honey. I can't lose you too."

"I am. I've made changes. I'm walking, fast as I can, up hills too, every morning. I'm trying to stick to Dr. Hillary's diet." She didn't mention the pretzels and chocolate chips.

"I did notice there were no snacks in the house."

"Yeah, well, I got a little carried away."

Booker crossed the distance between them and embraced her. "Please don't keep secrets from me. We need to see this thing through together."

Honey wasn't sure whether he meant secrets about her health, or secrets about Joe, or work, but she buried her face in his chest and promised.

CHAPTER TWENTY-TWO

HONEY DIDN'T GO to work that day, or the next, or the next. She found herself on a roller coaster of anxiety that swooped into medicated stupors only to climb to heart-pounding heights again. Her nights were filled with restless dreams, her days in a haze of fatigue and nameless fears.

Booker slipped from room to room silently, like the shadows that filled the spaces the sun abandoned on its circuit. Each evening, when the daylight was gone, and the electric lights turned on, he joined her in the living room. They watched TV instead of talking, although she couldn't tell you what they saw. Not crime dramas, but that's all she remembered.

Rosie stopped by Sweeter each day to make sure Angela was managing things and wasn't overwhelmed. Then she'd come by the house, make a report, and take Fury for a walk. The dog was delighted to get out of the dismal atmosphere he didn't understand and couldn't fix.

Ash called on Wednesday morning. It was good to hear from him, although Honey didn't have much to say. After a few minutes, she handed the phone to Booker. They talked longer, but not about Joe.

The snippets Honey heard revolved around the base, Ash's training, and possible deployment. Ash was his father's son. He knew intuitively how to comfort him.

After Booker hung up, he sat with head hung, knees wide, fingers steepled, and hands like arrows pointing toward Honey. She wished she knew what to say. Her version of comfort smelled like baking bread and hot chocolate and sounded like the clatter of dishes. But the kitchen seemed miles away.

Later that day, Willow showed up like an unexpected Kentucky snow flurry; her soft hands and soft words blanketed the house. Her presence was as comforting to Honey as Ash's call had been to Booker. They talked for a while, but most of the time was spent sipping Angela's chicken soup and watching old movies while Booker made phone calls. The family had to be informed.

"How's it going with Jonathan?" Honey asked when they paused *Strangers on a Train* to get cups of herb tea.

Willow colored, her cheeks turning a lovely shade of peach. "Go-od." She strung out the word as if it had two syllables.

"I'm gonna need more than that," Honey said.

"I really like him, Mom."

The kettle whistled, and Honey stayed quiet as she poured water into two cups with lavender-chamomile teabags inside them. She waited for Will to fill in the details. She did.

"He's smart and handsome, and he can cook. Did I tell you he can cook?"

"You did," Honey said.

"His family is loaded, too. I didn't tell you that, did I?"

"Yes, you did."

Willow picked up the teacups and walked into the living room. She sank into the chair that had always been hers. "I can't wait for you to meet him." She sipped the tea, and made a face. "Hot!"

Honey dropped onto the couch. "Be careful."

"Right."

Honey wasn't referring to the tea alone. Her attitudes might be old-fashioned, or maybe they came from growing up in a rural area, but worry niggled at her. She'd had some bad experiences with the wealthy kids in town when she was a kid. It was a prejudice that had stuck with her. "So, you're dating a rich boy."

"Yes, and no. Jonathan wasn't rich growing up. Just middle-class, like us. They didn't hit the jackpot until he was, like, a senior in high school. He's not stuck-up or anything."

Honey blew on her tea and took a tentative sip. It was hot, but the heat helped her feel something other than panic, and that was worth it. "That's good. And, I guess, if you marry him, I won't have to worry about you."

Willow shook her head. "I plan to have my own career whomever I marry. This isn't the 1950s."

"I know, sweetheart, but you're a musician. There's a reason the word 'starving' is attached to 'artist'."

"Thanks for the vote of confidence."

Honey closed her eyes. She wasn't handling this well. She loved Willow's music and was incredibly proud of her daughter's talent. However, Honey was a practical woman. She knew what it was to go without, something her children had never experienced. Something she never wanted them to experience. As long as he wasn't a snob, a rich boyfriend wasn't a bad thing for a musician to have.

"I hired someone at the shop," she changed the subject.

"You did? I'm sure she can't be as wonderful as I was to work with."

"Of course not, but she's pretty good."

"Tell me about her."

Honey filled Willow in on how Angela was doing, then segued into how they met and her unusual living circumstances.

"That's weird," Willow said when Honey was done.

"What's weird?"

"That she went from a marketing position with a startup in Irvine to a prepper compound in Black Star Canyon. Why wouldn't she try to get a job with another company? I mean, it sounds like she had a good resume. Why move to the boonies? It's like she was running from something."

Honey set her teacup on the coffee table with a thump. *Running from something,* she hadn't thought of that. "It occurred to me that she was being abused by someone at the ranch. She's got bruises. But they could be old ones."

When Honey told Angela about Chef Fabien, she'd said she knew someone like him. Maybe that someone was no longer in her life. She looked into Will's eyes. "Maybe she's hiding from an abusive ex."

"Could be. If so, you'd better be careful. Helping her could put you in danger. Those guys are nuts."

"I can't abandon her if she needs help."

"I didn't say abandon her. I said be careful." Willow moved to the couch, sat next to her mother, and put her arms around her. "I don't know what's going on with you, Mom, but I'm worried. If this girl is stressing you out, you need to get some distance."

"It's not her," Honey said. "In fact, she's alleviating stress. No, she's a sweet girl. I think you'd like her."

"Okay." Willow returned to her chair. "Just remember, she's not family. You don't owe her anything but a fair wage."

"Why would you say that?"

"Because I know you. You," Willow made air quotes, "'adopt' people. You're too nice sometimes."

"Thank you, I guess."

"And, Rosie told me she thinks you're getting too attached."

"Rosie said that, did she?"

Willow hid a smile behind her teacup. She sipped, then said. "Don't forget, she's not your daughter. I am."

They turned the movie on again, but Honey missed most of it. Her thoughts were far away in Black Star Canyon.

Willow stayed late despite the hour and a half drive ahead of her. Honey tried to talk her into spending the night, but she said she was so full of energy she wouldn't be able to sleep if you paid her. She flitted away right before midnight. The calm she'd brought melted in the heat of yet another anxiety attack.

* * *

Sunshine broke through the clouds late on Thursday. Honey had been dozing on the couch for most of the day, when she was jarred awake by the bell followed immediately by a barking fit. Rosie stood on the stoop, a pizza box in her hand.

"Veggie everything," she said.

"Yum," Honey said.

"Oh, come on. Pizza is only on the edge of okay. If I load it up with pepperoni it goes over the cliff."

Booker appeared in the hallway. "I knew I smelled something good. Are you sharing?"

"Of course." Rosie pushed by Honey and disappeared into the kitchen. "Eric is working late. Thought I'd have dinner with you guys."

Honey padded after her. "Nothing like inviting yourself over."

"She can invite herself any time she wants to if she brings pizza," Booker said, retrieving a stack of plates from the cupboard. "There hasn't been much food around here lately."

Rosie placed two slices of pizza on a plate and handed it to Booker. "Here you go."

He lifted the plate to his nose and sniffed. "Love green peppers and onion. Anybody care if I eat in front of the TV? There's a Clippers game on."

Rosie waved him away. "I want to talk to your wife anyway." She placed a plate in front of Honey.

Honey looked at it suspiciously. She hadn't eaten anything but toast, crackers, and Angela's soup since Tuesday. She and Willow had finished the soup the night before, which meant all she'd had today was. . . Was nothing. Her stomach growled at the thought.

She took a small bite, set it down, and said, "Tell me about how Angela has been doing at work."

Rosie pulled up a stool at the counter next to her. "Seems fine. She's good with customers. The place looks clean. Somebody was in yesterday, Becks, Bev?"

"Bets." Honey groaned the name. "I totally forgot her party."

"Well, she didn't seem upset."

"I don't know how she couldn't be. She was giving me a second chance as it was." Honey filled Rosie in on Lisa-Liza's aborted party and the email she'd received from Bets the next day.

"Angela pulled your fat out of the fire," Rosie said around a bite of pizza.

"She what?"

"She pulled your fat out of the fire."

Honey closed her eyes in frustration. "I heard you. I just don't know what you mean."

"I mean, she did the party, and based on the conversation I heard, she did a great job."

"I never asked her to do that party."

"She's a self-starter. That's good isn't it?"

Honey thought about her next words before she said them. "Yes, of course. She saved me from a very embarrassing situation, but it makes me uncomfortable."

"Because?"

"Because I haven't trained her to do cooking parties. Call me controlling, call me a micro-manager, but I want to know things are going to be done the way I want them done."

"Then you better tell her."

"I will, but I don't want to be negative. She did do me a favor coming in last minute."

"Tell her she did a great job keeping the shop going while you were out. I can attest to that. Thank her for covering for you while you were gone."

"Right, but how do I bring up the party?"

A worried frown creased Rosie's forehead. "I don't know, but don't make it seem like I was spying on her."

"No, no. I won't say anything about you, but I am going to have to have a talk with her when I go in tomorrow." She wouldn't let on that Rosie had been keeping an eye on things, because she might ask Rosie to do it again.

Funny, Booker had asked Angela to spy on Honey. Now Honey was hoping Rosie would watch Angela. Her life was beginning to sound like an espionage movie and it was only going to get worse. She had a feeling she and Booker would be spending more time with lawyers and police in the next few weeks than she ever had in her life.

CHAPTER TWENTY-THREE

ON FRIDAY MORNING the police returned their laptops. Honey eagerly logged into her work email to see what she'd missed. It was much of the usual, links to small appliance sales and recipe blogs she followed, but there was also an email from Bets.

Honey's hand hovered over the mouse. Rosie believed the party went well, but what if Bets was only trying to encourage Angela? What if she hadn't wanted to hurt the girl's feelings? The cooking class might have been a disaster. She opened the message and bit her lower lip.

Dear Honey,

I can't tell you how much we all enjoyed your protege, Angela. Although we were disappointed not to have you, and certainly hope you're feeling better, we were delighted with her. You have trained her well.

Two of the women who attended would like to have parties of their own, and it was all I could do to convince them that they should leave it up to you which one of you does the instructing. They were that smitten by Angela. I've added their email addresses below.

Thank you again for the wonderful class.
Best,
Bets

Honey reread the email to be sure she hadn't misunderstood it the first time. She hadn't. The class had gone well. Honey didn't know whether to be relieved or upset. In the end, she settled somewhere between the two.

She was grateful Angela covered for her. It was a brave thing to do. However, the girl hadn't had any training. What if she'd bombed? In some ways that would have been worse for Honey's reputation.

She set her laptop on the coffee table and walked into the kitchen, indecision sending her to the refrigerator. It was a bad habit. She opened the door and peered in at the meager contents.

Poor Booker. She hadn't shopped or cooked in a week. The cupboard was bare. There were a couple of eggs and a half loaf of bread, however. She fried an egg, ate it with a piece of toast and washed it down with a cup of herb tea. She'd stayed away from coffee religiously for the past three days. It hadn't seemed to help. Her anxiety had been off the charts, but she was sure caffeine would make it worse.

Breakfast had fortified her. After a walk and a shower, she thought she should go to Sweeter. She had a ton of paperwork to catch up on after taking three days off, and she'd rather talk things out with Angela face to face.

As she was washing the breakfast dishes, Booker breezed into the kitchen. He looked, maybe not happier, but more at peace anyway. It had been frustrating that the autopsy and investigation meant that Joe's body wouldn't be released for a few days. He'd been calling Carla daily, trying to plan a service, but they were all in limbo. "Good morning."

"Morning."

"You look better," he said.

"I feel better. I'm going to work."

His eyebrows pinched together. "I wish you'd go to the doctor."

"I saw Dr. Hillary a couple of weeks ago. I'm fine. I think it was the flu."

He didn't look convinced, but he didn't argue. "I spoke with a lawyer this morning before you got up."

"A lawyer?" Worry rippled through her. "Why do we need a lawyer?"

Booker poured himself a cup of coffee and took a sip before answering. "The police implied they're looking at us as suspects in Joe's death."

"That's ridiculous. Why would we kill Joe? Besides, you're a firefighter. You're part of the system. One of their own. A hero—"

Booker held up a hand. "They have to look at everyone who knew Joe. Not only did we know Joe, we live near the place he was killed. There are very few people who fit that description."

"Two, as far as I can count. You and me."

"I get three."

Honey turned off the tap and reached for a towel. "Who's the third?"

"Kirk Wickett."

"The cop?"

"Yup." Booker's jaw muscle jumped.

"Did he know Joe was in the area?"

"I don't know, but I know neither you nor I killed Joe. I know Kirk had an ax to grind with him."

Honey hung the dishtowel on the oven door to dry. "That's the most confusing part of the whole thing for me."

"There's a most confusing part? I thought the whole thing was confusing."

"How did anybody know Joe was here? In Orange County? And, what was he doing in Black Star?"

"All I can think is he came to see me."

"But why Black Star?"

Booker leaned on the counter and gazed out the kitchen window. "He liked it up there. The last two times he came to visit, we'd hiked in Black Star. I never told you this, but he asked me to borrow the cash at the falls."

"What?" Honey's face got hot. She remembered Joe's last visit. It was about a month, maybe six weeks, before he disappeared. She'd made his favorite carne asada burritos when he and Booker got back from their hike. She'd washed sheets and towels for him. She'd told him to come again anytime. The fact that he'd been planning to take advantage of Booker's generous spirit while she was playing the hostess made the betrayal feel even worse somehow.

Booker didn't seem to notice her upset. "Yeah, I know, I should have told you, but it was a moment. You know?" He gazed at her, his eyes pleading for understanding. "We talked about how he'd messed up, how he wanted to make things better, how worried he was for Carla and the girls. I really thought he'd do the right thing. Fifty thousand seemed a small price to rescue his family."

"I might have agreed if you'd asked me." Honey's voice was soft.

"I don't think so, babe. I love you, but you worry about money."

That shut her down. She knew Booker was right, but shouldn't that have made him think harder about what he'd done?

"Anyway, when we were sitting up there at the falls, Joe said, 'Let's plan to come here next year, first Saturday of the new year. I have a feeling I'll have the money to pay you back and then some by then. I'll pack a couple of beers, and we'll celebrate.'"

"Is that why you were so insistent about hiking in Black Star the day we went?"

Booker gave her a sad smile. "Yeah. I was desperate. I didn't really think he'd be there, but I was out of ideas."

"But you'd heard from him?"

"He'd sent me that one email, said something about hiking together, and I thought maybe he was trying to send me a message."

"Did he even send that email?"

Booker closed his eyes. "I don't know. I guess he didn't, based on the condition of his—" His voice caught. He swallowed and blinked several times. "But the email, it sounded like him."

"You told me it didn't, that it was introspective. Joe was a lot of things but introspective wasn't one of them."

"But the emailer knew things."

"That's what you said." Honey hoped he'd elaborate. She wanted to know about Vic and the events mentioned in the email, but it didn't seem the right time to ask. Not while Booker was in mourning.

"Who could have done this?"

They were back to the unanswerable questions.

"Did the police delete stuff from your computer?" Honey asked.

"Doesn't look like it. Why?"

"Can we go over the emails from Joe? List them by dates, see if we can figure out which are which?"

Booker shrugged. "I guess, but I'm sure the police have already done that."

"The lawyer will want that information," Honey said.

"Speaking of, she can meet with us tomorrow afternoon. Are you available?"

"I can be. Can she help us with the estate stuff, too, or do we need another lawyer for that?"

"What estate stuff?"

She shifted her weight. "He owed us fifty thousand dollars. If there's money. . ."

"If there's money, it goes to Carla and the girls." Joe's voice was flat, emotionless.

"Right, but if they found a sum in a bank account somewhere that didn't have Carla's name attached to it, it's probably ours."

"We'd have to take Carla to court to get it."

"She might give it to us."

They glared at each other for a long moment. It was a standoff. Honey changed the subject. "Don't you have to go in to the station? You left last shift early?"

He crossed the kitchen and put his mug in the sink. "I'm taking a week off. Bereavement."

Bereavement. In the mess of mystery surrounding Joe's death, not to mention her health issues, Honey kept forgetting that Booker had lost his little brother. She'd be beside herself if she lost Poppy or Birch, and Booker had been much closer to Joe than she was to her youngest siblings.

Without meaning to, she'd been making things harder on him not easier. She couldn't pretend to grieve over Joe, but she could give Booker some time and space to do his own grieving.

"When are the police going to release the body?"

"Maybe they have. I don't know. I'll call Carla again and see if she's got the funeral plans nailed down yet."

Neither said anything for a long minute. Honey broke the silence. "I'm going to head into Sweeter unless you need me for something."

She was glad she had Angela to mind the store. It looked like she'd be making a trip to Kentucky in the not too distant future.

* * *

Honey saw Angela through the window before she reached the door. The girl stood behind the counter. Her blond head bowed over the computer, her gaze fixed on its screen.

She glanced up when the doorbell jingled, a professional smile already affixed. When she recognized Honey her eyes widened, and the smile faded for a second, then it blossomed again. "You're here."

"I am," Honey said.

"I didn't know you were—"

Honey cut off what sounded like an apology. "Neither did I. You did the right thing coming in."

Angela bent and picked up her purse. "I can leave. I have the car."

"No. Stay. I'm so behind it'll be good to have someone manage customers."

Neither said anything for a second or two, then both spoke at once. "The place looks—" Honey started to say.

"Are you feeling—" Angela said.

They both laughed. "Okay, you go first," Honey said.

"I just wanted to know how you were feeling. I'm so," she inhaled and exhaled slowly, "so sorry for you guys. It must be terrible."

"Thank you," Honey said. "It is terrible. More terrible for Booker than for me. Joe was his brother, but it was a shock for me too. Now, my turn," she looked around the room. "The place looks nice. You took good care of things."

Angela's concerned expression disappeared into a broad grin. "You think so? I made a couple of changes. Nothing big." She hurried from behind the counter and crossed to the cookbook corner.

"I put the gadget bins here, by the cookbooks." She gestured toward them. "I figured people need new gadgets when they try new recipes, right?" She reached into a bin and pulled out a ginger press. "I mean, if you never made Thai food before, you probably don't have one of these."

Honey had always kept the gadget bins near the cash register. Popular wisdom dictated that shopkeepers put small items near the checkout. Once people have their wallet in hand, they're more likely to add to their order. She wasn't convinced the move was a good one, but she'd give it a try.

"I also moved the baking tins next to the casserole dishes." Angela sidestepped to the shelves of stoneware. "I don't know about you, but I bake cakes and brownies and all kinds of things in my casseroles. Especially the oblong ones."

Honey did not bake sweets in her casseroles, thank you. She'd give the gadgets a go, but the bakeware would return to its place. Since Angela was so enthusiastic about her innovations, Honey didn't have the heart to say anything about it at the moment though.

By the time Angela finished the tour of Honey's own shop showing her all the little changes, Honey was ready for a nap. She had to talk to her, enforce the chain of command, but not now. She couldn't face it now.

"Very innovative," she said, making a feeble attempt at enthusiasm and headed to her office. She halted in the doorway. It smelled wrong. There was something different in the air. It took her a full minute of sniffing to find the bag of chocolate macadamia nut flavored coffee by the coffee maker.

Honey enjoyed surprising combinations of foods. She liked trying unorthodox recipes, unfamiliar ethnic dishes. However, there were some things you didn't mess with. Coffee was one of them. She hated flavored coffee. Hated the idea of it, the taste of it, and above all the smell. She picked up the offensive grind and stowed it in a drawer hoping that would muffle the smell.

She turned away from the small kitchen area and viewed the room from another vantage point. That's when she saw the calendar. On the wall where her favorite mixing bowl clock used to be, was a huge, whiteboard monstrosity. Printed on it in a neat, loopy hand were events.

Honey reached it in two long strides and began to read: *J. Thompson Cooking Class, In-store Pressure Cooker demo, Patricia Howard Cooking Class, Vegetarian Event - get booth.* And, that was just for the end of January.

Honey stood, one hand over her mouth, the other on her hip. This could not continue. The front of the store was one thing, this was something else altogether. Angela had invaded her inner sanctum. She felt violated.

She was sure Angela had been trying to be helpful, but she'd gone too far. Willow's words from the other day floated into her mind. *Don't forget, she's not your daughter. I am.* Honey hadn't taken that seriously. She hadn't understood why her daughter would say such a thing until this moment.

Willow left, and Angela slid into the space she'd vacated. Willow—and Rosie—knew Will's leaving had left a hole not only in the business, but also in Honey. Although she hadn't meant to, she'd invited Angela to fill it. That had to be why the girl felt she had permission to do all this.

She needed to be more cautious. Not because Angela was a bad person, or even because there might be a dangerous guy out there looking for her, but because she was emotionally vulnerable. Angela was looking for a place to belong. Her mother had thrown her to an aunt who hadn't wanted her. Honey, sitting on her empty nest, must represent the mother Angela had never had. It wasn't fair for Honey to send her the wrong signals then get irritated when she blew through red lights.

"Angela," Honey called.

"Yes?" Her voice rang from the front of the store.

"Can you come here?"

A moment later the girl stood in the doorway, eyes wide and innocent. "Oh. I forgot to tell you about the calendar. Do you like it? I thought it would be really handy to have something on the wall where we could both see what was coming up."

Honey tore her eyes from the whiteboard. "Tell me about these events."

"A rep from the pressure cooker company called and offered to do the demo. I thought it sounded like a good idea, so I booked it. I read about the veggie fair in the paper. I think that would be a great opportunity for us, but I didn't reserve a booth. You have to pay upfront."

Thank God Angela didn't have access to a company credit card. "And the classes?"

"So the cooking classes came from Bets' party. They loved your Greek recipes, by the way. A-mazing food." She said amazing as if it were two words.

"How do you know I'm available on those dates?" Honey controlled her tone, kept it calm, casual.

"I don't, but I figured I could do the classes if you were busy." Angela's voice faltered. Her face clouded over. "Did I overstep?" she said.

"Yeah." Honey nodded slowly. "You did."

Angela's lower lip trembled. She bit it and held it with her teeth.

"I know you're trying to do a good job, and I appreciate that. I do. But you can't make these kinds of decisions for me. This is my shop, my business. I've been running it for a long time, and—right or wrong—I have my ways of doing things."

Tears threatened to spill from Angela's eyes. "I'm so sorry. It's just you were out and. . ."

Honey crossed the room in two strides and wrapped her arms around the girl. "Now, stop that. You're great. I don't know what I'd do without you. You got that? We're just rubbing off the rough edges, learning to work together."

Angela pulled out of Honey's embrace and rubbed her red eyes with the heel of her hand, making them even redder. "I'm so embarrassed."

"I didn't mean to make you cry."

"It's not you. I mean, it's not only you."

Honey perched on the edge of her desk. She knew she'd resolved to create a professional distance between herself and her new employee, but compassion overrode the decision. "What's going on?"

"Nothing. It's. . . Nothing."

Only it wasn't nothing. Angela had cried off the makeup around her eyes and Honey could see the discoloration of her skin clearly now. If those were bruises, they weren't old. Angela had been living at the ranch for months. Her problem wasn't in the past. It was a very present trouble.

CHAPTER TWENTY-FOUR

HONEY ASKED ANGELA to close the office door as she left then called Rosie. "Want to go hiking with me?" she said when Rosie answered.

"Wait. I think there's something wrong with my phone. Can you repeat that?" Rosie said.

"Very funny. You heard me. Want to go hiking after work?"

"Today?"

"Yes, today."

"Where?"

"Black Star." There was a long pause on the other end of the line. "Did you hear me?" Honey said.

"Yeah. You said Black Star. Is that a good idea?"

"Why not?"

"First of all, you were on the couch for three days. Should you be exerting yourself?"

"I feel fine, and the doctor said I'm supposed to exercise."

"The bigger issue is the police are looking at you and Booker as suspects in Joe's death. Are you sure you want to return to the scene of the crime?"

"I didn't commit a crime." Honey bristled. "Besides, I don't want to go to the falls."

"Where do you want to go?"

Honey lowered her voice. "I want to see if I can find the ranch Angela lives on."

Rosie lowered her voice too. "Why are we whispering?"

"She's in the front of the shop. I don't want her to hear me."

"Did you talk to her about the cooking class?"

"Yes, and so much more. I'll fill you in on the hike."

"I didn't say I'd go."

Honey lifted her gaze to the ceiling. "Will you?"

"I can't leave until four. I have a client appointment at two."

"That's okay."

"It gets dark early."

"We can bring flashlights."

Another long pause. "Okay. I'll come over as soon as I'm ready."

They hung up, and Honey got to work.

* * *

Angela clocked out at three. She was subdued, but no longer overtly upset. "See you tomorrow?" Honey called after her.

Angela stopped with her hand on the door handle. "You still want me?"

"Of course, I still want you. Don't be silly."

A look of relief softened her features. "Okay. See you in the morning."

Soon after, Honey locked the shop and headed home. Rosie met her at four, and they were at the parking lot of Black Star Canyon's fire trail by four twenty.

The sun was low in an orange-gold sky. "You sure you don't mind walking in the dark?" Rosie asked for the third time.

"I don't, but I'm starting to wonder if you do."

"I'm good, as long as we stay on the fire trail. I don't want to do a bunch of off-roading in the dark. That's a good way to turn an ankle."

"Fire road it is."

As they crossed the dirt parking area, Honey noted how few cars there were compared to the Saturday morning she was here with Booker. A frisson of nerves feathered over the skin of her arms. They had flashlights, and they weren't going far. They'd be fine.

At the end of the lot, a barricade blocked cars from entering the fire trail, but it was easily circled by pedestrians and bikers. This must be one of the locked gates Angela had referred to. What a strange life. She couldn't imagine living in a home that hid behind a series of gates each one leading to more and more inaccessible places.

As they passed the barricade, a vision of prison doors swinging shut behind her filled Honey's mind. The thought was claustrophobic.

"It's a nice night," Rosie said.

"The sky is beautiful," Honey said. She wasn't walking into a prison. She was walking into the wilderness, away from small tight places not into them.

"What happened with Angela?" Rosie said.

Honey filled her in on all the changes the girl had made in her absence. When she reached the part about the whiteboard, Rosie laughed. "She doesn't know you very well does she?"

Honey's lips tightened into a thin line. "What do you mean by that?"

"You and I have been friends for, what, ten years?"

"Something like that."

"I've taken care of your dog, your kids, your house more times than I can count. You have the key to my home. I have the key to yours. I've worked in the shop, run your register, and organized your window display. But I'd never mess with your kitchen or your office. And, I'd absolutely not mess with your calendar."

"She knows that now," Honey said.

The road spiked upward, and neither said anything for several steep minutes. When they crested the hill, Rosie said, "What's our mission? Why are we up here tonight?"

"I told you, I want to see if I can find the ranch." Honey's words came in short pants, but she wasn't as winded as the first time she'd hiked in Black Star. The exercise she'd been doing was beginning to pay off.

"But why?"

"I'm worried about Angela. That man she's living with, Rick, is weird. "

"Weird how?"

"Weird in almost every way. One," Honey began to tick points off on her fingers. "He's a prepper, aka paranoid. Two, he had a mental breakdown after his wife died. Three, something is going on with Angela. She has bruises on her knuckles and around her eyes, and her eyes are red all the time, like she's been crying. Four, he carries a rifle everywhere he goes—"

Rosie interrupted, "You think Rick might have something to do with Joe's death?"

"Maybe." The thought had occurred to Honey. "It does seem like a big coincidence that a dead body and an armed crazy man just happen to be in the same remote area."

"Did you mention your suspicions to the police?"

"I didn't. I was too busy having a panic attack. Besides, I assumed they'd think of it for themselves. Booker says everybody knows the residents up here carry firearms."

"You think Joe went to the falls to see Rick?"

"No. I think he wanted to think things through. He loved this place. Every time he came to visit, he'd wrangle Booker into hiking up here."

They turned a corner, and two mountain bikers came into view. A moment later, they whizzed past, heading for the parking lot. Honey glanced at the sky. It was crimson now, like the day's blood was pooling at the bottom of the world. Black Star made her think morbid thoughts.

"Why would Rick kill Joe?" Rosie's eyes narrowed as if puzzling through the theory.

"Because he's crazy. I thought we already established that," Honey said.

"Even crazy people need a motive."

"Booker says the people who live up here are gun-shy. There's been a lot of crime, a lot of vagrancy. Maybe he thought Joe was trouble."

They hiked on for nearly half a mile. The dirt road took on a reddish hue, and the air shimmered like rose wine in the dying light. Rosie broke the silence. "If you're suspicious of Rick and the ranch, why aren't you worried about Angela working for you?"

"I'm worried *for* her. Joe's death is police business. Angela is my business. She's like Fury. Picked up from a rescue shelter, bad puppyhood, but sweet-tempered underneath. If this Rick is bad news, she could be in danger."

"Did she tell you about her puppyhood?"

"A little bit. It wasn't good." Peter's assessment of Angela popped into Honey's mind. "Speaking of which, the night of the artist opening Peter made a comment about Angela. He said she looked like someone who could take care of herself, said she seemed like someone with a past. He implied he'd spent time with others like her. What was that about? Did Peter work with disadvantaged youths in his past?"

"Peter was a disadvantaged youth."

Honey stopped walking and turned to stare at Rosie. "Peter? Our pretentious Peter?"

"Close your mouth. You'll catch flies." Honey's jaw clamped shut. "Yes, our Peter. Why do you think he's so pretentious? It's called overcompensation."

Honey began to walk again. "What's his story?"

"I don't know the details. He doesn't like to talk about it. But I get the impression he blames his rocky childhood for his involvement in Manifest."

Peter had spent years working as a trainer for Manifest, a cult-like movement based in Seattle that masqueraded as a business coaching organization. He'd become disillusioned when Wes Fellman, the founder, was accused of sexual harassment by several female employees. Honey had followed the court case in the papers last year. She'd wondered then how a man as intelligent as Peter could have been taken in by a creep like Wes Fellman. A bad start in life could explain it.

Rosie had slowed while she was answering Honey's question. She trotted a couple of steps to catch up now. "What do you hope to learn by coming up here tonight?"

Honey walked a bit before answering. "Honestly? I don't know, but I have to do something."

"Why? Why do you have to do something? Angela is an employee, not a daughter, not a sister."

"I worked for a chef in Louisville who made my life miserable. He was my Wes Fellman, a charismatic, manipulative man. When it got so bad I had to leave, he blackballed me. I know what it's like to feel trapped by a powerful person. If Angela needs help getting out of Rick's house for whatever reason, I want to be there for her."

The road curved to reveal the same pockmarked row of signs Honey had seen the last time she'd been here. The women stopped, hands on hips, and stared. "Okay, I see what you mean," Rosie said. "Whoever lives here isn't Mr. Rogers."

"Nope. Never a beautiful day in this neighborhood."

Three more bikes raced past Honey and Rosie on their way down the hill. The sky was peppered with birds winging toward their nests. Everybody was headed home. Honey wondered at the wisdom of her plan. "Let's walk up the drive a bit," she said before she changed her mind.

Rosie's eyebrows shot up. "You want to visit the crazy guy who might have killed Joe?"

"No, I just want to see his place. Friar Philip said he lived behind a bullet-hole riddled sign. This has got to be it."

Rosie pivoted away from Honey as if she couldn't stand to share the same patch of road with her anymore. She stared at the hills surrounding them, now black against a navy-blue sky, then circled back. "I think the climb has affected the oxygen levels in your brain. Preppers are paranoid. They're worried people are going to steal their supplies. I'm sure he's got security, big dogs, something."

"How do you know so much about it?"

A ghost of a smile played across Rosie's mouth. "Reality show."

Honey snorted and skirted the "No Trespassing" signs. "I'll stay in the trees."

Rosie paused for a moment, then followed. Honey felt foolish slipping between the trees into their uneasy shadows. She had no idea what she was looking for, only a vague hope she'd recognize it when she saw it.

About a quarter mile in, the dirt drive dead-ended into a clearing. A white ranch-style house, small but surprisingly well-kept, a gray barn, and a long, low cinder block structure were nestled around it. A newish Ford F150 and a very old Honda Civic she recognized as the one Charlie drove were between the house and the barn.

"Someone is home," Rosie whispered.

The windows glowed with lamplight. Rather than looking sinister, the house appeared warm and cozy. For a crazy minute, Honey thought about walking up to the front door and inviting herself in for tea.

They hid behind the oaks, peering around trunks and branches until the sky lost all color, and the gray shadows turned black. There was nothing to see. She didn't sense danger. This could be a den of wolves, or it could be group of people cobbled together by misfortune living as far away from an unkind world as they could get. Honey turned toward the main road. "We can go."

Melancholy settled heavily on her. This had been a fool's errand. Why she'd believed she could waltz up Black Star Canyon and discover what was happening behind closed doors was now beyond her. There were no clues here, not to what was happening to Angela and not to who killed Joe.

Another depressing thought struck her. They might never know who killed Joe. Which meant Booker would always be a suspect. The police might not be able to prove him guilty, but that didn't mean they would believe he was innocent. Six-day-old meatloaf might not be bad, but it wasn't exactly appetizing. This kind of taint could impact his career. Emergency service workers had to operate as a team, have each other's backs. Trust could mean the difference between life and death.

The growl of an engine behind them made her jump. Her heart skittered around her chest like the lights crisscrossing the tree trunks surrounding them. Honey and Rosie hunkered down and watched the pickup truck bounce past. "Do you think he saw us?" Rosie said.

"He'd have stopped if he did." Honey said the words to reassure herself as well as Rosie. She didn't know if he would've stopped, but based on the pockmarked signs it seemed likely.

She waited until the pounding inside her rib cage slowed, then began walking toward the fire road again. Neither dared to turn on their flashlights, so the going was slow. It seemed much farther out than it had in, but long minutes later, they broke through the brush onto the main trail.

The moon had risen, and the road seemed bright after the darkness of the trees. They walked at a fast clip, not bothering to turn on their lights. Now that they could speak in normal tones, neither had anything to say. Rosie seemed to sense Honey's depression.

Two miles later, the barricade that separated the fire road and the parking lot appeared in the distance, its metal frame glinting in the moonlight. "Thank goodness," Rosie said. "I was starting to get the creeps. You're rubbing off on me."

"Me?"

"All that talk about crazy men and murder. It's worse than thinking about mountain lions, which really are here, by the way."

"I know. Booker told me."

As they drew closer to the gate, another engine's hum hit her ears. Honey glanced around and saw the bright cones of headlights. She picked up her pace. If that was Charlie, or Angela, or Zach, she didn't want them to see her, but there was nowhere to hide between here and her van.

The car came faster than she and Rosie could jog. Minutes after she first heard the engine, the car pulled up alongside them. A window rolled down. "Do you ladies need help?" a male voice said. It was Zach.

"Hey, don't I know you?" Zach's eyes narrowed; his jaw hardened.

Honey's mouth twitched into a brief smile. "I'm Honey Wells. Angela works for me."

His face cleared, but Honey had the sense that there were hidden wells of emotion behind the handsome features. "That's right. I saw you at the Abbey."

"Right. This is my friend, Rosie."

"Zach." He flashed a smile she thought was intended to be disarming. It wasn't. "What are you guys doing up here?" The question was pointed, not casual.

"Hiking," Honey said.

"Kind of late, isn't it?"

"Took us longer than we thought," Rosie said with a nervous laugh.

He gazed out his windshield before answering as if considering her words. "That happens." It sounded like a verdict, as if he'd weighed her words, and they'd passed whatever test he'd applied. "Do you need a ride?"

Honey shook her head. "Car is in the lot." She was surprised at the sense of relief the words gave her. The idea of getting into the car with Zach made her skin prickle.

"Okay, then." He tapped his forehead with two fingers in salute, gave them another smile that should have been charming. "Be careful hiking up here. It's dangerous after dark." His car crunched down the road, dust billowing up behind it.

Rosie fanned the air in front of her face. "Why do I feel like I just had an interview with one of Anne Rice's vampires?"

Zach's car slowed to a stop, and so did Honey. She didn't want to catch up to him. He got out of the vehicle and walked to the gate. A minute later, the gate gave a violent shudder. It groaned as he pushed it open, the sound loud in the quiet night. He drove through, got out of the car again, and shut it. There was a cost to living so far from civilization. Why were these people willing to pay it?

"Maybe you should be worried about Angela," Rosie said.

Honey glanced at her friend. Rosie had always been intuitive, but since her experiences last year, she'd become even more so. "I'm going to go see Friar Philip."

"Schedule an exorcism?"

"Funny. No, he knows the family. I asked him about them before, but he wouldn't say anything. Didn't want to gossip. But if Rick is dangerous, if Angela could be in trouble, I need to know."

They reached the gate. Honey gave it a wide berth as she walked around it.

"If Angela *is* trouble, you need to know that too," Rosie said as they climbed into the van.

They didn't talk much on the ride home. Honey's mind was occupied with the contradictory messages of the evening. She'd expected to find a guarded compound, a prison behind the gates, but the house seemed normal, pleasant even. Zach, the young man she'd thought so beautiful that day at the Abbey, now made the hair on her arms stand on end.

When she turned onto her own street, the suburban homes that lined it welcomed her like a hug, warm light spilling from their windows. She felt as if she was returning from another country. Her neighborhood, so predictable, so average, filled her with a sense of security. She parked and got out of the van. The familiar scent of dirt and grass and growing things was as comforting as a bowl of corn chowder on a cold day.

Rosie crossed the damp grass to her own front yard. She stopped when she reached her walkway. "Honey, be careful. Please. Angela is a big girl. She can take care of herself."

Helping her could put you in danger. Willow's caution from the other night rang through Honey's mind, and a tingle of apprehension sheeted over the skin on her arms. Not because of Rosie's warning. Or Willow's. Because she didn't intend to heed either one.

CHAPTER TWENTY-FIVE

THE ALARM WENT off at 5:30 on Sunday morning. Booker groaned, pulled a pillow over his head, and turned from Honey. She slipped out of bed and dressed as quietly as possible. She didn't want to wake him for many reasons, not the least being that she didn't want to explain why she was up so early.

The early morning mass at the Abbey was open to the public. Honey wasn't Catholic, but she planned to attend. She wanted to see Friar Philip before he got busy with his day.

She heard the bells peal as she turned onto the Abbey's long drive. St. Francis looked smaller and softer in the morning light; the set of his features friendlier. Instead of turning left toward the refectory as she usually did, she made a right and parked in front of the chapel.

Novices and friars huddled against the chill in their long robes, hurried through the wood doors. One of the salt and pepper twins, she couldn't remember if he was Owen or Reginald, held the door for her.

The interior of the building was surprisingly warm. Maybe because of the friars' austere lifestyle and the age of the chapel, Honey had expected it to be cold. But vents along the floor pumped out a steady stream of warm air. Sunlight glittered on stained glass windows and lit the room with color. She slid into a pew and drew in a deep breath.

An organ sounded. The congregants stood. Mass began. The hymns they sang were unfamiliar to her Pentecostal ears. The songs were older and filled with mystery, as was the flutter of movement around her. The people in the pews stood, knelt, and spoke their lines like the actors in a well-rehearsed play. As a child, she'd been taught rituals were a heathen invention, as was the repetition of rote prayers.

She disagreed. The prayers seemed filled with reverence; the memorization worshipful. She closed her eyes and allowed the peaceful atmosphere to permeate her soul.

She must have dozed. A draft of chilly air jarred her to attention. The chapel door was ajar, and the devout were exiting the building. A shadow fell across her pew. Honey looked up into the face of Friar Philip. "Good morning, Honey. Thinking of converting?"

"My Assemblies of God grandma would roll over in her grave if I did. I'm here to see you."

His eyebrows lifted, but he didn't ask why. "We can talk in my office."

Honey followed him past several saints, cozy in their niches, to the back of the sanctuary, through a small door, and into a hallway. Honey blinked. After the ancient service, stepping into the hallway with its electric lights blinking overhead was like stepping into a time machine. Friar Philip opened the third door they came to.

His office was roomy, lined with shelves of books and filled with tattered but comfortable looking furniture. The priest walked around a large oak desk and settled himself into a black leather chair. She took the chair opposite his.

"I assume we don't need the confessional," he said.

"This is perfect. I—"

He held up a hand to silence her. "One minute." He fished a cell phone from somewhere in the folds of his robe and typed onto the screen. When he finished, he placed his phone on the desk screen side down. "Now, what can I do for you."

"You know I've hired Angela?"

"She's not causing problems?"

Honey thought about the talk she'd had to have with the girl recently, but it wasn't relevant. "No, not at all. Actually, I'm worried about her."

A crease formed between his eyebrows. "Worried?"

"She. . .," Honey searched for the right words. She didn't want to bring up the bruises, not if she didn't have to. "Seems afraid of something, or someone."

"Afraid?"

"I know you don't like to divulge things about your congregants, but Rick sounds so strange. I want your opinion, is the ranch a good place for a young woman?"

Friar Philip leaned back in his chair and folded his hands over his abdomen. He stared into Honey's eyes for a long second. "Rick is an honest man." He paused long enough for her to wonder what that had to do with Angela, then said, "He was never involved in the business."

The business? The business Zach and Angela worked for in Irvine? Why would Rick be involved? Before she could ask, the office door opened. A young man carrying a tray shuffled in. Honey smelled the coffee before she saw it.

The novice placed the tray on the desk and shuffled out again. Friar Philip poured dark liquid from a carafe into two mugs and handed one to Honey. She shouldn't, but she sipped the coffee and sighed. It was wonderful.

"The family business, that's what Ralph liked to call it, until the SEC shut it down at the end of last year," Friar Philip continued.

Honey's thoughts spun. She'd been worrying about an older man exerting undue influence over Angela, or a romantic relationship gone bad, not lawsuits and SEC agents. It did explain why Angela might be hiding in the canyon, but it didn't explain the bruises. "Are she and Zach involved? A couple?"

Friar Philip turned his palms to the ceiling. "I don't know. Two such attractive young people thrown together. It's possible."

"What's he like?" Honey said.

"Zach is, unfortunately, more like his uncle than his parents liked to admit."

Confusion fizzed inside her. "His uncle?"

"Yes, Ralph Trumbull is Zach and Charlie's uncle, their mother's brother. Her name was April. She was a dear woman. Nothing like Ralph."

"You talk like you know Ralph well."

"I should. He and I attended high school together, played on the same football team."

It took Honey a moment to digest that information. She had a hard time imagining the priest ramming a helmeted head into his opponents.

"Grew up in Laguna Beach," Father Philip continued. "We lost touch, but April would fill me in on his doings periodically. She was proud of him when he started the company. It seemed he'd turned over a new leaf, made a success of himself."

"Turned over a new leaf?" Honey said.

"He was intelligent but never satisfied to climb ladders in prescribed ways. He saw himself as brighter, better than others. He was also a terrible bully. Surrounded himself with a gang of weak-minded thugs and controlled them with his tongue. Anyone who didn't bend to his will paid a price." A cloud crept over Friar Philip's face, and he stopped speaking. He seemed to have disappeared into a dark memory.

An alarm bell sounded in Honey's brain. Ralph was a bully. Zach was like his uncle. She waited what she hoped was a respectful amount of time, then said, "You said Zach is like his uncle?"

Friar Philip inhaled and exhaled through his nose before answering. "He attended boys' camp here at the Abbey every summer until he got old enough to refuse. He was unkind to the less popular boys. I believe April saw into his soul and sent him to us in the hopes the church could fix him. I'm sorry to say, we didn't. It ate her up inside, like the cancer."

"Is that what killed her? The cancer, I mean?"

"Yes, it was terrible. I visited often, brought her the sacraments. When she died, Rick became a broken man."

He glanced at Honey and locked eyes with her. "Rick is obsessed with the end times, stockpiles food, and totes a gun, but he isn't a bad man. On the contrary, it was love for his wife that threw him into that downward spiral."

Honey stared into her cup. Her coffee had grown cold. A greasy slick floated on its top. She stood. "I won't keep you, Father. I know how busy you are."

The priest stood as well. "I don't know how much help I've been."

"You've given me a lot to think about. Thank you for that." Honey turned toward the door but stopped. "Oh, I forgot to mention, Booker's brother, Joe, has died."

Friar Philip paled. "Joe's gone?"

"Yes." She paused, wondering how to tell him the rest of the story. It was such a strange one. "You remember when I told you we found the body of a hiker in Black Star?"

The priest's hand flew to his chest. "It was Joe?"

She nodded.

"I didn't know you were looking for him."

"We weren't. We had no idea. It's a shock."

Neither said anything for a beat, then Father Philip said, "I don't believe in coincidences."

Honey stiffened. Did he mean he thought she and Booker had something to do with Joe's death? Before she could confront him, the priest said, "The Lord must have led you there so Booker and the family would know where he was."

Her shoulders relaxed. "Maybe," she said.

He shook his head slowly, sadly. "What a tragedy. He was a good man. He made mistakes, but he was a good man."

Honey was surprised by his statement. Joe had helped her at the soup kitchen once or twice when he'd visited, but she had no idea he'd grown close to the priest. "I didn't know you knew him that well."

Friar Philip gave her a small smile. "He stopped by to talk when he was in town. I think I provided a small measure of comfort, hopefully a modicum of wisdom. I'd be happy to say a few words at the funeral if I'm needed."

Honey thanked him and left. As she retraced her steps through the sanctuary, she tried to follow the threads of all the things she'd learned but they ended in a tangle. A tangle that knotted around the trees of Black Star Canyon.

CHAPTER TWENTY-SIX

ON MONDAY MORNING Honey got to the shop before nine. She walked to her office without turning on the shop lights but turned on her computer. She'd take advantage of the quiet to get her mind back on her business. If she needed to take time off for Joe's funeral, she'd better set things up for Angela before she left. This time there would be no reason for her to get creative.

While her laptop booted up, she made herself a cup of herbal tea. She looked longingly at the coffeepot but exercised self-control. She'd had a half cup already, more than she should have.

As she finished the tea, the front doorbell chimed, and Angela's voice sang out over the noise. "Hello. Honey, are you here?"

Honey closed her browser. "Yes. In the office."

Angela appeared in the doorway. "You're in early."

"Still playing catch up."

"I brought you something." Angela held out a bag. Honey could smell the contents from where she sat. It was something sweet and warm, and her stomach growled in response. "Remember the date bars I made you?"

"Yes, they were great."

"I've been working on the recipe. I think these are even better."

"Sugar-free, gluten-free, and all that free stuff?" Honey asked.

"Of course. I care about your health."

"No cholesterol?"

"No cholesterol."

"As long as they're Charlie approved, I guess I have to try one. Where is Charlie these days? I haven't seen him in a while."

"He went to stay with an aunt. She lives closer to his school. Driving in from the canyon is a pain." As Angela placed the bag on the desk, the sleeve of her blouse rode up her arm, exposing an angry bruise that circled her wrist like a bracelet. She quickly pulled the sleeve down.

"Where'd you get that bruise?" Honey said.

"Closed a door on myself. I'm so clumsy." She gave a small shrug and a nervous laugh.

Honey didn't believe her. She was lying, just like Ash and Willow used to lie when they broke the rules, with a laugh and a shrug. Honey opened her mouth to call her on it but filled it with date bar instead.

Angela wasn't Willow or Ash. She wasn't Honey's child. She was an adult. Honey needed to respect her privacy, but her purple wrist and the fact that Charlie was gone unsettled her. Honey wondered if he'd been her protector.

"These are great." Honey held up a bar. Angela's first attempt had been okay, but these were delicious. "You sure there's no sugar in this?"

"Nope," Angela grinned.

Honey returned the grin. She'd made a decision. She would be a friend, an encourager, earn her trust. If the girl needed help, she might open up and talk to Honey. Meanwhile, she'd keep an eye on things. If it looked like Zach was abusing Angela, she'd step in.

Honey held out the bag of sweets. "Why don't you sit and have one with me? There's nobody out front."

Angela's head shook, a small, tight movement. "No. Those are for you. I already ate breakfast." The front door jangled, and she disappeared through the doorway and out into the shop.

Honey sighed. Once again, she thought of Fury. It had taken Booker and Honey weeks to win the dog over. But win him they had. She could do the same with Angela. It would just take time.

She clicked on her browser again. This time she went straight to email. One message stood out in the mailing list correspondences; it was from Joe. Rather, it was from Joe's account.

Honey's heart jogged in her chest, and she took several long, slow breaths the way she'd been taught. She wouldn't have a panic attack. She wouldn't.

She shouldn't have had coffee with Friar Philip, but it wasn't the caffeine that was affecting her now. It was fear. She clicked it open. There was only one line.

Back off.

Back off? Back off from what? Did the killer know she'd been prowling around in Black Star? Was it because she'd gone to talk to Friar Philip? If so, that meant he was close, watching her. Her heart went from a jog to a run.

She wanted to wipe out the message, pretend she hadn't seen it. Her hand on the mouse, she hovered over the delete option for a long moment but resisted. She let her hand drop to her desk. She needed to show this email to the police. If they saw it, maybe they could trace it. Maybe they'd believe her that she and Booker had nothing to do with Joe's death.

She shut her laptop, threw it in a tote bag, and headed into the shop area. Angela was showing a customer their inventory of kitchen knives, explaining the advantages of each brand. Honey hadn't planned to leave her alone in the shop today, but she had to show Booker the email.

"I'm going out for a bit," she said.

Angela glanced up from the box she was holding. "When will you be back?"

"Not long. An hour maybe. Do you have lunch plans?"

"Just some running around. I have the car today. But I can do it another time."

"No, you're good. I'll be back way before lunch."

Honey's hand shook as she pressed the key fob for the van. She slid behind the wheel and had to catch her breath. The act of walking to the lot, opening the door, and climbing inside made her feel as if she'd sprinted around a track.

The email had shaken her. It was terrifying to imagine Joe's murderer watching her. But this physical reaction was something more, something primal. Adrenaline flowed through her like a triple shot of espresso.

She drove home on high alert, slowly and carefully, because it was the exact opposite of what she wanted to do.

She wanted to step on the gas, race up the hills, screech around corners and get to Booker as quickly as possible.

It seemed an eternity before she parked next to her husband's pickup truck in the driveway. She wiped beads of perspiration from her forehead with the back of her hand and exited the van.

She threw open the front door. "Book." Her voice sounded shrill to her own ears.

"Hey." His voice came from somewhere deeper in the house. She followed the sound and found him in the dining room with his computer.

"Book." He looked at her with surprise. "Book, I need to talk to you."

"Sure. Sure, babe." He shoved the chair that was next to his away from the table. "Why don't you sit."

Honey collapsed into the chair. "I got another email from Joe's account." She pulled her laptop from her bag and booted it up while she filled him in on her Black Star hike on Friday evening, and her visit to Friar Philip on Sunday morning.

Booker's eyebrows drew closer and closer together as she spoke. Deep lines furrowed his forehead. "That was a foolish thing to do, woman," he said when she finished.

"I know. I know. That's why I didn't tell you about it."

"I thought we agreed—"

"We did, but you've been so upset about Joe. I figured I'd fill you in if there was anything worth filling you in on, but there wasn't. Until this." She put a hand on her laptop. "Now I'm worried about Angela living up there. I think Zach might be abusing her, and if he is the one who killed Joe—"

"Why would Zach kill Joe?" Booker said. "They didn't even know each other."

"Then how do you explain this" She turned her computer so he could read the email.

He stared at it for a long minute before saying, "It doesn't prove it was Zach."

"But this person knew I was in Black Star Canyon. The only person I saw up there was Zach."

"He might not be referring to your hike. I've been talking to some of the guys on the force in Lawrenceburg, seeing if I can figure out what Joe was involved in."

"What do you mean, *involved in?*"

"If we knew why he stole from the church, we might know who killed him. Joe might have played loose with the rules from time to time, but he wasn't stupid. That was a desperate act. He had to know he'd be caught eventually."

"You think someone pressured him or blackmailed him into taking the money? "

Booker ran a hand through his hair. "It's also possible he didn't pay off the church with the money I sent him because he decided to run. He could start over in Mexico with fifty-thousand."

Honey had assumed Joe was running from his responsibilities, from the law. It hadn't occurred to her that he might have been running from someone he feared.

"It could be when the money dried up, whoever he'd been paying threatened him, and he took off."

"And maybe that person followed him from Kentucky to California," Honey said.

"Right."

"But why would they email me?"

"Because you emailed them."

It was hard for Honey to think clearly with her heart racing, her breath coming in small thirsty bursts. She dropped her head into one hand. "You think?"

"Could be," he said.

"You think we've been on the wrong track all this time? Assuming it had to be someone from California who killed him?"

"My guess is Joe's death has its roots in Kentucky." Booker squeezed his hands into tight balls on the tabletop. "I got another email, too. It refers to things Joe did, bad things."

"Like what?" She thought about Officer Kirk's anger when he spoke Joe's name, and the allusions in the emails *Not Joe* sent to Booker. Something had happened in Joe's past; she'd known that for a while. She wanted to know what it was.

"When Joe was in high school, he was kind of wild."

Honey thought Joe had never stopped being kind of wild, but she held her tongue.

"He did drugs. He might have even dealt in a small way. You know, just to friends."

Friends don't sell drugs to friends, but she didn't say that either.

"I think this person knows about something Joe did, something that I didn't report."

"You think he held it over Joe's head, and now he's holding it over yours." It wasn't a question. She already knew the answer. The event was mentioned in both of the emails sent to Booker.

He gave a short nod.

"Do you have any idea who this person is? Could it be a family member of someone Joe hurt, or sold drugs to?"

"Kirk Wickett's cousin, Vic, died from a drug overdose. He was always suspicious Joe had something to do with her death."

Honey wanted to shout, *Did he*? But she resisted. "Why now? Why wait all these years?"

"I don't know. Maybe Kirk ran across some proof, something he could blackmail Joe with."

"Assuming Not Joe is Kirk," she said. "What does he want from you?"

"He wants money. What else?"

Why would Booker pay him? What had he done? Or, not done? The staccato beating on her ribs picked up speed. The faster her heart went, the more difficult it was to grab a breath. She wanted to ask him, but all she could do was moan.

Booker seemed to notice her discomfort for the first time. "You should rest."

"I can't stay. I have to get back." She gasped the words.

"That's not happening. Look at you." He stood, walked to the kitchen, and returned a moment later with water and a Xanax.

"I can't keep taking these things."

"How about a half?"

Panic rushed through her like a spooked horse. Which was more debilitating? The drug, or the attack? Maybe a half-pill was a good compromise. She took it and allowed Booker to lead her to the couch. "What are you going to do?" she said.

"The right thing. I'm going to get a hold of that detective. I'm going to show her the email and face the past. I've been running from it for too long."

CHAPTER TWENTY-SEVEN

THE HALF-PILL did its job and gentled the runaway horse within. It still stomped and flared its nostrils, but it had stopped bucking. Honey dozed for ten or fifteen minutes. When she woke, she thought she might be able to return to work in an hour or two, when the worst of the fuzziness wore off. She lay on the couch, thinking about getting up until the doorbell rang. Fury raced toward the sound.

Had Booker called the detective? Honey pushed herself onto an elbow, waited for her head to stop spinning then rose the rest of the way. The murmur of voices floating from the front hall were all wrong.

The woman's voice was higher and raspier than Detective Sylla's dry tones and didn't have the clipped rhythm of a British accent. Honey stood and walked into the kitchen where she could hear but not be seen. She seemed to be doing this a lot lately.

"Is she okay?" It was Angela.

"She only took half a pill. I'm sure she'll head to the shop after her nap."

"She won't go to the doctor?"

"No, she's pretty stubborn."

"What are we going to do about her?" Angela laughed softly.

Honey stopped short. The conversation was intimate. Like you'd have with a family member or a close friend.

Or, a lover.

Now, where had that thought come from?

Booker and Angela hardly knew each other, and Angela was Willow's age. Her husband wasn't a cheat, and he wasn't a dirty old man. But, still, she didn't like the tone of the conversation.

"I'd better get going," Angela said.

"Thanks for stopping. It was thoughtful of you." Honey could hear the smile in Booker's voice. She didn't like that either.

As the door closed, she walked to the living room again and slid next to the big picture window that looked onto the street. The Honda Charlie always drove was parked out front, but Charlie wasn't in it. Zach leaned against it; arms folded over his chest. He watched Angela walk toward him. His face was like granite, a carved likeness of cold beauty. They didn't speak. Angela pushed past him and entered the passenger side. A beat later, he circled the car, got in the driver's side. They drove away.

"You're up," Booker said. She hadn't heard him enter.

"Yeah." Honey searched his face for traces of guilt but saw none. "I overheard your conversation with Angela."

He dropped the bag of date bars on the coffee table. "She's worried about you."

"You two sound pretty close."

Booker drew his chin into his neck. "Close? What are you talking about?"

"Oh, you know, all in cahoots about me. I didn't realize you knew each other that well."

"Honey, are you jealous?"

Was she? Angela was a beautiful girl, but no. She didn't think Booker was interested in her that way. She was having a hard time putting her finger on the problem. "No," she finally said. "But I'd be careful if I were you. I'm afraid Angela doesn't understand how to have a healthy relationship with a man. She's being abused by someone, Rick or Zach."

Booker frowned. "If you think that, we should do something to help her."

"What can you do if a person doesn't want help?"

"How do you know she doesn't?"

"She had a bruise." Honey made a ring around her wrist. "Like someone had grabbed her hard. I've seen scrapes on her knuckles, too. Like maybe she's had to defend herself. She had a dark ring around one eye."

"Have you asked her about it?"

"I asked about her wrist. She said she closed a door on it."

"You don't believe her?"

"It was her right wrist. She's right-handed. I guess it's possible but doesn't seem likely. Plus, she told me it was a door with the same little laugh and shrug Willow and Ash used to use whenever they were lying to me."

"There's not much we can do if she won't admit she needs help."

"I guess I could offer her Willow's old room?" Honey phrased it like a question.

Booker gave her a long look. "In a pinch, for a short bit."

"Right, of course. Nothing permanent." Honey was surprised she even brought that up after her almost accusing Booker of being inappropriate with the girl.

Neither spoke for a long moment, then Booker said, "I'm going to the police station to talk to Detective Sylla. Want to come?"

She didn't, but she probably should.

"Angela said she's got things under control at the shop," he added.

"Let me comb my hair."

* * *

Forty-five minutes later, they sat in the waiting room in the Orange County Sheriff's Department on hard plastic chairs waiting for the detective. When they arrived, Sylla was out of the office. The desk sergeant let her know via radio Booker and Honey were there. She was on her way.

Before Honey finished responding to comments on Sweeter Than Honey's Facebook page, the glass front door opened, and a swirl of cool air circled the room. She turned to see Sylla enter, her movements lithe and catlike. Honey envied her natural athleticism. Although she was improving, Honey wasn't an athlete, natural or fabricated.

"Sorry for the wait," Sylla said reaching them.

Booker stood. "Didn't give you much warning."

"Right then. Let's go have a chat." She turned on her heel and led them down a linoleum-tiled hallway into an interview room. "Can I get you anything? Water? Terrible coffee?"

Booker and Honey declined. They settled themselves in another set of hard, plastic chairs, Booker and Honey on one side of the table, Sylla on the other. The detective pulled a tablet from a purse that looked like a postal bag. "So, you've heard from Impostor Joe again."

"Yes," Booker said. "He emailed me yesterday and Honey earlier today."

"What were the missives?"

Booker took a folded sheet of paper from his jacket pocket, smoothed it out, and pushed it toward her. "It's long, like the others. Essentially a blackmail letter. Impostor Joe, as you call him, wants money. My guess is that's what he's wanted all along. When he was posing as Joe, I think he thought his best bet was to play the brother card. Now that's off the table, so he's sunk to threats."

"What was the nature of the threat?"

Honey craned her neck toward the page. A sense of unreality filled her as she read it. She and Booker were paying for Joe's crimes, again. If she was going to pay for them, she wanted details.

It bothered her Booker hadn't given them to her before telling the police, but he probably would have if she hadn't gotten sick. She sat up straighter, preparing herself for the full story. Her heart thumped twice as if to remind her it was still there ready to run off the rails at any moment.

Booker stared at his hands that were clasping and unclasping on the table. "When Joe was in high school, he did some small-time dealing. Not for money. Just to make sure he always had drugs on hand for himself and for the girls. One of those girls, her name was Vic, overdosed. A lot of people blamed Joe."

Booker stopped talking as if he couldn't make himself continue. Sylla cleared her throat. "Was he to blame?"

Booker tipped his head to one side. "I blame myself."

"How's that?" Sylla said.

"I knew he was dealing. I didn't stop him."

"And you think Impostor Joe is blackmailing you because of that? Seems weak to me."

Booker glanced at her. "I knew he and Vic had a date the night she died. I told people he was with me, that we went to a movie. I lied."

"How old was Vic?"

"Eighteen, not a minor."

"And you were?"

"Twenty-one."

Sylla gave him a brief nod as if all that was good news. "Your role could be construed as aiding and abetting if it came to court."

"I believe it could. If it was proved that she died taking the drugs Joe gave her, it might be an involuntary manslaughter charge. There's no statute of limitations for involuntary manslaughter." Booker released his hands, rubbed them on his thigh.

"Surprised you didn't tell us about this earlier," Sylla said.

"I should have. I guess I didn't think it had any bearing. It was a long time ago."

"Sometimes things percolate longer than you'd imagine. I had a case once where a man killed his ex-wife twenty-five years after their divorce. She'd had an affair which ended the marriage, but both of them had remarried, successfully, I believe."

"What lit the fuse?" Honey said.

Sylla looked at her for the first time since they'd come into the interview room, an expression of mild surprise on her face as if she'd forgotten Honey was there. "His second wife died. He decided if he couldn't be happy any longer, neither could the ex. There was an odd logic to it."

"In any case," Booker said, "I think his killer must be from Lawrenceburg, our hometown. Who else would know about Vic?"

"Are there any other details you want to tell me now that might help the investigation?" Sylla rocked her chair onto two legs.

"Tell her about Kirk," Honey burst out.

Four eyes swiveled toward her. "Kirk?" Sylla said.

"Kirk Wickett. The dead girl was his cousin. He blamed Joe for her death." Honey looked at Booker for help.

His jaw tensed. "Joe didn't force pills down her throat."

Booker was a man of integrity, an upright guy. He was a hero, literally. He'd been recognized on several occasions for heroic acts of bravery in the line of duty. But when it came to Joe, he had a blind spot.

Sylla's eyes narrowed. "Kirk didn't mention he knew you in Kentucky."

There didn't seem to be an answer to that, so neither Honey nor Booker offered one. Sylla spoke again, "Tell me about the email you received."

Honey didn't realize Sylla was addressing her until the detective turned her gaze on her and raised her eyebrows. "Oh," she stammered. "Ah, two words: *Back off.*"

"Back off?"

"Yeah, just *back off.*"

"What did you take that to mean?"

"I don't know now, but when I read it, I assumed it had something to do with my visit to Black Star Friday night."

The two floating legs of Sylla's chair landed on the linoleum with a thump. "You went to Black Star?" Her eyes were wide and incredulous.

"I see now it wasn't the best idea, but at the time. . ."

"Why did you hike up Black Star, at least I assume you hiked?"

"Yes, I went with my neighbor." Honey tried to maintain a conversational tone.

"Why?"

"There's a man named Rick who has a ranch up there. It's kind of a prepper compound. The girl who works for me lives with him. I was worried about her, and I wanted to see the place."

"So, your hike had nothing to do with your brother-in-law's murder?" Sylla's tone registered disbelief.

"Maybe a little," Honey admitted. There was a long, pregnant-with-twins kind of pause. Honey squirmed in her seat. "I thought maybe Rick shot Joe for trespassing. The gate to his property is covered with No Trespassing signs."

Sylla nodded. "And they're full of bullet holes. I've seen them. Did anyone see you when you were up there?"

"Rick's son Zach."

Sylla stood, ending the conversation. "We'll be monitoring your email account but continue using it as usual. Yes?" She gestured toward the door, and Booker and Honey obediently moved in that direction.

"Oh," she said as they reached the hall. "We did get an IP address on the emails. They're coming from the Rancho Santa Margarita area."

"RSM?" Honey said. "Who do we know in RSM?"

"They may not be coming from Rancho proper. The IP addresses aren't exact. Some servers cover a broad area, particularly in less populated areas." Her gaze rested on Honey. "The emails could have come from Black Star Canyon. I'd stay away if I were you." Zach's cold, marble face filled Honey's mind.

CHAPTER TWENTY-EIGHT

Email dated: January 25th

Dear Booker,

SO, NOW YOU know I'm not Joe. It would have been better if you hadn't found out so soon, but as Joe always said, *It is what it is*. We have to move forward.

Joe talked so much about your family I feel like I know you. Many times, as I listened to his stories, I imagined being there with you at the big rectangular table on holidays, around the campfire on trips up the coast, at summer barbecues in your backyard. Sometimes I thought I could taste Honey's Thanksgiving turkey with the chestnut stuffing, hear Willow's lovely violin pieces. I laughed at Ash's jokes, even though I'm sure Joe didn't tell them as well.

I think he loved your family more than his own, but don't tell Kortney or Kelsie. They'd be heartbroken, and I know they're good girls. The problem is Carla's influence. I've heard enough to know she's a difficult woman.

But you were his hero. I'd like to start our new relationship on that note. Please know I admire you. I'm not out to screw you. I just want what's mine. I'll even settle for part of it. Ten thousand doesn't come close to clearing the slate, but it'll do.

Why should you pay me anything? I'm sure that's the question running through your mind. There are two reasons. I'll start by appealing to your better nature.

You and Joe were family. Did you know the word "family" comes from the Latin word for servant or slave? Today we think it's all about blood, but that's only a part of it. DNA doesn't bind us to each other; covenant does. I choose to serve you. You choose to serve me. Like a marriage contract— 'till death do us part.

But death doesn't really part us, does it? If Honey died with debt, it would become your debt. You and Joe had a contract as well. He was part of your tribe, and you embraced that responsibility.

The second reason you should pay me is Vic, but I won't press that point now. I'm holding out hope that you'll do the right thing because it is the right thing.

What happened with Vic changed my opinion of Joe, by the way. I liked him once, thought he was a stand-up guy. He wasn't. He was selfish and narcissistic. I don't feel bad about what happened to him. The only thing I feel bad about is that he left the planet without paying the debt he owed me.

Ultimately, I did you a favor, Booker. Joe already cost you plenty. It wouldn't have stopped. He'd have been a drain on you and yours for years. Ten thousand more seems a small price to pay to have that burden lifted from your shoulders.

If it makes you feel better, you can think of it as a gratuity for services rendered. If that doesn't work for you, think of it as your final act of service to your wayward brother. Let me know your thoughts, and we'll iron out the details. Please don't involve the police in this. It's a family matter.

Give my best to Honey and your lovely daughter, Willow.

Best,
Not Joe

CHAPTER TWENTY-NINE

"WHY DIDN'T YOU show me that email when you got it?" Honey said as soon as they got in Booker's truck.

"I didn't want to upset you."

A pain shot through Honey's forehead. She massaged it. "How does he know so much about our family? Why did he mention Willow at the end? It sounded like a threat."

"The real Joe, public records, Facebook. I don't know, Hon, there are a thousand ways someone can find out who we are, who our children are."

"I don't like it." Booker didn't bother responding to that. "The letter said not to involve the police. It implied something would happen to Will if we did. Don't you think? I mean why say, *don't get the police involved*, then, *give my best to Willow*, if that isn't what he meant?"

"Actually, it was something like give my best to Honey and Willow."

"Okay, then." Honey flipped her palms to the ceiling. "Do you want me or Willow to get hurt?"

"That's a stupid question, Hon." His tone was soothing.

The louder and more hysterical Honey got, the calmer and more controlled Booker became. It was the way they'd always been, the state of the Wells' union.

"Stupid? If I got an email that said, 'Don't talk to the police or Booker will be hurt,' guess what I wouldn't do?"

He didn't guess.

"I wouldn't go to the police, that's what I wouldn't do."

"Honey, you're not being reasonable. What should I have done? Paid the ten thousand?"

Honey massaged her forehead again. She was unreasonable, but she was so terrified by the threat to her daughter she couldn't think straight. "I'm going to call Willow."

She reached into her purse for her phone. Booker put a hand on her arm. "Don't. If you tell her what's happening, she'll want to come home. Solidarity and all that. You know her. She's safer in San Diego."

"We don't know where this maniac is."

"The emails are coming from the Rancho Santa Margarita area, not San Diego."

He had a point. She had to calm herself, think rationally, which was hard where her children were concerned. "Thank God Ash is in the military where he can't get hurt."

As soon as those words left her mouth, she realized how ridiculous they sounded. Booker smiled but had the common sense not to comment.

"If we don't call Willow, what do we do?"

Booker pulled into the driveway next to her van and turned off the engine. "The only suspect we have that makes any sense is Kirk, right?"

"Right."

"We understand Kirk's motive, at least sort of. But what about the timing? Why wait twenty years?"

"Sylla said things can percolate," Honey said.

"Maybe. But the email said Joe owed him. What if there was someone else? Someone who had a more recent beef, who was in a business venture with Joe?"

"What kind of business venture?"

"As I said before, if we knew what he did with all the money he took from the church, we'd know."

Honey climbed out of the truck. "I'm sure the police are looking into that."

Five minutes later, Booker sat at the dining room table, his laptop open in front of him.

"What are you doing?" Honey said.

"Rereading the emails." He stared at the screen for several minutes. "Here it is. The second one said he wanted me to invest in a downline."

"A multilevel marketing company?"

"Yup. And, Carla mentioned he tried to sell a case of snake oil to the mailman last year."

"What kind of snake oil?"

"I don't know. We should call Carla."

Honey ran to the front hall, found her purse where she'd dropped it next to the door, pulled out her phone and punched in Carla's number. As it rang, she looked at her watch. It was 3:30, 6:30 in Kentucky. Carla should be home from work.

She was. "Hey, Honey."

"Hey, Carla." Honey tried to modulate the tension in her voice. "Just checking up on you and the girls."

"That's sweet of you." Carla sounded weary. "We're doing okay. As well as can be expected. I'd planned to call Booker. We're cleared to ship Joe's body next week.

Thought you and he might accompany it. I mean, the body will ship in cargo, but I believe we can book you on the same flight."

"Oh." Honey was at a loss for words. Joe's funeral had been driven from her mind by their trip to the police station. "Sure. Just let us know."

"If he was going to die, I wish he'd have done it at home. Shipping mortal remains is complicated and expensive. I swear, the death industry's got you by the—"

"Carla," Honey interrupted her. She didn't want to hear, or think, about the death industry at the moment. "I actually called because I have a question for you."

"Shoot," Carla said.

"Was Joe involved in a multilevel marketing company?"

"He was. I'm surprised he didn't hound Booker about it."

"Must have figured Booker wouldn't be interested. Do you remember the name?"

"Do I remember? How could I forget. It was called Ageless, Inc. They made bars and shake mixes that were supposed to make you look twenty years younger. *Eat your way young.* That was their tagline. It didn't work. Trust me."

"When did he get involved with the company?"

"It was three years ago last October at a business fair in Irvine. I'm surprised you don't remember. It was right before Halloween. He stayed with you for the holiday. Kort and Kelsie were upset he was away."

Honey looked at Booker and mouthed, "October," and put three fingers up. "Do you remember because it was Halloween, or was there something else?"

"I remember because it was the beginning of the end. He'd gotten involved with other shady businesses before, but this one was different. All he could talk about was Clueless, Inc. that's what the girls called it. He started sinking all our money into *product.*" She said the word "product" like it was a curse word. "I had to move what was left of our savings into a private account or everything would've been gone.

"He was hopping a plane to John Wayne Airport every time he turned around. He always had some sales meeting or other to attend. He spent a fortune."

"He did mention he was in town for meetings, but I didn't ask a lot of questions," Honey said.

"I told him he was going to wear out his welcome with you. I thought maybe he'd stay home more, but he started booking hotel rooms. I had to hide the credit cards too."

Honey felt ill. She'd been focused on her frustrations with Joe and hadn't stopped to think about how hard it must have been for his family. "We had no idea, Carla. Maybe Booker could've talked some sense into him."

"I can't tell you how many people tried; our pastor, his friend Chuck, even my dad talked to him. If I'd have thought it would help, I'd have called Booker, don't you worry."

"I hope so," Honey said. "You know we're always here for you guys."

"I know you are. Can I tell you something? Just between us?"

"Of course."

"I was about to file for divorce, but then he disappeared."

Honey shot a look at Booker. "Divorce?"

"When the church confronted him about the money he stole, I was so ashamed. I'd thought he was seeing another woman, which was bad enough, but this was too much.

"I saw it clearly for the first time. He wasn't going to change. He was an addict. His addiction wasn't drugs, or alcohol, or porn, or overeating. His addiction was get-rich-quick schemes. He was a complete sucker for those things. Clueless, Inc was just the latest and the worst. I couldn't live with it anymore."

Honey had never thought about get-rich-quick schemes as addict-able, but why not? They were a form of gambling, and people got addicted to gambling. When addicts lost, they had to keep playing to earn back the losses. When they won, they got greedy for more. Like all addicts, they were never satisfied. It was a kind of gluttony.

"So, that's what he spent the money he took from the church on? On Ageless?"

"I don't know what else it could have been," Carla said.

"Have you talked to the police about this?"

"The Lawrenceburg police haven't asked me about anything. They came to tell me Joe was dead, and that's it. A detective from the Orange County Sheriff's department called but she didn't ask about Ageless."

Honey assumed it must have been Sylla. "What did she ask about?"

"Why I thought Joe disappeared, if he had any enemies, that kind of thing." Carla said.

"What did you say?"

"I told her about the embezzlement and gave her Pastor Kevin's phone number. I said I didn't think he had any enemies. Joe wasn't a good man, but he wasn't a terrible one either. Most people liked him."

Honey asked about the girls and talked as long as she felt she had to for decency's sake. She couldn't wait to discuss all this with Booker.

When Honey ended the call, she turned to Booker, put her hands on her hips, and said, "So he never mentioned a company called Ageless, Inc to you?"

"No. He said he was working on his investment portfolio. I should've asked more questions, but I was happy to see him thinking ahead for a change."

Booker stood and stretched. "Want a cup of coffee?" Honey widened her eyes at him. "Oh, sorry." He disappeared into the kitchen. A moment later, he returned with a bag in his hand. "What's this?"

"Those are sugar-free, gluten-free date bars Angela made for me."

"Oh." His face fell, and he rolled up the top of the bag.

"They're good. Try one."

"That's okay. Don't want to hog your treats."

Honey retrieved her laptop from her bag by the door. "We should find out what we can about Ageless."

Booker sat nearby with a cup of coffee and his computer. "Good idea."

The click of keys was the only sound for several minutes. "Nothing," Booker said.

"Me, either. I can't find anything specific." Honey straightened. She was running out of steam. The Xanax had worn off, leaving her feeling numb and sluggish.

Booker took a sip of coffee and set the mug down with a thump. "Wait a minute. What's this?"

"What's what?"

"I think the company is called Ageless Products, Inc, not Ageless, Inc. It's mentioned in a newspaper article about Ponzi schemes. They were one of a dozen companies closed by the government at the end of last year."

"Angela and Zach worked for an Irvine based company that was shut down by the SEC at the end of last year," Honey said.

Honey and Booker stared at each other for a long, silent minute. Booker reached for his cell phone.

"What are you doing?"

"Calling Sylla. Letting her know she needs to talk to Angela and Zach."

Honey perched on the edge of her chair. "Wait."

"Why wait?"

"Why would Zach or Angela kill Joe?"

"I don't know, but the Ageless connection is a glaring coincidence."

Honey thought about Angela, the bruises, the bloodshot eyes. Someone who lived at the ranch was violent, and Honey was pretty sure she knew who it was. If Zach thought Angela had leaked information that brought the cops to their door, what would he do to her? "I'm worried about Angela."

Booker picked up his phone. "Detective Sylla needs to know what we know."

Visions of the Branch Davidian Compound members shooting it out with government agents, of innocent women and children falling from gunfire raged in her mind. The situation in Black Star seemed so volatile.

If she said that, Booker would tell her not to overreact. To let the police sort it out. *Sort it out like they did in Waco, Texas?* She pushed the thought away and rehearsed the things she knew he'd say. He would tell her there were extenuating circumstances in Waco. She was sure that was true. He would tell her it was an anomaly. She was sure that was true as well. Booker believed in the system, and she believed in Booker.

However, he hadn't seen Angela's bruises.

Honey was in a quandary. When Joe's full story came out it was possible the death of the girl from his past would be revealed. It was also possible Booker's involvement, or lack of involvement, would be made public. His career could be compromised. Even though he'd been a young man then, a public servant who knew about something illegal and didn't report it might not be breaking any laws, but his integrity would certainly be questioned.

Warning Angela that the police were coming could be seen as aiding and abetting if Zach had something to do with Joe's death. Would people see this as a pattern in Booker's life? Could it appear that he put friends and family above the law?

Honey couldn't allow her sense of responsibility for Angela to make things worse for Booker, but she couldn't ignore it either. She chewed her bottom lip and came to a decision. She'd warn Angela, but she'd do it alone. What Booker didn't know couldn't get him in trouble.

CHAPTER THIRTY

"I'M GOING TO Sweeter," Honey said.

"Now?" Booker asked.

"It's only 4:15. I can let Angela go and close up myself. She's done so much overtime lately."

He squinted at her. "You feeling okay?"

"Yeah. The Xanax wore off hours ago."

Booker's gaze shifted to his laptop, and he set down his cell phone. "What time will you be home?" He seemed suddenly distracted, disinterested in the answer.

"Six-thirty latest." As she walked out the door, Booker sat frozen at the table, his gaze on the screen of his computer.

Angela was behind the counter, looking at a vendor catalog when Honey got to the shop. She glanced up, face lit with enthusiasm. "Have you seen these new manual food choppers? You pull a cord and the blade revolves. No electricity needed. They're cheap too. I bet we'd sell a lot of them with summer coming on. Good for camping, picnics—"

"Angela," Honey said.

Angela blinked. "Yes?"

"I have something I need to talk to you about." Animation bled from the girl's face leaving it pale and still. Her body tensed for fight or flight.

"You're not in trouble," Honey said. "Or maybe you are but not with me."

Angela didn't speak, but her shoulders relaxed.

"I don't know if you know this, but I went up to Black Star the other night. I wanted to see the ranch."

"You did?"

"Zach didn't tell you?"

She gave a small shake of her head.

"I got another email from Joe's account today. It told me to back off. The only person who knew I was in Black Star was Zach."

"You think Zach is the killer." It was a statement not a question.

"I think it's possible. I also think he's hurting you."

Her eyes widened in surprise.

"I suspect you're being abused. I've seen the bruises. I can tell you're not sleeping. Your eyes are bloodshot, and you're too pale. Angela, I'm worried about you."

Angela stared at the countertop.

Honey continued. "Booker and I discovered that Joe was involved with Ageless. That was Zach's uncle's company, the one you worked for, wasn't it?"

Angela's head jerked.

"The police know it now too. It may not be enough to arrest Zach, but it's enough to make them look at him long and hard. You don't need to be there when they do."

"Where would I go?" Her voice was soft, childlike.

"You can stay with us. At least until you find something more permanent. You can have Willow's old room."

"You'd do that for me?" She looked as if she was about to cry.

Honey crossed the room, reached out, and picked up the girl's hand. "Yes, of course."

"Zach scares me," Angela said.

Honey's chest ached with compassion. "Where is he now?"

"At work. He works at Jambalaya off El Toro Road."

Honey knew the restaurant. "Do you know when his shift is over?"

"Not for a couple of hours."

"Did he drop you off?"

Angela nodded.

"How about Rick?"

"Rick will be at home."

"I can take you to the ranch. We can get your stuff and be gone before Zach gets off work, but Rick will tell him where you've gone. Do you think he'll come after you?"

"I don't." She said the words slowly as if thinking them over. "Especially not if the police are looking at him." She locked gazes with Honey. "Are you sure, though? It's a big imposition. I hate to—"

Honey lifted a hand. "Stop.

Ten minutes later the two women were in Honey's van on their way to Black Star Canyon. "Do you have the gate keys?" Honey said.

"Yeah." Angela dug through her purse and pulled out a key chain.

The closer they got to the fire road; the less courageous Honey felt. It was all fine and good to play guardian angel in the safety of the city, but Black Star seemed wild and dangerous.

She noted how few cars were in the parking area as she drove up to the first gate. Not that it mattered. There wouldn't be any hikers or bikers down Rick's private road anyway. But it increased the tension she felt crawling across her shoulders.

Angela got out of the van, unlocked a padlock, and pushed the long arm of the gate. It shuddered then seemed to creak to life. Honey drove through but refused to watch it stutter shut behind her. It wasn't a trap, a prison door, or a coffin lid. It wasn't any of those things conjured up by her imagination. However, it seemed best not to look at it. Why feed her fears?

The drive up the hill was slow and dusty and, in some ways, more tiring than hiking the same distance. She was very aware of the awkwardness of her large vehicle, how difficult it would be to turn around and head back down, how trapped she felt by the gate she didn't have a key for.

A group of women on mountain bikes appeared on the horizon, and Honey pulled as far to the right of the road as she could and slowed. As they zoomed past, envy overtook her. They seemed so free with the wind in their faces. Maybe when all this was over, she'd look into joining the Trail Angels. Facing her fears seemed to be what was required of her of late. Why not that one?

"Here," Angela said. Honey had to hit the brakes hard, and the van slid in the soft dirt. She'd almost missed Rick's well-decorated gate. Angela got out of the van and went through the same process as she had at the lower gate. It had been nerve-wracking driving through the first entrance, but this was worse. She felt like she was entering the cave of a hungry animal.

Rick's private road was even bumpier than the fire trail. Her van was built for city streets. It skidded and lurched in the uneven dirt. She was relieved when she saw the clearing ahead, but only for a moment. The sight of Rick's pickup truck sent a new wave of anxiety through her.

"Are you sure Rick isn't going to try to stop you?" she said.

"No. Rick is in his own world. He doesn't much care what happens around him."

Honey circled the clearing and pointed the van toward the exit before turning off the engine. Angela paused with her hand on the door latch. "Are you coming in?"

Honey blew her bangs out of her eyes. "Sure." She didn't want to. She wanted to hunker in her car and wait, but sending Angela into the bear's lair alone seemed wrong. She hopped out of the van and headed toward the house.

The house didn't look quite as well-kept or homey in the daylight. Its white trim was peeling, the windows needed washing, and the front door harbored black scuff marks at the bottom as if someone regularly kicked it open with booted feet.

"Hey," Angela called as she entered. The sound of a television game show was the only response.

The interior was dim and musty. Buried in the trees as it was, the home didn't get much direct light. The light it did get had to fight its way through the film on the windows. Based on the smells, those windows weren't opened any more often than they were washed. Old beef stew, cooked cabbage, and mold assaulted Honey's nostrils.

Angela walked toward the rear of the building. "Rick?" Honey didn't follow her; she couldn't seem to make herself leave the proximity of the door. She watched Angela stop in a doorway halfway down a dark hall. "Just stopping home for a minute," she said to an invisible person.

Honey heard the low tones of a man but couldn't hear what he said.

"I will," Angela responded then continued down the hall.

Honey's gaze traveled the room as she waited. This must be the formal living room. There was a fireplace at its far end, above which was a family portrait. She crossed an oval braided rug to examine the photo. Like everything else in this house, it was coated with dust. Honey lifted it from the wall and swiped it with the sleeve of her shirt. Four smiling faces appeared.

The man looked to be in his early forties. His hair was dark. He wore a pair of jeans and a flannel shirt. He gazed at the camera through happy eyes. Next to him was a lovely, brown-haired woman. She also had on jeans and a flannel shirt, but her gaze was directed at the boys between them.

Honey would have recognized the boys' faces even if she hadn't been standing in their childhood home. Zach and Charlie were beautiful children. Charlie looked much the same. Zach had changed, however. The open and happy expression he wore as a child was gone now. She couldn't imagine the Zach she knew with such an expression.

A cough behind her made Honey spin. Rick stood in the entrance to the room. She only knew this must be Rick because this was his home. She would never have recognized the man from the picture over the mantel. He was as leathered as old roadkill.

"Who're you?" His voice was as dry and brittle as he was.

"I'm, ah, I'm Honey." She took a step toward him and stuck out a hand. "Angela's employer."

He glanced at her hand without interest. She dropped it to her side. "I brought Angela home so she could pick up a couple of things."

He stared at her for an uncomfortable minute, nodded, and shambled toward the sound of the television. Angela's assessment of him seemed correct. He was in a world of his own, a world of ghosts and shadows, a world that didn't include strangers or sunlight.

Honey paused before continuing her tour of the room. She didn't want to appear to be prying, although it didn't seem Rick cared much what she did. To the left of the fireplace was a bookshelf filled with volumes. She ran a finger over the books, reading the titles. Most seemed to revolve around the great outdoors. There were several Jack London books, Zane Grey westerns, nonfiction books about hiking, living in the wilderness, and creating a self-sustaining homestead. *Stalking the Wild Asparagus* caught her eye.

She pulled it from the shelf and leafed through it. Pictures of edible plants appeared on its pages. There were even recipes for things like fiddle leaf ferns and wild carrot roots. She'd stick to tame asparagus, thank you. She replaced the book.

On the next wall was an overstuffed couch covered in a plaid fabric that had gone out of style fifteen or twenty years ago. April had probably purchased it. Someone had decorated this room once with loving care. Shades of green and brown were brightened with rust and gold pillows. A lamp with a woodland scene shade sat on an end table next to the couch. It must have been a cozy retreat once. Now it seemed more like a shrine to the dead woman.

"Ready?" Honey jumped at the sound of Angela's voice. The girl had a backpack slung over one shoulder. A duffel bag hung from her other hand.

"Sure. Let's go."

Angela led the way, not bothering to say goodbye to Rick as she exited. They stowed the bags in the van, but instead of getting inside, Angela pointed at the narrow cinder block building. "I have to get something out of the shed."

The shed? It seemed too large for the name. Honey moved toward the driver's side of the car, thinking she'd start the engine, but Angela said. "You should see this."

She wasn't sure she wanted to see anything else on Rick's property. She'd been prepared to be afraid, to feel trapped. What she hadn't expected was the melancholy fog that draped the place like a shroud. She followed anyway.

Angela pulled a set of keys from her pocket and fitted one into the thick metal door of the structure. "This is his stockpile. It's kind of a trip."

The door swung open smoothly. Angela flipped a switch and three rows of florescent lights glowed overhead. Unlike the house, there wasn't a speck of dirt anywhere. The cool cement floor was swept clean. The air smelled fresh. Honey stepped inside.

The side walls were lined with metal shelving leaving about a four-foot-wide corridor between them. On the shelves were wood crates, small metal barrels, and glass jars filled with produce. Against the far wall were larger barrels Honey assumed contained water.

"Wow. There must be enough food in here for a year," Honey said.

"Five years for three people if it's rationed," Angela corrected her.

"He's convinced the end of the world is coming?"

Angela moved to the rear of the structure, pulled a stool out from under the shelving, and climbed up. "Something like that."

As she shuffled through boxes, Honey's gaze scanned the walls. There was something off-putting about this small structure stuffed floor to ceiling with food like an overfed person. She imagined how many people the Abbey could feed with this instead of stockpiling for a day that would most likely never come.

Chances were Rick would go to his grave leaving these supplies behind. She ran a finger along the label of a small barrel of rice. Maybe it would do somebody good someday.

Besides the rice there were burlap bags of dried beans and cases of beef jerky. She moved along the row reading labels. Two cardboard boxes were hidden behind the beef. She saw the words "chocolate nutri-shakes" on one. Curious to see what kind, she pushed aside a case of jerky. A tingle of nerves flowed from her spine along her arms. It read "Ageless Products, Inc."

Why should this make her nervous? She knew there was a connection between Ageless and this ranch, that the multilevel marketing was owned by Rick's brother-in-law. Still, there was something about seeing the actual evidence of the connection that made her heart race.

"We should get going," she said.

Angela climbed off the stool, a small paper bag in one hand. "I'm ready."

"Well, what do we have here?" Zach's voice came from behind Honey, and it raised the hair on the back of her neck. She didn't turn, not immediately. She sought Angela's gaze, but the girl looked over her head toward the doorway. Her face was hard and cold.

"Hey, Zach." Her tone matched her expression.

"Why would you bring her here?"

Angela didn't answer. She stood frozen in place, eyes fixed on something behind Honey.

Honey wanted to turn, to see what she saw, but her limbs seemed to have a will of their own. She couldn't make them move.

A whoosh of air next to her ear broke the spell, but it was too late. Something dark and smelling of plastic covered her face and tightened around her neck. She clawed at the hands that held it in place, but they were made of granite.

Air. There was none. She sucked desperately for a breath. Her mouth filled with plastic. Again and again and again. Then the world faded away.

CHAPTER THIRTY-ONE

Email Dated: January 27th

Dear Booker,

I HAVE TO say I'm really disappointed in you. I thought my arguments about kith and kin would be enough to get you to rise to the occasion. I didn't want to have to threaten. It's so cold, but here we are. You force my hand.

Joe wasn't the brother you believed him to be. In fact, through him you inherited more than debt, you inherited a familiar. The term comes from the same root word as family but refers to a servant spirit. Familiars are usually demons but sometimes ghosts of deceased persons. Their services are never free. Vic is your familiar.

You and he had a pact, never to talk about what happened that night. I'm sure you kept your side of the deal, because you have integrity. What you fail to realize is that Joe did not. He did speak. To me. In case you have any doubts about that, I will repeat the story in full.

One evening the summer before Joe's senior year of high school, he and a girl called Vic, short for Victoria, went to the river near your hometown of Lawrenceburg.

It was a sultry Kentucky night, the perfect kind of night to howl under the moon. He brought along his current drug of choice—Ecstasy. His plan was to get high and then get lucky.

Poor Vic had never done E before. It didn't agree with her, especially not after all the vodka they drank. Not a good idea to mix the two, but they did. She got sick. Real sick.

There were no cell phones then, so Joe left her where she was and ran for help. Stupid move, but Joe wasn't the sharpest knife in the drawer. He thought it would save time if he didn't have to drag her puking body to the car. What he didn't say, but I deduced from the fact that he'd driven his mother's new Honda Accord that evening, was he also didn't want up-chuck on the seats.

He drove to the closest gas station and called you. He should have called an ambulance, but maybe it wouldn't have made a difference. We'll never know.

Either way, by the time you arrived poor Vic was dead. So, what did you do? The upright, responsible member of the family? You left her where she'd be sure to be found in the morning, cleaned up any evidence of your brother's crime—because, yes, it was a crime—and took him home.

I realize you won't be in legal trouble if Vic's story comes out. I looked it up. It's not against the law to walk right on past a dead body and not let anyone know about it. There's also no proof that any of this happened the way I say it happened other than the words of a dead man, but you and I know the truth. It's not exactly the kind of thing you want to make public, is it? Not in your position.

Again, sorry to do this the hard way. Think of it as divine penance for your role in Vic's death.

I'll send instructions about where and how to leave the money when I hear from you. Oh, and don't get the police involved. I don't want this to impact your family any more than it has to. No sense getting Honey hurt.

Best,
Not Joe

CHAPTER THIRTY-TWO

"WE'VE GOT EVIDENCE, Book," Honey said.

"A couple of cases of Ageless shakes isn't evidence." Booker looked different. Honey stared at him for a long moment before she realized what it was. He looked younger. Much younger. Could it be the Ageless Products worked? He didn't look a day over thirty-five.

"But it's a physical link between Joe and Zach." She couldn't believe he didn't get that, wasn't as excited about what she'd found as she was.

Booker walked to the shelf, dug a bottle out, and twisted the top.

"What are you doing?" She almost screamed the words, then remembered she had to be quiet. Zach was around here somewhere. She lowered her voice to a whisper. "You're drinking the evidence."

Booker took a long swig and wiped his mouth. "Joe was right. We should invest in the stuff. It's amazing." He extended the bottle to Honey. She reached out to slap his hand away but slapped the bottle instead. It crashed to the floor.

Her eyes snapped open.

Darkness and silence enveloped her. Three heartbeats passed. "Look at that mess." It was Zach's voice.

"Sorry. I'll clean it up." Angela's voice.

"Don't let Dad see. He'll have a cow."

"He'll know anyway."

"It's only one jar."

"He counts everything every day."

The conversation halted. Honey heard the sweep of a broom and the scratch of glass shards on the cement floor. Five heartbeats passed.

"I don't know what you were thinking bringing her here," Zach said.

"We weren't going to stay, just pick up my clothes and stuff."

"Why? This is your home now." Zach sounded angry. Honey stiffened, afraid for the girl.

"Rick doesn't want me here."

"Rick doesn't want anybody anymore. It doesn't matter. He's not going to throw us out."

The swish of the broom on cement was her answer.

"Don't be like this, Ange." Zach's voice took on a whining tone. "We can make this work."

"It doesn't work for me."

"It's not plan A, I grant you that, but we both have jobs now."

"You know how long it's going to take us to save up the money we need?"

"What's the hurry?" The words rumbled from his chest, deep and suggestive.

Angela laughed, but it sounded nervous not amused. "It's this place. We're living out in the middle of nowhere. I want to be in town. I want to see people. I want to shop, and go out to restaurants, and get my hair done."

Honey noted Angela hadn't said anything to Zach about the police knowing about Joe's connection to his uncle's defunct company. She must have thought it was still a secret.

The angry edge returned to Zach's voice. "How long you think they'd keep you, anyway? How long before she doesn't like the way her husband is looking at you? Doesn't like the way you take over her life."

"Her husband isn't like that."

Angela didn't deny she'd take over Honey's life, only that Booker wasn't a lech. Honey thought about the girl's assertiveness at the shop. Her anxiety, already a dull throb, became a steady thrum.

"He's a guy, isn't he?" Zach said.

Something slapped to the floor; the sound reverberated in the dark. A shuffle of feet, then a grunt.

"Zach." Angela sounded upset, afraid maybe.

Honey sat up and moved toward the sound, a useless gesture. She couldn't protect Angela through the walls, but if she hadn't, she wouldn't have caught his next words. "Don't do this again. I'll take care of you."

"I appreciate that." Angela's voice was gentle but noncommittal. She was placating him.

Neither said anything for ten, eleven, twelve heartbeats. Zach broke the silence. "I'm going in. I'll keep Dad busy, so he doesn't see you dumping that."

"Okay."

Footsteps, more sweeps of the broom, the cascade of glass into a trash can, then quiet. Honey glanced around the darkened space she occupied. Her eyes had adjusted to the gloom, and she could now see a stripe of light where the walls of her shelter met the ceiling.

She sat on a cot in an enclosed section of the cinder block shed. A smooth wall separated her from Angela and Zach's voices. She could see the outline of a door in it. The other three walls of her cell were constructed of the same blocks as the storage area she'd seen earlier.

"Honey." Angela's voice whispered through the cracks around the door like a gentle wind.

Honey scrambled from the cot and knelt near the door. "I'm here." The words rasped through her throat.

"I'll get you out, don't worry."

"Call the police, get help."

"I will when I can, but Zach's going to watch me like a hawk for a while."

Honey thought about the hawk she'd seen circling the day she and Booker found Joe's body by the falls. At the time, it had made her think about the freedom of flight, now she felt sympathy for the prey it had been seeking. "This is crazy. Zach is crazy."

"He is, but I can handle him. At least, I can handle him until we get away."

Angela's words didn't fill Honey with confidence, but she had to trust her. What other choice did she have? "Booker will be looking for me," she said.

"I know. We need to leave before he thinks of coming here. It's not safe." Cold seeped into Honey's bones. She wrapped her arms around herself. "I'm going to have to play along with whatever Zach has planned. Make him think I'm on his side," Angela said.

"Whatever he has planned isn't going to be good for me," Honey said.

"I can handle him."

The phrase didn't sound any better the second time Honey heard it. She felt lightheaded. Her throat was raw. Symptoms of having a plastic bag jammed over her head she was sure. How long did it take to suffocate someone? Four minutes? Five?

She shuddered. She was grateful to be alive. No, she had no confidence that Angela could handle Zach. "I'm thirsty."

"I left water by the cot," Angela said. "There's also a bucket and a roll of toilet paper in the corner."

Honey gazed toward the bed and saw a glass bottle with a stopper on an upturned box. She reached for it, pushed out the stopper, and guzzled hungrily. Cool liquid slid down her dry throat soothing it. When she spoke again, her voice was clearer. "How long before we can leave?"

Before Angela could answer, Zach's voice invaded Honey's enclosure. "Who are you talking to?"

"No one." Angela's tone was defensive, too defensive. It belied the truth of her words.

"She's awake," he said. Angela didn't answer. "I know you're awake," Zach raised his voice.

"My husband will be looking for me," Honey repeated the only threat she could think of.

"He won't find you." Zach didn't sound concerned. "Come on, Angela. We need to get rid of the van."

Panic skittered over Honey's skin. "What are you going to do with my car?"

"I'll come as soon as I'm done cleaning up," Angela said.

"Hurry." His footsteps faded.

"What's he going to do?" Honey couldn't keep the fear from her voice. She was afraid she already knew. If he was Not Joe, his aim was money. He must be planning to use her for ransom, but she and Booker didn't have much left. They'd given most of their savings to Joe already.

"We can't talk now. It's not safe." Angela's voice grew softer as she spoke. She was walking away.

Honey's pulse pounded in her ears. "Don't leave me."

"I'll come back when he goes to bed." Honey heard the thud of a door, then nothing.

She crawled onto the cot and pulled the scratchy wool blanket around herself. She inhaled and exhaled slowly; the way Dr. Hillary had taught her. She wasn't in any present danger. Based on the strip of light circling her enclosure, Angela wouldn't return for a long while. She had time to think, to plan, if she could only calm her frantic imagination.

She had no idea what the statistics were about hostages being returned alive after ransoms were paid, but she didn't think they were good. Visions of Booker walking up Rick's long drive, a pack full of hundred-dollar bills in his hand, terrified rather than buoyed her. Why wouldn't Zach kill them both once he got the money? He'd murdered once.

Angela was her only hope. Angela and God. Angela, her name like an angel of God. She squeezed her eyes shut and breathed a prayer.

She turned her attention to her heart, willed it to beat slowly and evenly. Long moments later, she opened her eyes. There was a battery-operated lantern on the box. She didn't switch it on. Instead, she allowed her thoughts to paint pictures on the darkening walls around her.

With the van gone, she and Angela would have to hike out. She hoped the girl had the courage to escape. From her volunteer work at a battered women's shelter some years ago, she knew it often took a victim as many as seven or eight attempts to leave. How many times had Angela tried to leave Zach? Maybe rescuing Honey would give her the strength to do the right thing. She had to hang onto that, to make her plans. If she didn't, she'd lose her mind.

Her cell phone would be disposed of along with her car. Zach wouldn't take a chance on it being traced, but Angela had a cell phone. They could call for help as soon as they reached the fire road.

She imagined the line of sheriff department vehicles she and Booker had seen the day they'd found Joe—a caravan to the rescue. They would come for her. She'd be fine. Booker was calling Detective Sylla as she'd left the house that afternoon. She told herself these things over and over until she nodded off.

She woke with a start as if something had startled her, but when her eyelids fluttered open, she didn't hear a sound. The crack of light around the ceiling had turned from yellow to blue. It was night.

She lay there for several minutes feeling the lub-dub of her heart against her sternum. It was comforting, its sound the one every newborn was drawn to after being pulled from the cozy darkness of the womb. Bruiser, their dog before Fury, was a pup when they got him. The only way they could stop his howls at bedtime those first weeks was to put a clock in his bed. It mimicked the beat of his mother's heart.

It struck her now that her own heartbeat had become a source of stress. It had bucked and bolted and run through her chest in panic at the slightest provocation, which only made her more fearful. Yet here she was imprisoned by the man who'd murdered her brother-in-law, perhaps facing the same fate, and her heart was practically unperturbed. Why?

She'd practiced the breathing techniques Dr. Hillary had taught her numbers of times in the past month without much success. She hadn't had a Xanax since the half-pill she'd taken that morning, or yesterday morning. She'd lost track of time. Either way, it didn't make any sense, but now wasn't the time to puzzle over it. She needed to prepare herself.

When Angela came, they would head to the fire road. They wouldn't take the driveway, but dodge through the trees as she and Rosie had done last time they were here.

Rosie.

Another comforting thought.

When Booker noticed Honey was missing, he'd call Rosie. Rosie would think of this place. She'd suggest he look for her here. She was sure of it. Rosie hadn't felt safe here. Zach had put her on high alert. Her intuition had been correct. She'd share that intuition with Booker now.

Of course, chances were Zach was planning to contact Booker himself, ask for a ransom. Zach would also insist the police not be called. Would Booker agree to that? She didn't think so, besides he'd already called Detective Sylla.

Honey sat up; her heartbeat no longer as steady. Visions of the Branch Davidian firefight ran through her mind again. She wondered how many weapons were on this ranch. Plenty, she was sure. It could devolve into a shootout.

A light flipped on outside her door, and Honey froze. Could it be Angela coming to get her? She heard the shuffle of feet on the rough surface of the cement. It didn't sound like her light step, but it didn't sound like Zach's heavily booted one either. She scooted off the end of the cot and pressed one eye to the crack around the door. A sliver of floor, a bit of a metal barrel, the joint of a shelf; this was all she could see.

She stayed there, her breathing soft and shallow, until her legs began to cramp. Silently cursing, she pushed against the wall and massaged her protesting thighs. The shuffle came closer. She closed her eyes and listened. She heard breathing now, heavy and full of mucus. It had to be Rick.

She pivoted and peeked through the crack again. A leg, not in blue jeans like both Angela and Zach were wearing last she saw them, but dark blue cotton fabric. It was Rick.

What was he doing? Inventory? Angela had said he counted every jar and box on the shelves. The slide of his leather shoes shushed across the cement. He was close, just on the other side of the door.

"Damn," he muttered, then bent over. For a split-second, Honey saw the side of his grizzled head. He picked up something so small it was invisible to her eye. A shard of glass? Most likely. Now he knew something had broken in the storage shed.

Friar Philip's words, *Rick is a good man,* echoed in her memory. Honey opened her mouth to call out, but his eyes, cold and vacant, slid into her mind as well. She closed her mouth. No, she couldn't trust him. Zach was his son, his child. Honey was a stranger. Strangers meant danger to someone like Rick. His son would win in any contest between them.

A moment later Rick moved quickly toward the exit. She heard the heavy door thud closed and felt tension drain from her limbs. She collapsed against the wall again and waited.

Ten minutes passed, twenty, maybe more. She had no way of knowing the time. But at some point, she gave up hope that anyone would return that night. Her stomach rumbled. She hadn't eaten anything for hours, but despite the rumble she wasn't hungry. The thought of food made her throat constrict.

She crawled to the lantern near the bed, switched it on, and blinked in its glare. Once her eyes adjusted, she gazed around her prison, looking for what? A weapon? A way out?

Her gaze fell on the bucket. Her bladder squeezed in response. She slid off the bed and squatted over it. When she was finished, she rinsed her hands with a splash of water from the bottle. She was observing the niceties of polite society. How long before they disappeared, before they seemed meaningless, wasteful even?

She had to get free before Zach had a chance to contact Booker. That was the only way this thing had any chance of a happy ending. Where was Angela?

CHAPTER THIRTY-THREE

A BREEZE FLUTTERED across Honey's face. A hand gripped her ankle and shook it. Her eyes opened. Angela stood at the foot of the cot. "Wake up." She spoke in a harsh whisper.

Honey rubbed sleep from her eyes, shocked that she did sleep. There were so many times this past month she lay awake all night in her king-sized bed with its memory foam topped mattress on 800 thread count Egyptian cotton sheets in a temperature-controlled room. Yet here, on this lumpy cot with its itchy wool blankets in fear for her life, she'd dropped into unconsciousness like a stone.

"I'm sorry I didn't come last night. Rick missed that jar of beans I broke and threw a fit. He stayed up so late writing in his notebook, doing his calculations, I fell asleep. Here, I brought you this."

Angela tossed something wrapped in a paper towel onto the cot. Honey opened it. It was a peanut butter and jelly sandwich on white bread. Honey hadn't eaten soft over-processed white bread since she was a kid. She took a tentative bite, and hunger hit like a sledgehammer. She attacked the sandwich, washing down gooey bites with the end of her water bottle. "I was thinking about it," she said.

Angela's eyebrows raised in question.

"I think we should head straight for the trees, then when we get to the main road, we can call for help."

Angela's eyes narrowed. "Why not call from here?"

Honey set her water bottle aside. "I figured you'd want to be gone before the police show up. Like we talked about at the shop. If you're with me, escaping, they'll know you weren't part of. . . " Honey let her words dwindle away. She didn't want to say *Joe's murder.* Angela must not know what Zach had done. If she'd known, she would have left.

"It might be a while before we can leave," Angela said.

"Why?" Despair flowed through Honey. She wanted to leave now, find Booker, head off Zach's plans.

"Zach is—"

"Ange." Zach's voice cut off her words.

Her face hardened. "I've got to go."

"When are you coming back?"

"When I can." Angela hurried from the room and locked the door. It was evening before she returned. Honey had been here over twenty-four hours.

* * *

"We need to go, now." Angela entered without knocking.

Honey stood too quickly and grew dizzy for a minute. She'd been lying down almost the entire day listening for the sound of the police cars that never came. Hadn't Booker called Sylla? And if he had, why hadn't she come? Did she have something more important to do than investigate Joe's murder? Honey's disappearance?

"You have a cell phone with you, right?" Honey said. She wanted to call the police herself. First to scream for help, next to let them know what she thought of them.

Angela slipped one out of her rear pocket and held it up.

"You don't know where mine is, do you?" Honey's question was half-hearted. She didn't expect to see that phone again.

"Long gone." Angela pivoted and walked from the room.

Honey followed past the rows of provisions. Her gaze fell on the boxes of Ageless chocolate shakes, and her chest ached. It was the first time she'd felt grief for Joe. Maybe it was because she'd experienced violence, stared his killer in the face. Whatever he'd done, he hadn't deserved death.

The two women exited the building, but instead of rushing to the trees, Angela turned to close and lock the door. "It might buy us time," she explained over her shoulder.

Honey gazed around the clearing while she waited and noted her van was no longer parked near the house. Her hands clenched. Even when she reached safety, she knew the chances of having any of her property returned was slim. Her van, her purse, her cell phone, like her money, were history. Things were unimportant when compared to her life, but the empty spot made her violation seem more real.

Angela moved away from the shed and jerked her chin toward the trees. Honey hurried in that direction.

"Thief. Stop." Before they reached shelter, a voice boomed from the direction of the house. Honey darted a glance over her shoulder. Rick stood on the front porch wearing a pair of tattered sweatpants and a once-white t-shirt.

His hair, what he had left of it, rose from his head in tufts like he'd been tearing at it. "You stop right there. Angela, why'd you bring this thief to my house?"

Angela halted in her tracks. "Now, Rick. Honey didn't take anything from you."

"She did. I counted them beans. I put up twenty-five jars. There's been twenty-five jars every time I done my inventory. Until last night, that is." He pointed a trembling finger in Honey's direction. "That's one heck of a coincidence, girly."

"The jar fell on the floor. It broke." Angela kept her voice calm, modulated.

"I know that. What do you take me for?" He swayed.

Was he drunk?

"She was pawing around out there, looking through my supplies, probably planning to haul everything off in that van of hers. I'm not daft. I know what's what."

"No, Rick. Honey doesn't want your stuff. She's got plenty of her own." Angela locked gazes with Honey and turned toward the trees again. "We're going for a walk. We'll be back."

A shot cracked the evening air and shattered it like that glass jar. There was a flurry of flapping wings, then silence. Honey froze. Incomprehension, solid and thick, pressed in on her.

Another shot, and the dirt near her feet exploded. "Down," Angela grabbed her by the arm and threw her to the ground. "Trees," she hissed.

Honey crawled toward the trees, still not understanding, but obeying. A third shot rang behind her, and this time something pinged off one of the trees she'd been making for. She climbed to her feet, made a sharp left and darted toward a stand of oaks on the opposite side of the long drive.

"Rick," Angela screamed. "What are you doing? Put that gun down. You're going to kill someone."

"Thieves don't deserve to live. They steal the food right out of your mouth. What do you call that? It's worse than murder."

"Rick, we can go to the market. Get more. It's not worth shooting somebody over a jar of green beans."

His response was another bullet. This one ricocheted between two trees only feet behind Honey. She plastered herself against the far side of a trunk and tried to think. He'd lost his mind. He was a mad man with a loaded gun.

"Dad?" It was Zach's voice. Hope sparked in Honey's chest, but she didn't dare peek around the tree to see what was happening. "Dad, what are you doing?"

"Chasing off that thief," Rick said.

"Who? Angela?"

"No, not Angela." Rick's voice was filled with scorn. "That other one. The chef lady."

"Now, Dad, what would Honey want with your beans?" Zach spoke in the cheerful tones of a kindergarten teacher.

"You know as well as I do, supplies are dwindling out there. When they dwindle, that's when the thieves come. You should be helping me protect our stores, not arguing with me, boy.

It was apparent by Rick's answers that he believed an apocalypse had already occurred. The world had digressed into a *Walking Dead* scenario minus the zombies. Thank God for that. Honey couldn't imagine what he'd do her if he thought she was one of the undead.

Zach tried to get Rick to see reason while Rick raved about the dark things in his brain. As they conversed, Honey moved from tree to tree, seeking a hiding place in case Zach's attempts to get Rick's gun ended badly, and he started shooting again. The sun was heading toward the horizon, the evening shadows lengthening, but she needed someplace to hide until the dark descended. Rick's voice reached a fever pitch. "I'm doing this for you, Zach."

Fear pushed Honey forward. About five feet ahead, she noticed a tangle of vines covering something rectangular. Whatever it was didn't appear to be organic, despite the greenery on its top. She ran toward it, hoping it would create a barrier between her and any flying projectiles Rick might let loose.

As if on cue, a fourth shot echoed through the trees. She slid like a baseball player coming in to home and landed behind the object. It was a box. A large, green metal box with a complicated handle holding it shut. A bear box, at least that's what she thought it was. She had a vague memory of boxes like these from her one camping trip to Mammoth with the Scouts lo those many years ago.

Bear boxes were one of the reasons she'd never returned. That and sleeping on the ground. Her idea of a vacation included hotel maids, four-course meals, and drinks with little umbrellas sipped poolside. She had no need to protect s'mores from predators.

But now she was thrilled to see the heavy, metal structure. She even bet the sides of the box were bulletproof. They had to be strong to withstand a bear's claws, didn't they?

Rick and Zach's voices were increasing in volume. The men were moving in her direction. She peeked around the side of the box and saw Rick waving his gun in the air as Zach attempted to block his forward progress.

Honey grabbed the handle of the bear box and turned it. She didn't like the idea of crawling inside, but she liked the idea of getting shot even less. She pulled the door toward her in slow motion, hoping it wouldn't creak.

The smell—rotten and sweet—hit her before the door was fully ajar. It reached out and grabbed her by the throat. She gagged and slid away on her butt. An animal must have gotten trapped and died inside, a raccoon maybe. She remembered reading about their ability to unzip tents flaps, break into ice chests, and wreak all kinds of havoc at campgrounds.

She couldn't use the box, couldn't stand the odor of death. She glanced around for another hiding spot. The gun cracked, and a tree limb landed on the dirt not far from where she crouched. She scuttled to the metal structure again. She'd pull the raccoon out. A dead thing couldn't hurt her. It was the living that were lethal.

Keeping her face as far from the opening as she could, she reached an arm inside. Her fingers came to rest on something soft. Fur she supposed, although it wasn't as thick as she'd thought a raccoon's would be. She wrapped her hand around a foreleg and tugged. It didn't move. This animal was big. Bigger than your average raccoon.

Perhaps it wasn't a raccoon at all. Maybe Rick had once had a dog, and he'd stowed it in the box after it died waiting until the weather warmed to bury it. Or, maybe he'd shot a neighbor's dog and tossed it in the box to hide it. She wouldn't put it past him.

She gripped the limb more tightly, placed her heels against the rim of the box, and used her legs for leverage. This time the creature slid toward the opening. She dropped the limb and wiped her arm across her forehead. She was sweating now.

She could hear Zach's steady cajoling but knew it wasn't working because of the crunch of footsteps moving in her direction. Where was Angela? The thought crossed her mind but only for a moment. She didn't have time to worry about the girl.

"Come on, come on," she said aloud. This was taking too long. Not only did she have to pull the animal from the box, but she'd also have to bury it with leaves before she took its place.

She reached into the black space with both hands ignoring the smell, gripped the limb and threw herself backward into the dirt. The creature jolted from its grave and landed on top of her with a sickening crunch. Suppressing a squeal, she rolled it away and sat up.

Her hand slapped across her mouth almost of its own accord. She scuttled backward like a crab, bounced off a tree, skittered around it, flipped to all fours, rose to her feet, and ran. She no longer cared if anyone heard her. All she could think about was getting as far away as possible from the horror that was once Charlie.

CHAPTER THIRTY-FOUR

HONEY RAN BLINDLY for as many minutes as her heart and lungs would allow. When the burning in her thighs and the cramp in her side got too great to ignore, she slowed to a walk. Many minutes later, she stopped, tree trunk at her back, to catch her breath and get her bearings.

She had no idea where she was. She'd thought she was running in the direction of the fire trail, but it was nowhere in sight. When she and Rosie had hiked here, it hadn't taken long to get from Rick's house to the road, certainly not as long as she'd been running now.

She muttered a word she never used in polite company. She'd been in such a panic after seeing Charlie, she hadn't paid attention to directions.

Charlie. What had happened to the boy? Angela told her he'd left, gone to live with an aunt. Had she lied? The thought created a whirlpool of emotions within her.

Someone had murdered Charlie and stuffed his body into a bear box. If Angela knew about it and didn't report it, she was complicit in his death. An image of the girl's bruised wrist popped into Honey's mind. Bad things had happened to Angela here, maybe she'd been cowed into silence. Maybe she was afraid of winding up like Charlie. Maybe she hadn't known anything about his death.

Honey didn't know, couldn't know, the answers to those questions. She did know she had to get away from here. Honey pushed off the tree and started walking, slower this time, head up, eyes alert. She came to the rise of a small hill. The landscape sloped on the opposite side. Wasn't Rick's house higher than the fire road? She was almost certain it was. She headed downhill.

An uncomfortable feeling settled on her the farther she walked. It was guilt. She felt guilty about leaving Angela with those maniacs. Rick had lost his mind, and Zach was a ruthless narcissist according to Friar Philip. Charlie's body had shown her a vivid picture of the nightmare she was retreating from. The nightmare she'd deserted Angela in.

But what else could she do? She had no gun, no cell phone, no way to help the girl. Going back wouldn't accomplish anything other than delivering herself into Zach and Rick's hands. Besides, they weren't waving guns at Angela. It was Honey they were after.

The justifications didn't alleviate the guilt, but she moved ahead anyway. She would return with help. The police, Booker, someone had to be coming soon. She'd been missing for at least twenty-four hours. Leaving was the logical decision even if her emotions didn't agree.

She trudged on for several minutes more before the ground beneath her leveled out, and she could see a break in the trees ahead. Relief and joy bubbled up inside her, and she started to trot. A moment later, she broke into a run.

She burst through the last stand of trees and stopped short. Where was the fire road? All she saw was a house.

Rick's house. Somehow, she'd managed to circle his property and come up behind the homestead.

Her throat constricted. Tears sprang into her eyes. She retreated into the cover of trees and collapsed onto a boulder.

She'd read about people walking in circles when lost in the woods but never experienced it herself. Of course, she wasn't much of an outdoorsy girl. The last time she got lost was in the Disneyland parking lot.

She dropped her head into one hand and allowed herself to wallow for three or four minutes, then wiped her nose with the sleeve of her shirt and stood. This didn't change a thing.

In fact, it was good. She knew where she was, and more importantly, she knew where the fire road was from here. The other bonus was Rick and Zach *didn't* know where she was. She was sure the last thing either of them expected was that she would double back to the house.

But where were they? That was the question. She didn't want to blunder into them.

The house was still. They must all be out looking for her. She didn't think anyone was inside, but she darted from tree to tree as she made her way around the side to the front of the house. She paused when she had a good view of the clearing.

Both vehicles—Rick's pickup and Zach's Honda— were parked near the barn. Charlie loved to drive that car. That's what Angela had said. The thought gave her a pang. He was a sweet kid. A funny kid. Obviously in love with Angela.

Anger slipped into the mix of emotions jockeying for position inside her. She wanted Zach to pay for what he did to Charlie, and to Joe, but first she had to get out of here.

Nobody was in sight. Honey slid as silently as she knew how to the rear of the barn and peered through a window. Hay covered a wide-planked floor. Two goats dozed in a pen.

She darted from the barn to the cinder block shed she'd spent the night in and paused for a breath. She was about to cross the driveway to the trees on the far side when she heard the stomp of booted feet. The hair on her arms sprang to attention.

"She'll be back," Rick said. "She'll be back, and she'll rob us blind."

Zach and Rick came into view. Rick, still waving his gun in the air, led the way while Zach trudged behind him, not bothering to argue. Honey flattened herself against the wall of the shed.

"Did you find her?" Angela's voice came from another direction. Honey sucked in a breath. The girl must have been in the house. She could have gotten to her before Zach and Rick returned.

"No." Zach sounded resigned.

Rick muttered unintelligible things as he and Zach passed by the shed. Honey assumed they were about her. The men and Angela met in front of the house. Honey couldn't see them from where she stood, but she could hear them.

"What are we going to do?" That was Angela.

"I don't know. I need to think," Zach said.

"Think, think, think. That's all you do," Rick said. "We need action." His voice fell into a rumble again.

Zach and Angela seemed to be ignoring him. "We only have two hours," Angela said.

Two hours until what? Had they set up a ransom drop? Was Booker on his way?

"We gotta find her," Zach said.

"That's what I'm saying." Rick's voice rose from its rumble.

"I'll take the truck, drive to the parking lot. She's got to go that way," Zach said.

"I'll come with you," Rick said.

"No, Dad. You stay here."

"I'm not staying here while you drive my vehicle down the hill. It's dangerous out there. You're going to need backup."

"I'll be fine."

"Rick." Angela's voice was calm. "You need to go inside, have a glass of water, and get some rest. You're upset."

"I may be upset, but I'm not tired." He spat the words. "I want to protect my son, protect my property. I knew this would happen. The more things fall apart out there, the more people that will come looking. Come stealing. We've got to. . ." His voice descended into a mumbled hum.

"Can you take Dad inside? Settle him down? I'll find Honey," Zach said.

"Sure," Angela said.

The fact that she and Zach seemed to be working together, on the same team, bothered Honey. Had Angela ever planned to leave with Honey? Or had Zach changed her mind? Was she playing along with him until it was safe for her to escape? Honey shut her eyes as if she could shut out the questions screaming in her brain.

The truck started and bounced down the dirt drive toward the fire road. When the noise of the engine died away, Honey heard Angela say, "Let's go inside."

"I'm not gonna," Rick said.

"You are."

Honey heard the scuffle of feet and a yelp. "Like I said, you are." Angela's voice was cold and hard. It didn't sound like her.

"What're you gonna do? Shoot me?" Rick said.

"Yeah." A shot rang out.

A split-second later, a grunt and a thud.

The sour taste of panic crept up Honey's throat. Had Angela shot Rick? Or had she been shot? Honey slipped to the side of the shed where she could see what was happening.

Rick lay on his side, a pool of red growing around him. Angela stood, legs wide, the gun in her hand.

Honey gripped the wall with tense fingers. What should she do? It could have been self-defense. She might have snapped from the months of abuse; been so desperate to escape she'd killed one of her captors.

If that was the case, Honey should reveal herself. Talk the gun out of the girl's hands. There must be some phone service out here. They could call an ambulance, get help before Zach returned.

She stepped away from the building and opened her mouth to call out. Angela lobbed a kick into Rick's gut so violent he screamed and folded in half. Honey's mouth clamped shut.

She threw herself against the shed wall. What was happening? Had she completely misjudged this girl? Several visions played across the screen of Honey's mind in rapid succession: Angela dousing Marco with a bowl of salsa. Angela dismissing the smitten Charlie with a wave. Angela taking over Honey's shop. Her office. Her schedule.

Realization hit her with as much force as the kick that hit Rick. Angela had been playing Honey all along.

A gurgle rose from Rick's throat. He coughed. Honey heard the thud of Angela's foot making contact with the old man again. A wet sound came from between his lips. The wet sound became a rattle, a wheeze of escaping air, then there was silence. He was dead. He must be dead.

If it wasn't for Rick's sturdy cinder block wall, Honey's legs would have given way. She had trusted this girl. Had been about to take her into her home. Angela had been her hope of escape, then her responsibility. She'd felt guilty for running out on her.

The conversation Rick and Angela had outside Honey's room the night before returned in clarifying detail.

How long you think they'd keep you, anyway? How long before she doesn't like the way her husband is looking at you? Doesn't like the way you take over her life.

At the time, Honey had noticed Angela hadn't denied that she wanted to take over Honey's life, but she'd shuffled that aside. Hadn't thought it was important.

Don't do this again. I'll take care of you. That's what Zach had said. Honey thought it was the kind of statement an abuser made to lure his victim into another round of violence. Viewing it in the light of what had happened, it took on a different meaning. Those may have been simple words from a man in love.

Honey didn't know this new Angela at all, and from what she'd seen, she didn't want to. What would happen when Zach returned and found his father dead in the dirt? She didn't want to be around to find out. She slid away from the storage shed into the trees and ran.

CHAPTER THIRTY-FIVE

Email dated: January 28

Dear Booker,

YOU CAN'T IGNORE me. I'm sure you've realized by now that your wife is missing. Well, she's not really missing because I have her. I tried to do this the nice way, then the easy way. I even resorted to the hard way, but none of them worked. I wish you hadn't pushed me to this—the terrible way.

Don't laugh. These words are trite, overused and oh, so Hollywood, but I mean them sincerely. If you ever want to see Honey again, you'll do exactly what I tell you to. I feel silly, overdramatic, just typing those sentences, but I'm not sure how else to say it.

The thing is, I like your wife, and I don't want to hurt her, so please, please cooperate. Don't throw on your superhero cape and fly to the rescue, just do as I say.

Here's the plan, I'll put it in bullet points so you don't miss a step:

- Go to your mailbox. Inside you'll find an unmarked envelope.

- Inside the envelope is a money order made out to you from Joe for $50,000. He was planning to pay you what he owed you, by the way.
- Take the money order to the bank and cash it.
- Bring the cash to The Indian Village site in Black Star Canyon at 8:00 tonight. You know the spot, where the mountain men slaughtered the Native Americans—a little theatrical, I know.
- Put the money into the grinding holes in the big rock.
- Go to the California Oak to the left of the rock where Honey will be handcuffed.
- As soon as I count the cash, I'll throw the keys to the cuffs in your direction.

There you go. Simple plan. You give me the money you've already kissed goodbye, and I give you your wife. I'll be there, by the way, with my gun trained on Honey's head the whole time. If you miss a step, if you fail to deposit the cash in the grinding holes, if you do anything other than what I've outlined above, I'll shoot her. Then I'll shoot you.

Side note, did you know that being a horse thief was punishable by death at the time the natives were killed? I think those mountain men felt completely justified in their actions. It's all about perspective.

Here's where I get to say another one of those standard ransom letter lines: If you get the police involved, you'll never see Honey again. I know this rubs against your grain since you're part of the system. But you were able to see your way clear to breaking the rules once, with Vic.

Think about Vic now. Remember what her cold, dead face looked like in the glare of a full moon. You don't want to see that same pallor on your wife's face. I mention Vic as both a cautionary tale and also so you will think twice before you forward this email to that detective. Do you want her to know what you did? I'm guessing not.

See you tomorrow night.

Best,
Not Joe

CHAPTER THIRTY-SIX

FEAR RIPPLED OVER Honey's skin like waves of icy water. She stayed closer to the driveway than she was comfortable doing, but she feared losing her way again. If Zach returned, she'd see the truck. It was only if Angela came looking for her that she had to worry.

The kick looped in her mind. Angela pulling her foot back and launching it into the old man's gut, again and again. It was violent and even worse, it was unnecessary. He was down, no threat. He wasn't getting up again. It was cruel. Angela was cruel.

Which raised another question, one Honey hadn't had time to ponder before. She was running for her life. She felt swells of adrenaline rising in her, but she wasn't debilitated. The adrenaline was doing its job. The world was in sharp focus, her senses heightened. She was filled with energy. These sensations were nothing like the ones she experienced when having an anxiety attack.

Why wasn't she having an anxiety attack? Unless the attacks had something to do with Angela.

The realization that Angela was. . . Was what? Evil? She hated to use that word. It was an archaic word. One she usually reserved for devils, human and supernatural.

Hitler was evil. Beelzebub was evil. Yet, knowing that Angela's beautiful, innocent face hid such a cruel and devious soul made the word appropriate.

A shriek broke into her thoughts. Honey crouched behind a tree, heart slamming into her rib cage. The flap of wings followed, and she saw an owl make its way across a darkening sky. Her heartbeat gradually came under control. She pushed herself to her feet using a trunk for support and resumed her trek to the road.

This.

This was an example of what she'd been thinking about. She'd been frightened, badly. Her heart had responded to the fright, but once she realized she wasn't in danger it slowed. Why hadn't that been her experience for the past month?

Her first panic attack came before she hired Angela. It hadn't had anything to do with the girl. It was a response to finding Joe, to the loss of their savings, to the stress and overwork she'd experienced trying to replace it. But Angela knew about it. Could she have decided to keep those attacks coming?

The second attack came after Honey drank coffee with the stevia Angela had given her, and eaten one of her homemade date bars. She'd assumed caffeine was part of the problem and cut out coffee.

She'd gotten better. Then Angela brought her the second batch of date bars, and the attacks returned.

The worst bout lasted for three days. Three days in which she hadn't seen Angela. Her theory was falling apart. The girl couldn't have had anything—wait. The chicken soup. She'd brought chicken soup. The attacks didn't stop until the chicken soup was gone.

Booker hated chicken soup, so he never ate any, but Willow had. So, it couldn't be.

Honey's imagination was out of control because of what she'd seen Angela do to Rick. The girl was evil, but she couldn't control Honey's body.

Will's words from the night she visited intruded into Honey's thoughts. *I couldn't sleep if you paid me.* It had been midnight. Willow had a long day. She should have been tired, but she wasn't.

Willow had also had a reaction to the soup. It hadn't been as dramatic as the reactions Honey had, but her daughter wasn't suffering from panic attacks.

Angela had been poisoning Honey. The truth hit her like a slap. But why? Why would she want to make Honey sick? What was the point?

Zach's words: *Doesn't like the way you take over her life.* Take over her life. Was that what she'd wanted? Honey's life?

The trees ended abruptly, and Honey, lost in thought, almost blundered onto the fire road. She staggered to a stop and hid behind the last tree. Her gaze swept as far as she could see in either direction. She had to plan the next leg of the journey, stay focused on the moment. The revelations about Angela had crowded out more immediate concerns.

The trees ended a short distance away. After that, she'd have to walk on the road, at least for a while. She'd be exposed.

What else could she do? She couldn't stay holed up in the trees all night. She had no cell phone. Waiting until daylight would only make it more likely that Angela and Zach would find her.

She shivered. Whether it was against the cold or from the thought of meeting Angela, she wasn't sure. Most likely it was both. She had to keep moving to stay warm and to put distance between herself and the girl.

Her progress on the road was much faster. She was able to pick up her pace without worrying about tripping over rocks or tree roots. The moon was full, or close to full. It was low in the sky and lit the path before her like a beacon. She wondered what time it was. The sun had set hours ago, but it went down early in the winter. It must be close to eight. Honey broke into a trot.

Only a couple of miles and she'd reach Silverado Canyon Road. When she got there, she could try to flag a passing motorist. Maybe she'd run into Booker. It wasn't much of a plan, but it was one, and having a plan gave her hope.

She turned a corner and paused. The hills rose around her like prison walls. There were cities on the other side of them. Cities that twinkled like a universe of stars. This place, wild and haunted, hid behind its walls while the people outside sat in their living rooms watching Netflix and picking popcorn out of their teeth.

She jogged on, anxious to return to the mundane.

Zach had scared her. She'd sensed the feral in him. But Angela scared her more, because she hadn't sensed the feral in her. Rattlesnakes weren't as terrifying to

Honey as recluse spiders. The first announced its danger. The second hid. Angela was a recluse spider.

Had they killed Joe together? Revelations sparked to life in her brain like the lights beyond the canyon walls. Angela must have known Joe if Zach knew him. Why hadn't Honey thought of that before? Angela and Zach both worked for Ageless.

Carla had thought Joe was seeing another woman. Maybe he had been. Maybe Angela was that woman.

The more she thought about it, the more likely it seemed. Angela had the ability to read people, to understand what it was they craved, to spot their weakness. Wasn't that what she'd done with Honey? She'd sailed into Honey's life, sensed and filled the void Willow had left.

Joe would have been vulnerable to Angela. Her brother-in-law needed attention and praise like an alcoholic needed booze. Zach wouldn't fill that hole, but Angela would. Angela would tell him whatever he wanted to hear, just as she'd done with Honey.

Take over her life. Zach's words nagged at her. They were the key to understanding Angela, Honey was sure of that. But she couldn't find the right door.

The break of branches on Honey's left made her jump. She cowered and gazed around with anxious eyes but there was nowhere to run. A second later a deer bounded onto the fire road. It paused, eyes and nostrils wide, then bounced across.

Honey watched its progress as it leaped over rocks and skidded past bushes until it disappeared into the night. The deer was made for this landscape. She wasn't.

She was more fit than she'd been when she and Booker had made the fateful hike. That day everything had hurt. She hurt tonight, but from much more than sore feet and weak muscles. She'd suffered a lot of abuse in the past twenty-four hours.

She rounded a bend and skidded to a stop. Rick's truck blocked the road. Through the windshield, she saw Zach's eyes glistening in the moonlight.

Her gaze skittered to the left and the right. A dirt cliff rose above her on one side. The land fell away, steep, rocky, and treacherous on the other. He'd picked the perfect spot to barricade the road.

Honey pivoted and ran. She heard the drop of boots on gravel, then the steady thudding of steps behind her. She'd had a head start, but Zach was gaining on her quickly. She heard his panting breaths now, his footsteps growing louder.

Her thighs burned with her uphill effort. Her own breaths came in shallow gasps. Her chest ached. A hand closed around her arm like a bear trap.

The stop was so abrupt, she stumbled and fell, catching herself with her hands. Gravel bit into her palms, then her knees. Zach threw himself on her. She flattened onto the road, and sharp rocks pierced her cheek.

"That's it." He grunted the words.

They lay that way for a long moment, Zach breathing heavily into her hair, her sucking air from between the rocks of the road. His weight lifted. He slid onto the trail beside her. She thought about running again, but the uselessness of it stopped her. She needed to conserve the small amount of strength she had.

"Let's go." He grabbed her arm again and yanked her up. Her back screamed in protest.

"Zach," she said. He pulled her toward the truck. "Zach," she repeated his name. "Angela killed your father." He stopped so suddenly, she fell into his chest. "What?"

"She killed Rick," Honey repeated the information.

A long pause, then, "You're lying."

Honey turned to face him. "I'm not lying. She shot him." His face was impossible to read in the dim light. "She didn't have a gun."

"She took Rick's." His jaw tensed, too tight for speech. Honey continued, the words falling from her in a torrent. "She shot him. It was horrible. There's something wrong with her Zach. You can't trust her. I know you think you love her, but—"

His slap made her head jerk to the side. "Shut up. Just shut up."

Honey righted her head and stared into his eyes. He didn't want to believe her. "We can go back. You can see for yourself."

Zach ran for the truck, dragging Honey behind him. She tripped and jogged and tripped again. When they reached the vehicle, he threw open the passenger side door, shoved her in, then drew a gun from the waistband of his pants. "If you move, I'll kill you."

Honey believed him. She sat quietly as he entered the truck, put it in gear and tore up the road.

CHAPTER THIRTY-SEVEN

RICK'S BODY WAS gone when they pulled up to the house. All that remained of the man was a stain, black in the gloom. Honey didn't point it out. She watched as Zach's gaze traveled to the dark patch on the ground and away as if he couldn't bear to look.

He got out of the truck, never pointing the muzzle of the gun anywhere but at Honey's head. He circled the vehicle, opened her door, and gestured with the weapon for her to exit. Honey hopped out and walked in front of him toward the house. When they got there, Zach reached around her and turned the doorknob.

The smells of cabbage, mold, and meat oozed through the open door. Honey almost gagged. A random thought flitted through her mind: she would never make a New England boiled dinner again.

They stepped into the too bright, too warm room. "Zach." Angela rushed toward them, a flurry of shampoo-lemony sweet, bright hair and threw herself at him. His hands raised as if in surrender, the right still gripping his gun.

"It was terrible. Zach, I'm so sorry. I tried to stop the bleeding. I tried. . ." Her words were buried by sobs. She was an amazing actor, so convincing Honey had to remind herself what she'd seen Angela do to Rick.

Zach's face was hard, however. His eyes trained on something over the girl's head. Honey followed his gaze. A form lay on the plaid couch, a cheerful red blanket thrown over it.

"He's dead?" Zach said. Angela nodded without taking her face from his chest. "How?"

She took one step away. "I wanted to take him into the house, get him settled like you said, but he wouldn't go. He tried to head out after you. I was scared for him." Her voice broke.

She covered her face with her hands for a moment, seemed to pull herself together then dropped her arms to her sides. "I shouldn't have, I guess, but I tried to get the gun." She turned pleading eyes on his face. "I didn't know what he'd planned. He was delusional. You know how he gets."

Zach gave a small nod. She continued. "Anyway, we struggled and somehow. . ." Her words choked off. She bit her lip, inhaled and exhaled. "The gun went off." Angela stepped toward him again and wept on his shirt.

Zach's free hand hovered in the air for a moment then fluttered to her shoulder like a wounded bird. "It's not your fault." The words seemed to be torn from him.

"It's not true," Honey said.

Angela stilled. Zach stiffened.

"What she said, it's not true," Honey said again.

Angela lifted her head and gazed at Honey through tear-filled eyes.

"I was hiding behind the shed," Honey said. "I saw the whole thing. I saw you kick him, Angela."

Zach's reaction was visceral. His hands moved to Angela's shoulders, and he shoved her away. "You kicked him?"

"No, Zach, no. I would never. She's trying to get between us."

Honey tried to capture his eyes with hers. "Listen to me, Zach. I'm telling you the truth. Angela shot your father and kicked him while he was dying."

His fingers tightened around Angela's shoulders. "You did that?"

"Of course not. I'm telling you, she's making things up, trying to get between us."

"You kicked him like you kicked Joe?"

Kicked Joe? The knowledge almost made Honey double over. She hadn't liked Joe, but he was family.

"No, no, no. Don't listen to her." Angela broke free from his grasp and backed toward the couch where Rick's body lay.

"How did she know you kicked Joe then?" Zach asked.

"She doesn't know anything," Angela said.

"She pulled that from air?"

"Yes. No. I don't know. Maybe the police told her Joe'd been kicked. Maybe she just thought it up. I didn't shoot Rick. I didn't kick him. I tried to save him." She held out her hands, palms up, beseeching him.

Zach's jaw worked. Honey could see he wanted to believe her. This was Angela's power. She'd become the woman Zach wanted, needed. If he believed Honey, the fantasy would burst like an overfull blister.

"Did you kill Joe together?" Honey said.

Both sets of eyes turned toward her. Neither said anything for a long moment. Angela broke the silence. "We don't have time for this, Zach. It's almost eight o'clock."

"What happens at eight?" Honey said.

Again, they ignored her. Angela took a tentative step toward him. "We need that money, now more than ever. We have to leave town. The police know about Joe and Ageless."

The realization of what they must be discussing trickled down Honey's back like ice water. It was her ransom. They must have a plan to meet Booker somewhere, to get money from him.

After what she'd seen, she now knew with a certainty neither she nor Booker would live through it. Angela and Zach had killed Joe. They'd probably killed Charlie, and Angela had killed Rick. What would stop them from getting rid of Honey and Booker?

"Why did you kill Charlie?" Honey asked.

Zach's head turned toward her in slow motion. Surprise lit his eyes. "Charlie?" The name was a whisper. "Charlie's dead?"

"I found his body in the bear box," Honey said.

"She's lying." Angela's words darted from her mouth like a snake's tongue. "Don't listen to her Zach. She's playing you."

He didn't move. Even his breath seemed to cease. He'd turned to granite again. The only thing that showed his humanity was his eyes. Pain, acceptance, then resolve flickered there in turns. "Let's take a look."

"We don't have time. It's almost eight." Angela's tone became wheedling.

"It'll only take a minute."

She folded her arms across her chest. "If you go out there, don't bother coming back. I can't be with a man who doesn't trust me."

"I've never trusted you, Angela. Watch her." He gestured at Honey with his gun and left.

Anger blazed in Angela's face, in her posture. Her mouth tightened. Her shoulders lifted. Her hands clenched. How had Honey ever thought her beautiful? She was hideous. A Medusa. "What is wrong with you?"

"With me?" Honey was so shocked by the question, she couldn't answer it.

"Yes," she hissed the word. "We were going to escape. Together. Then you take off and leave me alone with—" She pointed toward the couch and its burden. "He was crazy. I told you that. I did what I did for both of us."

The blatant lie was staggering. "For both of us?" Honey found herself repeating Angela's words because she had no original ones.

"I'm trying to get us both out of here alive, then you tell Zach I killed his father. If he believes you, he'll kill me. Then how are you going to get out of here?"

Honey was reeling. Could this be true? Could it be that Angela was attempting to orchestrate their escape, and Honey ruined her plan?

Angela paced to one end of the living room and back again, hand on her chin. "Okay, okay. We can salvage this. When he returns you need to tell him you didn't see the whole thing with Rick. Tell him that you knew about

me kicking Joe because the forensic guys could tell—
there were broken ribs or something. You made it up to
save yourself."

"What changed my mind?"

Angela stopped moving and glared at Honey. "I don't
know. Do I have to do everything? You and I talked
while he was gone, and I explained things, and you
realized you'd misunderstood what you'd seen."

"But why would I tell him that? Angela, you are
taking me somewhere at eight to collect a ransom for
kidnapping me. You'll probably kill me after you get the
money. There's no incentive for me to defend you."

In two quick strides she stood before Honey, her face
only inches away. "Do you want me to get you out of this
or don't you?"

Honey faltered. Was she wrong about Angela?
Correction, of course she was wrong about Angela. She'd
imagined the girl was like Willow. Hadn't she said that to
anyone who'd listen? She'd used those exact words;
Angela is so much like Willow.

She'd believed that because that's what Angela
wanted her to believe. It was how the girl invaded
people's lives. She was a parasite. She attached herself to
her host and sucked their life into herself because she had
no life of her own.

This didn't mean she wasn't sincere about helping
Honey escape, however. She may very well want to leave
this place with Honey so she could continue to cannibalize
her. What was the best play? Was it better to create a rift
between her captors, or trust Angela one last time?

Before she could decide, the front door slammed against the wall, and Zach entered with a blast of rage and cold air. "Why did you kill Charlie?"

Angela didn't speak. She'd obviously not thought through this part of her plan.

"Charlie wouldn't have hurt you. He wouldn't have hurt anyone."

"He heard us talking about Joe. He knew we killed him," Angela said.

"He wouldn't have said anything," Zach said.

There it was. They'd killed Joe. Honey had known it, but hearing it come from their mouths set her on her heels.

"But he was going to leave." Angela's voice rose to a screech. "Going to leave *me*." She said the last word as if Zach should understand.

"You still had me." Zach's voice was soft and sad. Honey noted he'd used the past tense—still *had* me.

Angela must have noticed it too. She gripped the front of his flannel shirt. "He was going to leave me." She repeated, her words low and guttural.

Three things happened in quick succession. A shot rang out. Zach's eyes widened in surprise. Angela caught him as his legs weakened and lowered him to the floor. His gun clattered to the ground next to him. "You're not leaving," she said.

Zach clutched his stomach with both hands. Blood oozed from between his fingers. Honey flattened herself against the wall.

Angela looked at the gun in her hand with a surprised expression, almost as if she hadn't expected it to do the damage it had. She wiped it clean on the hem of her shirt, and wrapped Zach's bloody hand around it. Honey assumed it was Rick's weapon, the one that had killed him.

Angela picked up Zach's gun, and put it in the waistband of her jeans. Then she locked gazes with Honey. "Let's go."

"Ange." Zach breathed her name. She didn't seem to hear.

Honey stepped around the dying man and opened the door. Angela followed her into the cool night air.

CHAPTER THIRTY-EIGHT

ANGELA DIRECTED HONEY to sit in the passenger seat of the truck and climbed into the driver's side. This was the second time Honey was held at gunpoint by a driver in this vehicle. Angela, like Zach before her, drove with one hand while the other held the gun on Honey.

Honey hadn't belted in. If this were a movie it would have been her chance to escape. She'd reach over, grab the steering wheel, and send them into a tree. Or she'd grab the gun and wrestle it away. Or she'd pop open her own door, roll out of the moving vehicle and crawl into the cover of trees before Angela had time to take aim.

None of those things were going to happen. Honey wasn't a stunt woman. She was a middle-aged chef with too much padding. She was certain any of those actions would result in disaster. No, her best bet seemed to be to go along for the ride. If Booker was wherever they were going, it would be two against one. Even if the one did have a gun, it would be better odds than if she tackled Angela alone. Still, she felt better with her seat belt unlatched.

When they reached the fire road, Angela turned right instead of left. Left headed down the mountain to civilization. Right would take them farther into the wilderness.

The truck bounced along the uneven surface, making Honey nauseous. She tried to focus on the night sky to relieve the symptoms. The only food she'd eaten in the past twenty-four hours was the peanut butter and jelly sandwich Angela had brought her that morning. She wouldn't eat or drink anything offered by Angela again. Despite the queasiness, the emptiness of her stomach made her feel light and alert. She told herself this was a good thing.

"What was in the stevia and the date bars?" she asked.

Angela didn't respond for a moment, then she said, "Caffeine. I bought capsules."

Honey was confused. "Caffeine isn't poisonous."

"Depends on how much you take," Angela said. "But I wasn't trying to kill you. I just wanted you to need me."

"Need you?" Honey didn't understand.

Angela's face softened into childlike lines. "When you were sick, you needed me. I helped you. Really helped."

Honey inhaled, attempting to control the rage that threatened to erupt from her. Did this girl have any clue how that level of anxiety made a person feel? It was a kind of torture.

It was cruel, but it was also ingenious. Honey had assumed the caffeine hit was another panic attack. Since panic attacks terrified her, it was enough to bring one on. "You put it in the chicken soup too." It wasn't a question. Honey was stating what she now knew to be the truth.

"Yeah. Seemed like a good way to keep you out of the shop for a couple of days."

"Why did you want me out of the shop?"

Angela's gaze slid toward Honey, then to the road. "I wanted you to see how necessary I was. I knew I could run your business better than you were running it. The changes I made were smart, efficient, but I don't think you appreciated them."

The last sentence dripped bitterness.

"It's my business. I run it the way I run it."

"I liked the shop. I liked teaching the class. I thought maybe I could become a partner, maybe take things over one day. But I wasn't thinking clearly. That wasn't why I was there."

"Why were you there?"

"The money order. I needed Booker's ID, his social, something, so we could cash it. I was trying to get close. Get inside your world. When Zach and I heard you found Joe's body we were sure you knew who it was, that you'd been looking for him. Zach panicked, tried to break into your house a couple of times, but your dog is really noisy."

That explained the nights Fury had growled at the windows and the doors. The thought that Zach had been hiding in the shadows of her backyard raised the hair on Honey's arms.

"Once Joe was identified, it wouldn't be long before the police knew he had an Ageless account. We had to get out of town," Angela said.

"So why didn't you?"

"Leave?"

"Yeah, leave."

"We were broke. Ralph took everything the Feds hadn't and went to Mexico."

The truck hit a rock. Honey placed a hand on the ceiling to keep herself from hitting her head. "But you emailed Booker asking for money before we even found Joe." Honey was trying to sort this out. Angela seemed to be talking in circles.

"Yeah, I was grasping. I thought since Booker had given Joe money once, he might do it again. I'd have asked for it in cash this time, though."

"We thought Joe was alive," Honey said.

"That was a side benefit. Nobody was looking for him as long as they believed he was alive and well and running."

Both women were quiet for a bumpy quarter of a mile. Angela spoke first. "You know what I regret the most?"

Honey couldn't imagine. Killing Joe? Killing Rick, or Charlie, or Zach? The possibilities were endless, so she shook her head.

"That I can't stay on at Sweeter."

Honey had to stifle a laugh.

"No, really," Angela said. "I thought we worked well together. I was good for you, for the business. Better than Willow ever was."

Better than Willow ever was? Honey wondered what would have happened to her daughter if things had gone on the way they were, if she'd never discovered who Angela really was. Would Willow have met the same fate as Charlie?

"For a while, I thought I might be able to make the police think Zach had killed Joe on his own, that I was an innocent victim." Angela pulled a sad, pathetic face that made Honey want to slap her. She'd been taken in by that face once. No more.

"Doesn't it bother you? Taking what doesn't belong to you? Taking lives?" Honey said. It was a stupid question. There was something missing inside Angela, the something that experienced compassion.

"The money Booker is bringing tonight is mine. I earned it." Her voice was clipped.

Honey didn't bother stifling her laugh this time. "Booker's money, my money, is yours?"

"That money order should have been made out to me." She glanced at Honey again. "That's all I asked Booker for. Just the $50,000. I could have cleaned you out. Your husband would pay whatever I asked." She said it as if Honey should be grateful.

"I don't understand," Honey said. "Joe borrowed $50,000 from us. He was about to reimburse us, but somehow that money is yours?"

Angela grimaced, her lips thin and angry. How had Honey never noticed her incisors before? They were so prominent, like a wolf's or a vampire's. "Joe promised me he'd take me away as soon as he could afford it. He knew how Ralph was treating me."

"Ralph?" Honey's eyebrows arched. She'd thought Angela and Zach were lovers.

"Right. He was mean." She glanced at Honey like she was looking for sympathy. "Joe said he'd rescue me as soon as he could afford it."

But Joe had decided to reimburse his brother instead of making good on his promise. Knowing what she now knew about Angela, Honey realized that was his fatal decision. "Why did he change his mind?"

Angela lifted one shoulder and let it drop in a half shrug. "He found out about the business. That it wasn't what Ralph said it was."

Honey waited several beats for Angela to continue.

"He got all mad and stuffy and said how we were ruining people's lives, and he couldn't believe he'd been a part of it. He was going to tell the Feds everything he knew."

"But the company was already shut down, wasn't it?"

"Yeah, but Zach and I were under investigation."

"So, you killed him?" Honey's words were soft.

Angela pulled to the side of the road and turned off the engine. She didn't answer the question. Instead, she said, "Get out."

Honey gazed out the window. There was nothing but dark sky and empty land. She couldn't see anyone or anything that warranted stopping. Fear slid down her backbone, through her loins, and made her thighs feel weak. Was Angela going to kill her here? "Why are we stopping?"

Angela opened her door and climbed out. "We have an errand."

Honey exited the truck, her eyes scanning the terrain for a way of escape. It appeared they were in a meadow, only a handful of trees sprinkled the landscape. Not enough for cover.

Angela was next to her, poking the gun into her ribs before she could form a plan. They walked off the road onto a footpath, followed it for a short distance, then came to an area of large flat rocks.

Honey recognized the place from pictures Booker had shown her when he was trying to get her interested in hiking. It was a historic site called The Indian Village, famous because of the massacre that had taken place here decades before. This was the hub of the ghost stories that revolved around Black Star. Honey hugged herself.

From a distance, it almost seemed the area was paved, but she knew from things she'd read it was covered with flat boulders. When they drew close to the largest of the rocks, she could see deep holes dotting its surface. This had once been the natives' kitchen. The women had used natural divots in the rock to grind acorns and other seeds. Over time, the motion wore away the stone, creating the deep, smooth cup-like impressions that were there now.

"Stand over there." Angela gestured toward a lone tree. Honey obeyed. She leaned against the trunk for support and felt the itch of bark through her shirt. It was uncomfortable, but she wanted to be uncomfortable. She needed to remind herself of the danger she was in.

Angela's mood had turned. She acted as if they were two friends on a nature walk. It was easy to accept the fantasies Angela projected, but Honey had seen what happened to others who'd done that.

Then Angela pulled a pair of handcuffs from the backpack she carried. The illusion of friendship was shattered. "Wrap your arms around the trunk."

Honey did, and Angela slid the cuffs onto her wrists and clicked them shut. She walked away when she was done, disappearing into the tall brush behind the stones.

Honey inhaled the sage and dust of the area, listened to the night birds call to one another, and tried to calm herself. Booker would come, and they'd most likely die. But at least she'd see her husband one last time.

It was lonely here. The abandoned workspace pried open hollow places in Honey's heart. She felt a kindred spirit with the women who'd worked with their hands to feed their families. Sensational stories were spun about this site, but it didn't feel sensational to her, only sad.

The mountain men who had opened fire on the men, women, and children were the pirates of their day— pirates without ships. Their god was their belly. They were unscrupulous, willing to do whatever was necessary to fill the emptiness in their guts from the long months in the wilderness.

She could imagine the Native Americans screaming in fear, running for their lives, falling to the ground with the grease of horse meat on their chins. Honey shivered.

The sound of booted feet crossing the sand snapped her to attention. In the light of the rising moon, she saw Booker. He walked in slow, deliberate steps to the flat stone.

"Book," she said.

He raised his hands as if to show whoever was watching, that he had no weapon. He stepped onto the flat rock and placed a hand into his jacket pocket. Honey could see the roll of bills from where she stood. He knelt and shoved it into a grinding hole, then repeated the process four times with four more rolls of bills. When he was done, he walked toward Honey.

Angela scurried to the rock as soon he stepped off it. She pointed her flashlight into one of the grinding holes, then moved to the next, then the next.

Booker reached Honey and wrapped himself around her. She said his name, but he shushed her and repeated the shushing sound as if he was comforting a crying child. Honey thought he was comforting himself.

Angela crouched low, held the flashlight between her teeth, and unrolled a wad of bills. She counted the money and, seemingly satisfied, rolled it up again. She did the same with the four other rolls.

A wave of nerves and nausea washed over Honey. Angela had her ransom; therefore she and Booker no longer had value. Honey began to slide around the tree, hoping Booker would follow. It was scant cover, but she wanted to put something between her and Angela.

Angela stood. "Thank you."

Booker stepped away from his wife. "The key."

"You know, I think I lost it." She pulled a gun from the waistband of her jeans and raised it. Honey had known Angela never intended to allow them to live.

A shadow separated itself from a Manzanita tree on Honey's right. Angela's gun swiveled toward it. The black shape sprang forward and became a man.

CHAPTER THIRTY-NINE

SHOTS BROKE THE quiet. *Be careful, be careful, be careful.* The words might have left her mouth, they might not have. She wasn't sure. Booker crumpled to the ground. Then Honey did scream.

Angela bolted from the rocks and into the brush where she'd been hiding, a deer leaping into the dark. The shadow man followed.

"No, help him. Help Booker," she yelled after his retreating back. But he was a hound on the scent. Driven. Gone.

"Book, are you okay? Book?" She pressed her chest into the tree, trying to still the drumbeat behind her ribs so she could hear his answer. "Book?" she said again.

The answer came. A moan. No words, just a deep exhale of breath, but it was the most beautiful poetry she'd ever heard. He was alive. Booker was alive.

"Who was that? Booker, do you know? Who went after Angela?"

Her husband hissed air in and out of his lips before answering. "Kirk. Kirk Wickett. I brought him with me."

Kirk. The man who'd once topped Booker's suspect list was now their hope. But it made sense. Bringing a cop, one cop, with him was Booker's compromise between meeting the ransom demands and working within the system he'd devoted his life to. She wanted to ask how this strange partnership came to be, but she could hear her husband's labored breaths.

Quiet reigned for several minutes; then Honey heard a laugh. A laugh. So incongruous in the tension of the moment. Who would laugh here and now?

She stiffened. The crunch of tires. More laughter. Staccato bursts of conversation. Bikers. Mountain bikers were headed this way.

"Hey!" she called out. "Hey, help me here!"

"There's someone there," a voice behind her said. Honey's head swiveled toward the sound. She watched three bikers pull up to the rock. One, a well-muscled woman in bike shorts and a helmet, dismounted.

"Here. We're here," Honey said. The woman, her steps awkward in cleated shoes, jogged toward her and crouched at Booker's side. "Are you okay? Sir, have you been hurt?"

"He's been shot," Honey said.

The other women dropped their bikes near the rock and ran toward them.

"It's my husband. Please call 911," Honey said.

"Did you shoot him?" a woman in a bright orange jersey asked.

Honey couldn't tell if she was making a joke but gestured at her hands tethered around the tree. "No."

The third biker, a woman in black, pulled a phone from a backpack and paced between the tree and the flat rock, presumably trying to find a signal. After several trips, she disappeared in the direction of the road.

The orange jersey woman joined the muscular woman and knelt next to Booker.

Muscles stood. "She's a nurse," she said, gesturing to Orange Jersey. "She'll know what to do until help gets here. Are you okay?"

"Yeah," Honey said. She'd been held at gunpoint, slapped, threatened, and poisoned with caffeine. She'd been lost in the woods, dragged through the wilderness, and had seen two men murdered. But the words, *she'll know what to do until help gets here,* were like a balm soothing every pain she'd experienced. *Until help gets here.* Help would come. The nightmare was over.

Muscles walked around the tree and examined Honey's cuffed wrists. "Geez." It was all she said, but Honey thought that about covered it.

Another gunshot shook the air. Muscles and Orange Jersey hit the dirt. Booker was already down. But Honey couldn't escape. She was propped up like a target at a shooting range. She hugged the tree and moaned. She was done. Exhausted. Defeated. Terrified.

Moments after the ringing echoes quieted, footsteps could be heard moving toward them. *It had to be Kirk. Please, let it be Kirk.* Honey squeezed her eyes shut. She couldn't bear it if it wasn't him. Better not to see at all.

"Police. It's okay." Kirk's voice nudged her eyes open. His uniform was clear in the moonlight. She felt the women near her exhale.

He limped across the rock and joined the nurse at Booker's side. "How is he?"

Before she could answer, the woman in black returned to the group. "The police and a helicopter ambulance are on their way."

"Good," the nurse in the orange jersey said. "The bleeding is under control, but he needs medical attention."

Kirk levered himself into a standing position, and Honey saw a stain, dark and wet, on his pants leg. "You've been hit."

"It's not bad," he said.

The nurse moved toward him anyway. The muscular woman stepped between Honey and her view of Kirk. She'd dragged a pack to the tree and handed Honey a tube that was connected to it. "Suck on this," she said.

The water was warm and tasted of plastic, but it was the best thing Honey had ever had. She drank until the tube made whistling noises, and the flow slowed.

"What happened to you?" the woman asked when Honey finished.

"It's a long story." One she didn't have the strength to tell at the moment. Tears welled into her eyes. "I wish I could see him."

"He's right here." Muscles stepped aside so Honey could view Booker's still form. A spandex jacket made a makeshift tourniquet. It wrapped around his shoulder. His eyes were closed, his face pale, but his breathing appeared steady.

"He was wearing a vest," Orange Jersey said.

"A bulletproof vest?" The question was inane. Of course she'd meant a bulletproof vest, but the news was so staggering, so good, Honey struggled to believe it. Good things hadn't been happening much lately.

"Yes," the nurse said. "Probably saved his life. From what I can tell, in the dark with a flashlight, there's a bullet in his shoulder. I don't think it's life-threatening, but don't quote me on that. In my professional opinion, he'll hold."

Muscles smiled. Her teeth gleamed in the dark. "You see? He'll hold. And help is on its way."

The sound of a helicopter, blades slashing through the night sky, confirmed her words. Help was here.

CHAPTER FORTY

HONEY'S WOUNDS WERE superficial. Her biggest problem was dehydration. After transferring an IV bag of fluids into her, they released her.

The police weren't as easy on her as the doctors had been. Honey had repeated her story at least three times. Once to one of the uniform cops who'd arrived on the trail at about the same time as the Air Ambulance, once to the policewoman who drove her to the hospital, and once more to Detective Sylla as the IV fluids pumped into her.

The bodies of Zach, Rick, and Charlie had been found exactly where Honey had said they'd be. The police had also found Joe's laptop in the house, strong evidence that Angela, or Angela and Zach, had indeed killed him and written the emails in his name. There was an APB out on her, but so far she was the only one who hadn't been found.

Willow sat with Honey in the waiting room until they got word Booker's surgery had been a success. He was sleeping off the anesthesia in post-op and was expected to make a full recovery. The doctor recommended Honey go home and get some rest herself. There would be plenty of time to sit by his bedside in the days ahead.

Willow drove her home. As they pulled onto the street, sadness gripped Honey. From a block away her house looked forlorn and abandoned. Maybe because neither her van nor Booker's truck were parked in the driveway, maybe because she knew Booker wouldn't be home for days, but she couldn't shake the melancholy. As soon as she exited Willow's car, she heard a howl. Fury. The poor thing had been alone in the house for hours. She'd forgotten all about him.

Willow looked at her. "He's fine, Mom."

Honey nodded. "I hope Booker left the back door open so he could get out and go to the bathroom."

"I'm sure he did."

Honey hurried to the front, not sure at all. Booker worried about break-ins and may not have thought he'd be gone long. When she reached the door, she stopped short. "I don't have my keys." They were in her purse, which was in her van, which was Lord knew where. The thought tightened her throat. The nightmare might be over, but nothing was the same.

Willow put a hand on her arm and squeezed. "I've got my key." She stepped around her mother and inserted it into the lock. Fury howled again. The sound was so lonely, so bereft, that tears sprang into Honey's eyes.

"It's okay, Fury," Willow called out as she stepped across the threshold.

It struck Honey something was wrong before she entered. Fury wasn't at the door flipping somersaults, that was one problem. Booker always left the entryway light on for the dog. It was out, problem number two. But it was the scent of lemon shampoo that made her want to turn and run. She reached for Willow to pull her back, but it was too late.

"I'll feed him, and then I'll make sandwiches—" A rush of bright hair and glinting steel cut off Willow's words. Honey flew into the entryway to find Angela holding a knife to her daughter's throat. It was one of Honey's favorites. An eight-inch, carbon steel blade that she kept razor sharp.

Terror flowed over her like an acid wash. She'd thought she'd felt fear when she'd been held in the shed, when she'd faced the barrel of a gun, when she'd heard the shot and seen Booker fall, but she hadn't. Not compared with this. This was an agonizing fear that made all other fears fade away like the echoes of a bad dream. Seeing her child, her baby, with that blade so close to her jugular made Honey want to scream, and weep, and tear her hair. She did none of those things.

"No." She whispered the word.

Angela stared at her through blue eyes as wide and angelic as a child's. "No, what? No, you're in denial about my presence in your house? No, you don't want me to hurt your precious Willow?"

Honey swallowed. Her saliva was thick and viscous, her lips dry. "Don't hurt Will."

"I find that annoying." Angela jerked Honey's daughter against her. Willow cried out. "Everything with you is Willow this and Willow that. She's not that awesome, you know? I tried very hard to be the daughter you always wanted, but *Willow*. . ." She spat the name like it was a piece of rotten fruit. "She doesn't even make an effort."

Honey held up her hands in a gesture of surrender. Placate. She had to placate the girl. "You were great. I appreciated all you did for me. I'm sorry if I didn't tell you that enough."

Angela laughed. "Appreciated me? You were almost ready to fire me. You didn't like the way I taught your cooking class. Didn't like the way I reorganized the shop. Didn't like the wall calendar." She took the knife from Willow's throat and used it to emphasize her points. "I went above and beyond for you, lady."

Willow caught Honey's gaze and tensed. She was going to fight. Honey could see it in her eyes. She shook her head, an almost imperceptible movement. This wasn't the time. Will didn't know how fast Angela was, or how brutal.

Angela must have read the situation. The knife returned to Willow's neck. "Don't do anything stupid."

The dog let loose a volley of frantic barks that ended with another hopeless yowl. "Can we go into the living room and talk? Maybe let Fury loose?" Honey kept her tone even, as if any abrupt movement might detonate the girl.

"Sure." Angela pushed Willow along in front of her and shoved her onto the couch. Honey exhaled and fell into a chair; her legs had become jelly. They weren't out of danger, she knew that, but now that the knife was no longer at her daughter's throat she could think more clearly.

"Why are you here?" Honey heard the measured notes of her own voice, the calm words, and wondered who'd uttered them.

Angela spun to face her. "That's rich. Why am I here? I'm here because you invited me. You said I could have Willow's room, remember? Besides, now, thanks to you, I have nowhere else to go."

Surprise took Honey off guard. "Thanks to me?"

Angela gave a small shake of her head. "If it weren't for you, I wouldn't have had to get rid of Rick and Zach."

Honey didn't bother contradicting that logic. Angela wasn't well, which she'd known for a while, but the unreality she lived in was deeper than Honey had realized.

"You owe me," the girl said.

"My mother felt sorry for you. She tried to help you. She doesn't owe you a thing," Willow said.

Fear tripped up Honey's spine. "Willow." Didn't she realize how dangerous it was to antagonize Angela?

Angela pointed the knife toward Willow. "You need to shut up."

Willow opened her mouth, but Honey intercepted her. "What do you want?" she said.

"I want a place to stay for a couple of days. The police are looking for me. I figure every day goes by they don't find me, the less pressing finding me is going to be. I want to turn into a cold case."

A couple of days. Honey didn't think she could live under this stress for a couple of hours, never mind days. A whimper rose in her throat, but she refused to let it out. "The police will come looking for me if I don't show up at the hospital."

"So, you'll go to the hospital. Willow can stay here and keep me company."

Honey didn't respond. As long as her daughter was here, Angela held the cards. She'd do whatever she had to do.

"Do you have duct tape?" Angela said.

"What for?" Willow said.

Honey jumped up. "I think so. In the garage."

"Get it. I'll stay here with your darling daughter."

Honey paused. She didn't want to leave the two of them alone together.

"Now," Angela roared.

She was angry. *Don't make Angela angry.* Honey had seen what happened when Angela was angry. She ran to the garage, grabbed a roll of tape from the workbench, and jogged to the living room again. She held out the roll.

Angela took it and handed it to Willow. "Tape her hands."

Willow's chin jutted forward in that stubborn movement Honey knew so well. "Here." Honey thrust her hands out in front of her. Willow paused then reached for her mother's wrists.

Angela stepped close and touched Willow's neck with the knife. "Behind her back, stupid."

Honey pivoted, and Willow began to wrap her wrists. Honey had sensed Angela's animosity toward her daughter, but it had been contained. Now it was blatant, out in full force. Terror rippled over her skin again. Honey had to pour oil on these turbulent waters. She couldn't, wouldn't, allow Willow to be hurt.

"More," Angela said.

Willow wrapped another layer.

Angela shoved Honey into a chair. "Ankles."

Willow's eyes reflected the storm cloud inside her. She was furious. Fury was a dangerous emotion. As if on cue, the dog howled.

"For goodness sake, can I please let the dog out of wherever you've put him?" Willow said.

Angela moved her knife hand ever-so-slightly, and Willow winced. A moment later a trickle of blood slid down her neck. Willow dropped to her knees and began taping her mother's ankles.

"Now you." Angela took the tape from Willow, yanked her to her feet, and began wrapping her wrists. When finished, she pushed Willow toward the other easy chair, taped her ankles then stood. "I need sleep. I'm dead on my feet."

She stretched out on the couch, placed the knife on her chest, and crossed her arms over it. The pose made Honey think about vampires again. "You should sleep too," Angela said and closed her eyes.

Honey stared until she saw the rise and fall of Angela's chest. The jokes she and Booker used to make about wakeful terrors and sleeping angels when they checked on Ash and Willow after tucking them into bed at night came to mind. As she gazed at Angela, she thought those jokes had never seemed so true and never less humorous.

CHAPTER FORTY-ONE

THE PAIN WOKE Honey. Her head had fallen forward onto her chest and locked in position as she'd slept. Her neck muscles spasmed when she moved. She shifted in the chair. Her entire body screamed. She needed a hot bath, a massage, painkillers, and a night in her own bed.

Daylight had dwindled as they slept. The last rays of the sun slanted through the windows and fell on Angela's slumbering form. Despite the bruises and dirt on her face, she looked like a princess, a sleeping beauty waiting for her prince.

Honey's eyes cut to Willow. Her gaze was sharp. It didn't appear that she'd slept at all.

"Sorry." Honey mouthed the word.

Willow gave a small shake of her head. "Better," she mouthed.

Honey knew what she meant. Even though her body hurt, her mind was more alert. The sleep had done her good. She needed a plan, a strategy to get them out of this, but in the state of exhaustion she'd been in, it hadn't been possible to come up with one.

"You two talking about me behind my back?" Angela's eyes were open. The princess image was wiped away by the inhuman coldness of her face.

They didn't answer.

She sat up. "Hungry?" She asked as if they'd just popped over for a visit.

Willow shook her head.

"No," Honey said.

"Well, I'm starved. Why don't you. . ." She gazed at Honey and adopted a cowboy accent. "Rustle me up some grub." She smiled at her own humor.

"There's not a lot in the house," Honey said automatically, not because it was true, but because she never served company leftovers or canned tuna. She realized how silly her words were as soon as they left her mouth.

Angela cocked her head to one side. "Next you're going to suggest DoorDash. Not happening. I'm sure you can find something in there." She gestured to the kitchen.

As if in response to their voices, Fury whimpered from somewhere in the house. "Can I please give the dog water at least?" Honey said.

Angela stood, stretched and walked to Honey's chair. She lifted the knife, and Honey shrank away. "How are you going to cook or water the dog or do anything if I don't cut the tape?"

Honey lifted her ankles first, when those were free, she stood and turned her back so Angela could free her wrists as well. Blood rushed to her extremities. She rubbed her wrists. "Where is Fury?" she said.

"He's in the master bathroom. I figured if he made a mess, that was the place to do it." Angela grinned at her. "See, I'm not all bad."

Honey headed upstairs. Fury must have heard her coming. His whines became frantic as she approached the bathroom. His claws scrabbled at the door. She opened it, and a black ball of fur threw itself at her.

Honey sat on the floor, leaned against the side of her bed, and let the dog leap around her. He bounded in then out of her lap, not able to make up his mind where he wanted to be. He disappeared into the bathroom for a moment, then reemerged with one of Booker's dirty socks in his mouth. He pulled it into her lap, settled down, and nibbled nervously.

"Poor baby." She stroked his head and cooed at him until Angela yelled up the stairs.

Honey pushed herself to her feet using the bed for support and walked into the bathroom. Fury slunk behind her. He'd lifted his leg on one side of the toilet and dropped a pile on the other. "It's okay, boy. What were you supposed to do?"

She grabbed a roll of paper towels and a bottle of disinfectant from under the sink and cleaned up the mess. As she bent to replace the supplies, her gaze fell on a bottle sitting on the counter. It was her Xanax. An idea popped into her head like a light bulb switching on.

"Honey, what are you doing up there?" Angela screamed from below.

"Fury pooped all over the place. I'm cleaning it up," she yelled.

"Hurry up."

Honey opened the pill bottle, shook five pills into her hand then slipped them into her jeans pocket. She closed the bottle, but put it in the medicine cabinet behind her face wash. She didn't want to risk Angela seeing it.

Quickly, she walked into her bedroom, emptied the dish Booker kept on his dresser for change and keys, brought it to the bathroom, and filled it with water. Fury started drinking before she placed it on the floor. She used the toilet, then refilled his bowl, and shut him into the bathroom again. The despair in his eyes almost made her bring him down with her, but she thought about the knife in Angela's hand. He was safer here.

When she got downstairs, Angela was sitting on the couch, reading a cookbook. Willow was in her chair in restraints. "You need to take your kid to the potty," Angela said without looking up.

"I have to pee," Willow said.

Honey turned to Angela. "I can't carry her."

Angela heaved an exaggerated sigh, picked up the knife, and walked to Willow's chair. She flicked the blade across the tape at her ankles carelessly. Its tip scratched Willow's skin, and a ribbon of red appeared.

Willow's jaw tightened, but she didn't cry out. She'd been raised with a brother whose whole goal in life had been to join the Marine Corps. They'd played army since she was six years old. Both her children took martial arts classes from ages ten to eighteen. Angela shouldn't underestimate Willow. If she got free, she could do damage. At least, she'd try. Another reason Honey had to take care of Angela herself.

When they reached the bathroom, Honey helped Willow yank down her jeans. Her daughter's face flamed. Not with embarrassment. Honey was her mother, she'd diapered that butt, as she was fond of reminding her children. No, Will was humiliated because she needed help. She was one of the most independent and resourceful people Honey knew.

While Willow relieved herself, Honey reached into her pocket and pulled out the Xanax. She showed it to her daughter and whispered, "Don't eat the tuna." Willow nodded.

"I'll make tuna melts," Honey said when they reentered the living room.

"Sounds good," Angela said.

"Grilled cheese for me," Willow said.

Angela looked up from her book. "Picky eater?"

Willow shrugged. "I don't like tuna."

Honey disappeared into the kitchen. She pulled a can from the pantry, and celery and an apple from the fridge. She could see the girls from the island, which meant they could see her. Instead of setting up her workstation there as she usually did, she moved to a smaller area next to the sink. Here she could block Angela's view with her body, but still glance over her shoulder to keep tabs on her.

Angela appeared to be engrossed in the cookbook, so she slipped the pills from her pocket onto a cutting board. She used the flat side of her chef's knife to smash them into a powder. Then she pushed the powder into a teacup and got to work making tuna salad.

She filled a bowl with greens and topped it with tuna for herself. Then she grabbed the teacup and poured the pulverized Xanax into the remainder of the fish.

"Is it almost ready?" Angela stood on the other side of the kitchen island.

Honey glanced into the bowl of tuna salad. A pile of white powder sat on top. She grabbed a fork and began mashing. "Yes. Just have to make the sandwich. I'm hurrying."

"Have any crackers, or pickles, or anything to munch on?"

"There are pickles in the fridge." Honey was about to get them for Angela, but noticed the top of the cutting board was coated with white powder. She pivoted, hiding it with her body and gestured to the refrigerator.

While Angela rummaged inside, Honey wiped down the cutting board with a sponge. "Grab the bread while you're in there, will you?" She tried to keep her tone casual.

Angela tossed the bread to her and left the kitchen with the jar of pickles in her hand. Honey finished the sandwiches quickly, making a grilled cheese for Willow and a tuna melt for Angela. She put all three meals on a tray and carried them into the living room.

"How am I supposed to eat?" Willow said when Honey put the grilled cheese on a side table.

"Your mom can feed you like she did when you were little," Angela said.

Honey perched on the arm of Willow's chair and fed her in between bites of her own lunch. She wasn't hungry, but knew she needed to eat. She'd only had Angela's sandwich in the past two days. She no longer felt light and alert. She felt weak.

Angela inhaled the sandwich and half the jar of pickles. When she was done, she glanced at Honey. "Got any cookies?"

"There might be a date bar left." Honey's tone was droll.

"Thanks, no. I'm feeling energized enough," Angela said.

Willow's gaze darted between the two of them without understanding.

Honey picked up their empty plates, carted them into the kitchen, and pulled a box of gingersnaps from the cupboard. She carried them to the living room, handed them to Angela, and resumed her seat.

Honey watched as Angela popped a cookie into her mouth, picked up the cookbook again, and began leafing through it. "You should make this cioppino for me before I leave."

"I don't have the ingredients." Honey fought to keep her tone casual. She studied Angela's face for signs that the Xanax was working.

"You could pick them up when you go see Booker." Angela spoke clearly, no slur to her words. How long before the drug took effect?

Honey tried to remember her own reaction to it. Of course, now she knew that every time she'd taken it, she'd had mega doses of caffeine racing through her system. She had no idea what the effects would have been without the stimulant.

Angela ate another cookie and another. She'd downed at least five before the first yawn hit her. Three more cookies and she yawned again, wider and longer this time. She set down the gingersnaps and stood. "Come here," she said to Honey. Honey obeyed. Angela taped her wrists again but left her ankles loose. "Don't do anything stupid. I'll be right back."

She headed for the guest bathroom. It was only a short way down the hall. Honey watched her close the door behind herself. What if she passed out in the bathroom?

Willow leaped from her chair and strode toward the kitchen. "What are you doing?" Honey said in a stage whisper.

"Getting loose," Willow said. "There's gotta be something in there we can use to cut the tape."

"Why don't we—"

The sound of retching stopped her words. Willow spun around, their gazes met, then turned toward the closed bathroom door in unison. Despair and fear in equal measure coursed through Honey. What would Angela do now? How would she punish them? "How did she know?"

Willow stood stock still until the retching stopped. She didn't speak until they heard the sound of the toilet flushing. "Maybe she doesn't."

Honey gave a small shake of her head. "Of course she does. Why else would she puke?"

"Because she's bulimic."

"Bulimic?"

"Yeah. I thought that as soon as I saw her."

"Why?"

"My old roommate was bulimic. Angela had the same pale complexion, bruises on her arms, eating half a box of cookies, but it's the fingers that give them away." Honey thought about the scrape marks on Willow's knuckles. "It's called Russell's sign. It's from. . ." Willow shoved two fingers into her mouth.

"I thought she was being abused."

The door to the bathroom slammed open. Willow looked at her chair but didn't bother racing over to it. She wouldn't have made it in time anyway. Angela reentered the room seconds later. "What are you doing?" She stared at Willow.

"I'm thirsty," Willow said. "I thought I'd flip on the faucet and stick my head under."

Honey sucked in a breath and waited for Angela to fly into a rage, to accuse them of trying to poison her. Before she had the chance to do anything, the doorbell rang.

CHAPTER FORTY-TWO

HONEY AND WILLOW stared at Angela. The girl paled, but that was the only sign that the bell concerned her. "Come here," she finally said, her eyes trained on Honey. She lifted the knife that had become a part of her and sliced through the tape on Honey's wrists.

"Answer the door. Get rid of whoever it is. Me and my friend," she waggled the knife blade, "will be with Willow."

A weight dropped on Honey's shoulders as she walked the short hall to the front door. She was walking the plank, walking to the hangman's noose. Dread drilled down on her with each step heavier and heavier. If she made a mistake, said the wrong thing. . . No. She couldn't think of that. Willow would be fine. By the time she reached the door, the effort it took to open it was herculean.

She turned the knob, pulled the door ajar, and Fury broke into a volley of barks from the upstairs bath.

"Hey." Rosie stood on the stoop, her eyebrows forming a question mark. "How're you doing? I didn't want to come over earlier in case you were sleeping. I knew Willow was here to take care of you, but—" she paused. "Where's Fury?"

"Upstairs," Honey said, the truth always easier than a lie.

She realized the difficulty of that truth as soon as Rosie said, "Why is he upstairs?"

"Ah." Honey tried to think of a logical reason to lock her dog into the master bathroom. "He was sick. Puking. I didn't want him to mess on the rugs." She improvised.

Rosie's face collapsed into a frown. She wasn't buying it.

Honey pleaded with her eyes for her friend to intuit the situation. Rosie, her perceptive friend, her friend who saw people as colors that throbbed with meaning. If anyone could understand her nonverbal communication, surely it would be Rosie.

"Sick?" Rosie said. "Do you want me to take him to the vet? You use the same vet we do, right? He might just be upset. It's been an upsetting. . ." Her words dried up. "Oh," she said. She knew something was wrong, and that something wasn't Fury.

"He'll be fine. Probably ate something," Honey said.

"Right."

They stared at each other for several seconds, tension moving in the air between them like static electricity, until Honey realized the silence wasn't a good thing. Silence would send a message to Angela; one she didn't want to send.

"I'm exhausted," she said. *You need to leave. Get help*, she tried to communicate with her eyes.

"Of course. Is there anything you need?" Rosie's face said, *I've got it. I understand.* Honey was sure that's what her face said.

"I'm good." Honey communicated, *Thank you. Thank you.*

"I'll check in with you guys later." *I'll bring help soon.*

"Later would be great." Honey closed the door and rested her forehead against it. Rosie knew. She might not know everything, might not know the details, but she knew Honey was in trouble. She'd bring help.

Honey returned to the living room, to Angela and to Willow, hope like a small flame in her chest. Angela re-taped her hands, and she sat and waited.

* * *

Minutes that felt like hours passed with no ill effects from the Xanax. Angela must have thrown it all up. Honey tried to comfort herself with the thought that Rosie would bring help. However, the longer she sat without hearing sirens on the street outside, the more her doubts grew. Maybe Rosie hadn't understood.

There were more pills in the medicine cabinet. That was her other hope. Her backup plan. But if Willow was right, if Angela was bulimic, wouldn't she throw up everything she ate?

Angela wandered into the kitchen, got a glass of wine, and brought it to the couch. Wine. Wine would work.

"I'd offer you some vino, but it's hard to drink with your hands tied." She flipped on the TV.

"I need to feed Fury," Honey said. "He hasn't eaten today." The dog had stopped whining. It was worrying her. But, more than that, she could get the rest of the Xanax when she was upstairs, maybe slip it into Angela's second glass of wine.

After scrolling through the stations, Angela settled on *Man vs. Wild*. It wasn't the show Honey would've picked. What she wouldn't have given for a camera crew following her around Black Star Canyon. "He'll live. You can feed him in the morning."

Honey opened her mouth to protest but closed it again. She didn't want to seem overanxious.

"Why are you being so cruel?" Willow spoke up.

Honey tried to catch her daughter's eye, willing her to stop. Willow didn't stop. "He's just a little dog. He's scared. He's hungry. Why not let him come down?"

Angela silenced Bear Grylls and glared at Willow for a long moment. "Fine." She threw the remote onto the coffee table and marched upstairs. Honey sank into her chair, deflated. Now she would have no reason to go to the master bath.

A moment later, Fury raced into the room, a bundle of frantic energy. He threw himself first at Honey, then Willow, then Honey again. Angela appeared behind him. She pulled the knife from the pocket of a big sweater she'd taken from Honey's closet and cut the tape from Honey's hands and feet. "Feed him."

Honey rubbed her wrists, then stood. She didn't look at Willow, didn't want her to see the disappointment in her eyes. There was no point. She plodded to the kitchen, Fury at her heels.

As she fixed the dog's food, she heard the TV resume. Bear addressed the camera, explaining how to filter your own urine for drinking purposes. That was something to be thankful for anyway. She'd never had to drink her own piss. It was the small things in life.

Tomorrow was another day, as Scarlett O'Hara said. Perhaps in the morning, Angela would let her shower and dress before going to the hospital, and she could get more pills then. If she put them in the girl's morning coffee, they might stay down.

She put Fury's food on the floor, and he devoured it in seconds. She thought about giving him a second bowl but picked up his dish instead. He'd been without food for quite a while. She didn't want him to throw up.

She took the bowl to the sink, washed it, and set it on a towel to dry. Then she grabbed the dishes they'd dirtied earlier and washed those.

As she turned to dry her hands, she saw the wine bottle Angela had opened. It was Honey's last bottle of Red Ravish. Figures. The girl would pick the most expensive wine she had.

A short laugh escaped her lips. Angela had taken over her home, had tried to kill her husband, was threatening her daughter, had ditched her van somewhere, had stolen $50,000, and Honey got annoyed over a bottle of wine. Once a foodie, always a foodie.

She corked it, cleaned up the spills Angela had left on the counter, and made her way to the living room. When she entered, Willow shot her a wide-eyed look and mouthed, "Shhhh." Then jerked her chin toward Angela.

The girl's chin rested on her chest. Her eyes were closed. Her breathing steady. Angela was asleep.

Honey felt paralyzed. She was free. Angela was asleep. And, suddenly, she didn't know what to do. The knife lay on the coffee table next to the wine glass. She could reach over and take it, but what if Angela woke up?

What if she did?

If Honey had the knife, she would be the one who was armed.

Honey crept around the couch and stood next to the coffee table. The clip, clip of Fury's claws followed her. She shot him a glance, willing him to be quiet. He wagged in response.

Honey leaned forward and placed a hand on the knife. Angela didn't move. Honey slid the blade millimeter by agonizing millimeter toward the edge of the table, never taking her eyes from the sleeping girl. No movement. She wrapped her fingers around the handle.

The doorbell obliterated the silence.

Honey yanked the knife off the table. Fury raced to the front door, his barks echoing off the walls. She shifted the knife and held it like she planned to de-bone a chicken. Adrenaline, like tainted stevia, flooded her veins. She anchored herself, stance wide, ready for a fight. Angela wouldn't walk away this time.

But Angela never moved.

"Honey?" She barely heard Rosie's voice through the pounding of blood in her ears.

"In here." Willow called from somewhere far away.

"Mom. It worked. She's out." Willow's words telescoped toward her, but she couldn't comprehend their meaning.

"She's in shock," Rosie said. A moment later, Honey felt warm fingers pry the knife from her cold ones. Hands led her to a chair.

She wasn't sure how long she sat like that. By the time she came to herself, her living room was filled with people. One paramedic examined the sleeping beauty on the couch, leaning over her like Prince Charming ready to bestow a kiss. Two more rolled a gurney close.

A glass of something cool filled her hand. Honey turned to see where the gift had come from. Detective Sylla squatted next to her chair. "Drink up. The sugar will help."

Honey raised the juice to her lips obediently. Sylla was right. Within minutes she was able to tell her what had happened. Her words, halting at first, gathered strength and speed. Sylla typed quickly, only asking questions when Honey's narrative slowed.

"Willow," Honey said, suddenly remembering her daughter. Her gaze darted around the room and found her daughter. She and a paramedic sat close, speaking in low voices. The paramedic cleaned the dried blood from her neck with gauze.

"She's okay," Sylla said. "Better than you." She flashed Honey a bright white smile. "Was wondering if you needed a trip to hospital, but I think maybe you're better off here."

Honey leaned her head on the chair. "Yes, here. I'm fine now." But a thought made her sit bolt upright. "Booker?"

"Last I heard he was doing fine, but why don't you call and check up on him? You'll scare the life out of him if you run in looking like this."

Thirty minutes later, the living room was empty. The paramedics had wheeled Angela away to a stomach pump. The police had gotten their statements and left. Willow had gone upstairs to call the hospital to check on her father. Only Fury sat curled into a tight knot in Honey's lap. She closed her eyes and sank into the peace of the moment.

Rosie wandered into the room, both hands filled. "Look what I found." She placed a glass of red wine in Honey's hand. "Red Ravish," she said.

She curled up on the couch, feet underneath her, and sipped her own glass. "The Xanax in the tuna salad was pretty brilliant," she said.

Honey downed a gulp of her wine. "Don't tell anybody." Rosie's eyebrows raised. "I'm a chef. Nobody will trust my cooking again."

"Dad is good." Willow entered, a bandage on her throat. "Hey. Where's mine?"

"In the kitchen. I can get you some." Rosie leaned forward to stand.

"No, sit. I'll get it. I'm sick of sitting." Willow walked into the kitchen and returned a minute later, her own glass of wine in hand. "He woke up and asked about you." She looked at her mother. "When he heard you were fine, he went out again. The floor nurse said we shouldn't bug him until morning."

As much as Honey wanted to see Booker, she was relieved. The tension of the past two days had drained out of her and left her limp and weak. She couldn't have driven to the hospital in her current condition.

"I'm ordering pizza," Willow said.

"Pizza?" Honey parroted the word as if trying to remember what it was. It seemed a long time since she'd eaten any.

"I'll make it a veggie everything," Willow said, mistaking her mother's question for argument. "But I need carbs." She turned her gaze on Rosie. "You'll stay?"

"Only if we can watch a chick flick."

"Only if it's funny. If it's not funny, I'm not watching it," Honey said.

"Veggie everything, funny movie, got it," Willow said.

"You have more wine?" Rosie asked.

"Of course," Honey said, and closed her eyes again so she could feel the comfort surrounding her. She was safe. More important, Willow and Booker were safe. That knowledge grew inside her and became larger and larger until it was a solid presence. A presence that satisfied something deep inside of her that hadn't been satisfied since her mother died. It filled her being, splashed over into her living room, and flooded her entire home.

She opened her eyes. She'd be able to sleep tonight. To function tomorrow. They were safe.

CHAPTER FORTY-THREE

HONEY COASTED PAST the gate and into the lot of Black Star Canyon. Tracey wheeled alongside. "Good riding," she said. Tracey was the well-muscled Trail Angel who'd found Honey and Booker that night a month ago. A week after the ordeal, she'd wandered into Honey's shop to see how everyone was doing. Sweeter than Honey had been mentioned in the *Orange County Register*'s article about the event.

Before Tracey left that day, Honey had surprised herself by agreeing to a beginner's ride with the Trail Angels the following Saturday. Tracey had an old bike she could lend her. All Honey had to do was show up.

It was scary, but not nearly as scary as being weak and helpless. Honey had been on six rides since and had grown more confident with each. She'd gained physical strength more quickly than she'd imagined possible, but that wasn't the greatest gain. The greatest gain was the emotional reserves she sensed from so many in the group. These were strong women in more ways than one. After everything she'd been through, she was ready to join their ranks. As a bonus, she was also losing weight and getting her cholesterol under control.

She smiled as she remembered Charlie's disbelief that there could be such a thing as good cholesterol, but it was a sad smile.

Honey pulled her bike up to her new SUV. The police had found her van in a gully way up Black Star almost to Beek's Place. A family of raccoons had moved in and done what raccoons do to things. It was no longer fit to drive even if she could get the smell out, so she'd bought a new Toyota 4Runner. She hung her bike, another new purchase, on a rack extending from its hatch.

"Want to get a taco?" Tracey said.

"No. Can't," Honey said. "Willow is bringing her boyfriend, Jonathan, home to meet us."

"Fun. Are you cooking for everybody, or going out?"

"Jonathan is barbecuing his famous ribs. I'm making salads."

"Sounds amazing. What time should I be there?" Tracey threw her bike in the bed of her pickup, then turned to Honey and grinned. "Seriously, have fun. I hope you like him."

"He sounds wonderful. He's attentive, thoughtful, has a good job, and he's a foodie."

"If Willow breaks up with him, give him my number, will you?" Tracey climbed into her truck. "See you next week? Wednesday?"

"I'll be there." Honey planned to close up shop early and head to Laguna with the girls. When Booker's medical bills started rolling in, she'd had a realization. Even with good benefits, doctors were expensive. Exercise had to be a priority.

* * *

Honey's cell phone rang before she turned off the engine. It was Friar Philip. "Honey, wondering if I can impose."

"You're never an imposition, Father."

"Father Ambrose has come down with a cold. Would you be able to cook for the pantry on Monday? The guests miss you."

"I'll be there," she said. They decided on the menu, what Honey would bring and what would be waiting for her, and hung up. Honey hadn't hired anyone to replace Angela yet, but she hadn't hesitated even though she'd have to close the shop for the morning. She didn't mind. Not anymore.

Honey had decided money wasn't the great security blanket she'd once thought. Money hadn't saved her from Zach or Angela. In fact, money had placed her in greater danger. What had saved her were the people in her life who cared.

The day after Honey told Friar Philip about Joe's death, he had contacted Booker to offer his condolences. In the course of the conversation he'd explained that Joe had visited him on his last trip to Orange County and had confessed his affair with Angela. Booker realized she, either alone or with Zach's help, must have been Joe's killer and the one who held his wife prisoner.

He'd taken that information to Sylla and begged her not to send a battalion of deputies to the canyon, but to send only him and Kirk Wickett. She'd agreed if both men stayed in radio contact and wore Kevlar vests.

Booker and Kirk had risked their lives to save Honey. Willow would have if she'd had the chance. Rosie had understood her unspoken pleas and brought help. Even Fury had done his part, preventing Zach's early break-in attempts.

Poor Rick. Honey had sympathy for the man even if he had tried to shoot her. His stockpiles of food were his security just as Honey's savings account had been hers. It was a delusion. The jars and boxes and barrels hadn't defended him from Angela any more than the $50,000 had defended Honey.

No. Loved ones, people who cared, that's what sanctuaries were constructed of. Honey switched off the engine and headed into her home.

Willow and Jonathan arrived just as Honey finished drying her hair. She heard Fury's joyful greeting from the bedroom, checked her lipstick, and walked downstairs to meet the man who'd graduated from not-a-complete-loser status.

Everyone was huddled in the kitchen, leaning on cupboards and counters as usual. Why everyone insisted on standing in the kitchen when there were perfectly good chairs only feet away, she never understood. To annoy her. That was the only explanation she could come up with.

Willow ran to hug her as she entered, then took her hand and drew her toward a young man leaning against Honey's spice drawer. Will was beaming. "Mom, this is Jonathan. Jonathan, my mom, Honey."

He was cute. Honey knew she shouldn't objectify the guy. She was sure he was so much more than his handsome face, thick head of brown hair salted with sunlights, and broad shoulders, but, hey, first impressions were good. She shook hands with him and liked his strong, but not bone-crushing, grip.

"Willow talks about you all the time," he said. "She's so proud of you."

"Proud?" A knot formed in Honey's stomach. Images of Angela holding a knife to her daughter's throat haunted her dreams. "I almost got her killed."

Willow squeezed her hand. "You saved my life, Mom."

"If I hadn't hired—" her throat constricted, and she couldn't continue.

"Dad and I were after you to hire somebody," Willow said.

"You couldn't have known," Booker said, his voice raised. Honey knew he meant to be encouraging, but he sounded angry.

Honey shook her head. "I should have known."

It didn't seem as if Booker heard her. He crossed his arms over his chest and stared at the floor. "If we're attributing blame, I think it falls squarely on my shoulders. I knew who Joe was. I tried to whitewash his behavior, but I knew who he was. I knew the kind of people he associated with."

"Joe was sorry. He came to Orange County to make things right." Honey couldn't believe she was defending Joe to Booker.

"How do you make something like that right?"

Booker's body had almost completely healed from the bullet wound, but his psyche was still fractured. Honey often found him sitting, staring into space, his old enthusiasm gone, the bright flame of his personality reduced to a smoldering wick. "Don't—"

Jonathan interrupted her with a soft voice. "It sounds like Angela may have borderline personality disorder. It's fairly common in people who struggle with eating disorders. They are masters at hiding things they don't want people to know. You can't blame yourselves, either of you."

"Jonathan has a cousin like Angela." Willow barked an ironic laugh. "Well, she never killed anybody."

Jonathan's mouth twitched. "That we know of."

"But the family worries about her. I mean, not that she'll kill anybody. She's a nice person. Not like Angela that way." Willow's eyes widened. "I think I need to shut up."

"What Will's saying is half my aunt and uncle's retirement account has gone toward treatment centers and therapy. It's been rough on them," Jonathan said. "But that's what you do, right? It's family."

Booker's gaze shot to Jonathan's face.

"Yes," Honey said trying to catch Booker's eye. "I haven't always understood that. Maybe it was growing up in a big family. We struggled financially, and there were so many of us it was every man for himself. Especially at mealtimes. You could lose your hand reaching for the breadbasket."

Booker's mouth tipped into a half-grin. "She's not kidding. I've eaten meals with the Baumgarten clan."

"Speaking of food," Willow said.

Jonathan clapped his hands together. "I should start the ribs if we want to eat sometime today."

"Right." Booker pushed himself off the counter he'd been leaning against.

"Lead me to your grill," Jonathan said.

The men disappeared into the backyard, and Honey began pulling salad ingredients from the refrigerator.

"So, how are you guys?" Willow said. "Really?"

Honey didn't meet her gaze. "We're okay."

"Dad?"

Honey dumped an armload of vegetables into the sink and began running water over them. She wasn't sure how much she should say. She was worried about Booker, but she didn't want to transfer that worry to her daughter. "He's struggling, but he'll figure it out. Your dad is the strongest man I know. I was glad Ash could get away for the funeral. He's good for your dad."

"Dad took Uncle Joe's death hard," Will said.

"I thought the trip home would help. Closure and all that."

"It was good to see everybody."

"It was, but I'm not sure it did much to mend what Joe's death broke."

They worked in silence for a while. Honey washing lettuce, carrots, cucumbers, and green onion. Willow patting them dry. The men's voices rumbled through the window. Honey was about to comment that Jonathan and Booker seemed to be getting along when a laugh floated in from the yard. It was Booker. A second later, Jonathan's guffaw joined her husband's.

Honey moved to the window and gazed out. The two men stood next to the grill, beers in hand. Jonathan was regaling Booker with a story that must have been hysterical. Booker's face was raised to the sky, his mouth open in a hardy laugh. Honey grinned in response.

Willow stepped next to her. "He's pretty amazing, isn't he?"

Honey wasn't sure if she meant her father or her boyfriend, but she agreed on both counts. "Yeah."

"Jonathan reminds me of Ash." Willow waved a hand as if trying to erase her words. "Not in some Greek tragedy, creepy kind of way. Just his sense of humor. He's upbeat, optimistic. When I get all musician melancholy, he cracks a joke, and it blows away."

Honey saw something sparkle on her daughter's uplifted hand. She reached for it. "What's this?"

Willow tried to suppress a smile. "I was going to tell you right away, but everything got so serious."

"Booker," Honey yelled through the window.

"Yes, Hon," he said.

Honey dragged Willow toward the sliding glass door by her finger. "You need to see this."

Booker's eyes grew wide. Jonathan crossed the patio and put a protective arm around Willow's shoulders. "I wanted to wait until you tasted the ribs," he said.

Willow sparkled almost as brightly as the diamond on her finger. "Jonathan proposed. I said yes."

Honey was frozen in place, the cascade of emotions that washed over her too great to navigate. Joy and excitement tempered by loss and concern. They hadn't been dating long. Willow hardly knew him. She and Booker had just met him.

Booker saved the moment. "That's great news, sweetheart." He wrapped his arms around Willow, then slapped a hand on Jonathan's shoulder while shaking his hand with the other. "If you hurt her in any way, I'll kill you," he said with something between a smile and a snarl.

"Book," Honey said. "He didn't mean that." But as she hugged the couple, she thought he just might.

"You and Dad didn't date all that long, did you?" Willow said as if she sensed her mother's concerns.

"No, but we knew each other forever. We dated in high school." Willow's jaw muscles clenched like Booker's did when he was getting stubborn. Honey dropped it. Her daughter was an adult. Jonathan seemed like a great guy. He came from a good family.

The ribs were excellent. You could tell a lot about a person by the food they prepared. He was a good cook, his process professional, and his food delicious. Honey had to admit she liked what she saw. Not that she fully trusted herself yet.

The way Angela had fooled her had drilled into Honey's affections like a tick on a dog, had left her doubting herself. But she hadn't seen Booker in such a good mood since Joe's death, and that was something.

Honey began clearing dishes from the outdoor picnic table. "I made apple crisp for dessert."

Booker groaned. "If I eat one more thing, I'm going to explode."

Jonathan stood to help. "I saved room."

"Can you two sit for a minute," Willow said.

Honey set down the plates in her hand and perched on the edge of her chair.

Willow pulled Jonathan into his seat. "We have more news. News you're going to be excited about."

"We're moving back to Orange County," Jonathan said.

Booker's face erupted in a broad grin. "You're coming home?"

Willow's head bobbed as Jonathan gave them the details. "The bad news is my dad had a stroke. He and my mom need help, so I started applying for jobs in the area."

"He got an offer, a great offer," Willow said.

Jonathan tipped his head, a humble gesture. "It's good, but it's better that I'll be around to take some of the pressure off my sister. She's a bit overwhelmed."

"But what about your job?" Honey asked Willow.

"I'm going to finish the school year in San Diego, but I've been applying to schools up here for the fall. I've already had interest. I don't think it will be as difficult to find something now that I have a teaching gig on my resume."

Honey wasn't thrilled about Willow leaving a good job, but the excitement of having her daughter close again diluted the disappointment. Honey watched Booker's face as Will and Jonathan filled them in on their plans. The lines that had been etched on his forehead for months softened. The downturned bow of his mouth lifted. The shadows in his blue eyes cleared. He'd be okay. They were all going to be okay.

All those empty places in Honey's heart, the hollows Angela had filled with her poison, would mend. There was something about being pinched between death's fingers that now made her world feel big and full. Sure, there were things she wanted. She wanted to move to the next level in her business. She wanted Booker to be his old happy self. She wanted to write a cookbook, find a publisher, and hit bestseller lists. But she was satisfied with the way things were.

"Want another splash of wine?" Honey picked up the almost empty bottle and held it up for Willow to view. "Where's your glass?"

Willow smiled. "I don't have one."

Honey's brow furrowed. "You're not drinking wine?" Willow loved wine. She'd considered becoming a sommelier at one time in her life.

"Nope. I'm going to check on the guys." She flashed another enigmatic smile and walked out the backdoor.

No wine. Engaged. Honey put a hand on her lips. Was her life about to become even more full?

Join Greta Boris's readers community at
www.GretaBoris.com for free stories, new release
information, and more.

THE
SEVEN
DEADLY
SINS

THE
COLOR
OF ENVY

GRETA BORIS

And the good Master said: "This circle scourges
The sin of envy. . ."

And as unto the blind the sun comes not.
So to the shades, of whom just now I spake,
Heaven's light will not be bounteous of itself;
For all their lids an iron wire transpierces,
And sews them up. . .

From the Second Terrace of *Purgatorio*
***The Divine Comedy* of Dante Alighieri**

CHAPTER ONE

SATURDAY, MARCH 17TH

THE BUSH SHOOK and emitted strange snuffling noises. "Hurry up," Kate said and pulled her coat more closely around herself. She wished she was better prepared for the weather, but Jake had acted like it was an emergency. The dog was five months and not as house broken as she wished, so if Jake wanted out, she took him out. But the dog sniffed more than peed, and that was the truth.

Kate tugged the leash, and Jake trotted out from under the bush and onto the gravel path. "Are you going to go, or what?" Jake didn't answer, only dragged her to the next stand of bushes and resumed his olfactory research.

It was early, five-thirty. The sun had just begun to climb from beneath the horizon. Morning fog muted the little light and warmth it offered. She shivered.

Jake had jumped onto her bed and awakened her with a volley of slobbery kisses. Once she was up, he ran in circles from the front door, to her, and back, emitting the frantic yips that she'd learned the hard way meant he had to go. She slid her feet into flip flops, pulled a jacket over her thin cotton pajamas, and took him. Her clothes were scant protection against the wet chill.

Kate had made a left onto her street and walked two blocks to a path leading into the park adjacent to her Seattle neighborhood. She'd trudged along Jake's favorite route, patiently waiting for him to do his business, but now all she could think about was warmth and coffee.

"Okay, that's it. We're going home," she said to the dog and started to turn, but paused. The silhouette of a man moved toward her. She didn't want to see anyone. Not this early. Not in her pajamas. She made her way to a small cutoff ahead on the right. She'd take that, circle to the main path and get behind the man.

The cutoff was narrow and not well groomed. Soggy branches reached across it. Weeds poked up through the dirt. She avoided the foliage as best as she could with Jake pulling her this way and that. But her feet were sopping wet after a few yards. She cursed herself for procrastinating about obedience classes. Jake wasn't easy to manage.

A snap behind her echoed in the quiet morning. She glanced over her shoulder. The man she'd seen had followed her onto the cutoff. *Followed her.* She was overreacting. The dim light and lack of people in the park made her feel vulnerable. He'd probably been intending to come this way all along. But she picked up her pace anyway.

Soon the crunch of boots grew louder, closer. A thin prick of anxiety traveled up her spine. She began to jog, her shoes flipping mud onto her calves. Was it her imagination or were the heavy steps matching hers?

Jake frisked beside her, jumping and biting at the leash in her hand, happy with the new game. Kate stumbled over a tree root, righted herself, and looked behind her again. The man was so close now, she could see his beard, brown and curling. The rest of his face was invisible, covered by a black hoodie.

The cutoff opened onto the main path. She bolted forward, branches slapping wet stripes across her pajamas. She burst into the open area and looked left then right for another person. Somewhere to run. Safety.

There was a bench a few yards up the path. On it lay a reclining figure. Probably a homeless person holed up in the park for the night. Normally she'd give someone like that a wide berth, but this morning anybody was better than nobody. She ran to the bench. "Hey, wake up. Please." Her words were quiet pants.

Kate eyed the place where the cutoff had joined the gravel road, but the man hadn't appeared. Maybe he was hanging back because he'd seen the person on the bench too. "Can I sit with you? I don't want to be alone. I think someone is following me."

The sleeping person was dressed in dark slacks and a print top. It was a female. Kate felt a surge of relief. A shaft of early morning sun, shone in her eyes but she could still make out the outlines of the woman, and the open book that covered her face as if she'd fallen asleep reading. Jake sniffed at the figure and whined.

Kate put out a hand and touched the woman's legs pushing them to the side ever so slightly so she could perch on the edge of the bench. The homeless lady didn't acknowledge the shove. She must be sleeping off one heck of a blow. "I'm sorry. But I need to sit here for a while, until I'm sure he's gone," Kate said.

She settled herself on the bench and scanned the bushes. Jake sat at her feet and scratched himself. Long minutes passed, and Kate's heart rate began to slow. Jake curled into a ball and fell asleep. The man must be gone, but she would wait a bit longer to be sure.

When the sun began to warm the gravel path with watery rays, she decided it was safe to travel. She pivoted on the bench. "Well, thanks, not that you even know the good deed you did," she said to the still form. Kate put a hand on the bench readying herself to rise, then she saw it.

The hands resting on the sleeping figure's stomach weren't hands at all. The cuffs of the floral blouse lay empty. A jolt of adrenaline shot through her. Kate's heart thudded. Probably an accident. Probably why the woman was homeless. Nothing to be afraid of. But she jerked upward, an awkward movement, and jarred the woman's legs. The figure's arms fell open. The book slid to the ground.

Kate screamed. But not because the homeless woman's face was horrible. Because it wasn't there.

CHAPTER TWO

Monday, October 2nd

THE FORTRESS WAS being invaded. Rosie slowed as she made the sharp turn onto Cliff Drive. A moving van sat in front of the large stone house. Well-muscled men carried an expensive replica of a French settee, circa 1890, through an open door.

Rosie craned her neck to get a peek inside. She'd never been in the fortress and had always wondered what the interior looked like. The house had stood sentry on that cliff overlooking the small cove beneath for forty years. All its inhabitants had been rich, reclusive, and mysterious—her dream clients.

A horn tooted behind her. A woman in a Mercedes SUV threw up her hands in exasperation. Rosie stepped on the gas. She'd seen all she was going to anyway. Based on her glimpse of the furniture in the van, the new owners were like those of the past.

She'd have to get a hold of Gwen Bishop to find out more. Gwen was a Realtor and knew the neighborhood. She'd listed a house on this same street two years ago, and although it had been a terrible experience it had opened doors for her.

That home, although only three blocks south of the fortress, couldn't have been more different. Rosie drove past it slowly, noticing the changes that had been made since the days of its notoriety. Money had been spent, it was obvious. But despite the improvements, the place made her shudder. The owners couldn't pay her enough to take that project on. Not that they'd asked. On the flip side, she'd redecorate the fortress for a song just for a chance to see the interior and brag about the job.

Rosie navigated her way through the tight streets and onto the Coast Highway, next stop, the Nightshade Gallery. One of her clients had seen a painting in the window and wanted her to look at it, see what she thought.

Rarely did anything from Nightshade work in the homes she decorated. The art Peter carried was dark and disturbing, the opposite of Rosie's style. She prided herself on creating open, fresh, and comfortable spaces. But she would look, so she could tell her client why she didn't want it.

She parked behind the building and trudged through the alley toward the highway. Normally she'd enter the gallery from the rear entrance. She and Peter Stiller were friends, but not because they had similar taste. She'd met him through a marketing mastermind group he used to run. The group was too pseudo-spiritual for her to stick with. But they'd connected, and he referred business to her regularly. And she recommended him to anyone who might like the unusual art he specialized in.

However, today she wanted to see the window display as her clients had seen it. She made a left on

Coast Highway and walked to the main entrance. She picked out the painting immediately—a magenta dahlia.

At first glance it was lovely, so real you could feel the drops of water on its petals. She understood why her clients thought it would look beautiful in their home. Rosie had chosen creamy white for the walls and pale wood for the flooring. These formed the backdrop for the antique furniture the couple had accumulated on trips to New England. Deep, saturated jewel tones were a perfect complement.

Rosie stepped up to the glass and examined the painting. She knew the kind of surprises Peter's art held. It took a second for her to find what was hidden in this one. A worm, so fat and swollen with blood it was hardly distinguishable from the magenta flower.

She tracked a slender, green slime trail from the worm to the corner of the painting. A dead beetle, small enough to be overlooked, lay on its back, feet in the air. In its belly was a red gash from which mammalian looking entrails protruded.

Her client had missed this, Rosie was sure. She pulled her phone from her purse and snapped a picture of the worm and its victim. She'd text it to her with the recommendation to keep looking. As she replaced her cell in her purse, the front door of the gallery opened. Peter thrust out his head.

"Are you coming in? Or are you just going to stand there?"

She gave him a half smile. "Have any coffee made?"

"Was Leonardo Catholic?"

She followed him into the dim interior of the gallery. Peter, small, pale, and partial to black clothing and low lighting, almost disappeared as he moved deeper into the shop. Black, the color of mystery and hidden things, was the perfect hue for him. "So who are you going to talk out of buying one of my paintings this time?"

"You don't know her," Rosie said. "She and her husband were in town for dinner and saw the dahlia. But for the worm and the beetle, it would be perfect."

"But for the worm and the beetle you could buy it online from a paint-by-numbers artist. I don't carry frivolous art."

Rosie sat in a purple Victorian-era chair. It wasn't comfortable. Vicky hadn't believed in creature comforts. But it was authentic. "Then you can't complain when I don't encourage my client to hang it over her couch."

He waved a hand in the air, fanning away the subject. "Did you hear?"

"Hear what?"

"Someone bought the fortress."

"I just drove by it. I saw the moving van."

Peter set two small, china cups on a low table and took a seat in the matching chair across from hers. "I know who the new owner is." He gave her a smug smile and raised his cup to his lips. Peter liked to be in control. Rosie guessed it was what her husband referred to as "small man's syndrome." Eric believed short men made up for their stature by puffing up what they did have.

"Are you going to tell me? Or make me beg?" Rosie said.

He set down his cup, dabbed at his mouth with a napkin and reclined in his chair. "Jacob Rinehart."

"You're kidding?" Rosie had expected a Hollywood producer or business mogul, not an author. At least, not an author who was a household name. She felt a pang of disappointment. She wouldn't have to call Gwen after all. "How did you find that out?"

"I know his publicist. She's one of my best customers."

That Jacob Rinehart's publicist would enjoy the kind of art Peter sold didn't surprise Rosie. Rinehart wrote macabre, gritty books. She'd read his first novel, *Cage*, but never tackled another. *Cage* had given her enough nightmares. Six months ago there had been a real-life murder tied to one of his books. Another reason to avoid his novels.

"It's the perfect house for him. He can decorate it like one of his stories, complete with a dungeon in the basement," she said.

Peter shook his head. "By all accounts he's a very nice man, a gentle soul."

"That's hard to believe."

"Thriller and horror writers are some of the nicest people you'll ever meet. It's the romance authors you have to watch out for."

Rosie laughed.

"You think I'm joking? Jacob was so disturbed by the murder, so distraught that someone would mimic the crime he imagined, he couldn't write. Complete block."

"But I bet it sold a lot of books."

"You are a cynic, Rosie Ring. That's a terrible thing to say. Cecily-his publicist—said he was tortured by the idea he was responsible."

"I'm not saying he was happy about the crime, but I'm sure the attention he got helped pay for that big house." Rosie took a sip of her coffee. It was excellent. Thank goodness Peter's taste in java was better than his taste in art.

Peter shrugged. "He moved here from Seattle to get away from it all."

"The murder was like the ones in his second book, right?"

"No. That was *Deep*. Everybody drowned in that book. It was like the ones in the third, *Pillory*. Gruesome. Very upsetting."

"Eric thinks it was the Mexican mafia and not related to the book at all. He thinks the publisher exploited the murder to boost sales."

"Your husband might be right, but my understanding is the mob mutilates the bodies of its victims and sends the heads to their families or their gangs as a warning. This was quite neat. Head and hands severed and never found."

Rosie replaced her cup with a shaky hand. It clattered onto its saucer. Talking about murder and dismemberment wasn't pleasant anywhere, but here in Peter's gallery it was intolerable. She glanced around at the paintings closest to her.

Most were like the dahlia—nice enough at first. But the field of poppies dripped blood. The lovely dark-haired woman in the portrait had dead eyes and blue lips. And the crystal waterfall hid a demented, demonic face. Nothing in Peter's shop was as it seemed. Including Peter.

Rosie stood. "Thanks for the coffee."

"Leaving so soon?"

"I have to get going."

Peter walked her to the door. "I'll tell Cecily about you. I'm sure Rinehart will redecorate."

"Why don't you wait on that? Let me think about it."

"What's there to think about? It would be a great job for you, money, prestige. What's the downside?"

"Rinehart. He's the downside."

"I told you, Cecily said he's a terrific guy."

Rosie didn't want to talk about it anymore. "Just give me a few days."

Peter shrugged. "You want to lose another job to Twila, take your time."

She tightened her mouth. "I'm going to have to talk to Eric."

"You're a very good wife, Rosie. But you're also a very good interior designer. I think it's time to step out of Eric's shadow."

Rosie flushed. She couldn't stand it when Peter psychoanalyzed her. He'd made his money as a success guru with a New Age coaching organization called Manifest. About five years ago, accusations of sexual impropriety against the founder shut it down. Peter moved to Laguna, bought the gallery, stocked it, and retired to become an art dealer. But sometimes he reverted to his roots.

As much as she disliked his intrusion into her psyche, she didn't argue with him. She did feel more comfortable staying in the background. A bad habit left over from her stay-at-home-mom days, but she pushed past that tendency every day. No, that wasn't why she was undecided about having Peter promote her to Rinehart.

The reason was twofold. She felt cautious about working with someone whose mind traveled such twisted roads. But, more importantly, Eric would hate the idea.

There had been a death associated with his own company around the same time the killing in Seattle had taken place. Time might heal wounds, but six months wasn't long enough to mend the ravages of murder.

THE SEVEN DEADLY SINS

By Greta Boris

Available wherever fine books are sold.

Lightning Source UK Ltd.
Milton Keynes UK
UKHW011520050620
364505UK00003B/602